the best of both

CHELSIE LYNN

trigger warning

I wrote this book with every intention that it would be light, fluffy, and ridiculous. However, I am aware that there is some triggering content within the pages of this silly little book, and I want to be respectful of that.

With that being said, if you have experienced the death of a parent or a grandparent, these themes are discussed in this book. Additionally, this book contains open door spice, meaning there is on page sexual content and significant discussion of sexual activities. Please protect your peace while reading my loves. If you come across other triggers that I did not consider, please let me know so I can update this list!

Happy reading smoot sloots!

macy

CONCUSSION INDUCING STAGE
ELEVATORS: 14 MACY: 0

"HARPER! Watch your—"

Clang!

Dammit! You'd think after months of planning, countless rehearsals, and dozens of sold out concerts, I'd have learned by now to duck my fucking head as I get into the small elevator that raises me onto the stage. But alas, I now have a goose egg the size of fucking Los Angeles on the crown of my skull that has been slowly growing since we started this damn tour. And it *definitely* doesn't help that I'm currently nursing just a bit of the tequila flu.

"Fourteen shows on this tour, and she *still* runs into that thing. Maybe we should get her checked out in case there's any lasting damage affecting her memory." My older brother, Chase, snickers at me from down the hall with my best friend, Stella. She laughs alongside him, like I knew she would, because even though those two literally never see eye to eye on anything, the one thing they can agree on is making fun of me. As my tour manager and publicist, Chase generally tries to keep me out of trouble, but he will never miss a chance to tease me when given the opportunity.

1

I don't have time to properly snipe at him, so instead, I take the super mature route and flip him the bird while sticking out my tongue. Having satisfied my inner child, I adjust my headset microphone to make sure my wine red wig is in place. I'd hate for Chase to have something else to hound me for, and my wig slipping mid-show would definitely fuel his "Harper is an irresponsible mess" fire that has been slowly burning brighter and brighter over the last few months. Sometimes, I swear that maintaining a secret identity is more trouble than it's worth.

When I first started my singing career, I was just turning seventeen and I knew very little about what it really meant to be a celebrity. My family was always supportive of my dreams, but they worried that being in the spotlight would force me to give up any semblance of a normal life. I knew chasing stardom would be risky, and I agreed that I wasn't totally ready to say goodbye to being a teenager just yet.

So, after many teenage hormone fueled meltdowns and lots of family meetings, Chase and I came up with the idea of me living a double life. It was mostly Chase's brainchild, but even I could admit that it was a good idea. I would come up with an elaborate disguise that would hide any distinguishable features well enough that I would still be able to go out in public like a normal person while I navigated my new expectations.

At the time, I was thrilled that I would get to be the best of both versions of myself. But lately, I've been wondering if it's time to leave normal life behind and embrace life fully as Harper Bloom. I spend ninety percent of my time as her anyway, so what's the harm in moving forward with telling my secret?

"Nice Harp," Chase gripes with an eye roll but continues

chuckling despite his irritation. He loves me, even though I tend to drive him a little crazy. "You better–" He gets cut off as the elevator begins to rise, and I plaster the megawatt smile on my face that the infamous Harper Bloom is known for, amongst other things that will remain unmentioned for now. Lord knows my name has been splashed across the tabloids enough times, but there's no need to get into the gory details just yet.

I know that I will probably get another earful from Chase after the show, but for now I can't worry about his cranky ass. My show is about to start, and I shake off anything that doesn't directly involve singing my heart out in front of thousands of people and shaking my ass on stage.

I absolutely love performing, and right now, it's time to do what I do best.

"Goodnight, Houston! You've been amazing! Get home safe, and remember, don't do anything I wouldn't do!" I add with a saucy wink. I blow a kiss to the crowd and flounce off the stage, heading toward my dressing room for a quick touch up and outfit change before the meet and greet with the VIP ticket holders.

I could probably use a shower and a chance to wash my hair that's been sweating underneath this damn wig for hours on end, but unfortunately, I don't have that kind of time. It's always a super quick turn around between when the concert ends and the meet and greet begins, so a wet wipe cleanse will have to work for now. Thank God my wig soaks up most of my sweat, so I still have beautiful hair. It's the little things in life I guess.

"Harper! Get your ass over here NOW!" Chase booms at me as I saunter down the stadium hallway, almost making it to my dressing room before he catches up with me. To be honest, I'm a little shocked he wasn't waiting for me on stage right to start laying into me the second my big toe crossed the threshold to backstage. I should really give him some credit for giving me a few extra minutes of peace before laying the smack down, but something tells me he wouldn't appreciate the humor in my gratitude. I stop in my tracks and let out a sigh before turning toward him with a saccharine smile on my face.

"Oh, hey Ace! Sounded pretty good out there tonight, huh? Turns out I'm *pretty* good at this pop star business, am I right?" I toss his way with a smirk, knowing full well he's about to go absolutely berserk on my ass, but I'm unable to stop the sass from rolling off of my tongue. What can I say? Pissing off Chase is basically my second job as his little sister. Plus, he's been up my ass lately, so he totally deserves it.

"Cut the shit, Harper. What was with that last comment up there? 'Don't do anything I wouldn't do?' It's almost like you *want* Leopold Regis to write another scathing clickbait piece about you," Chase chastises with a face that clearly reads I am getting on his last damn nerve. He's being a total dick, but I can tell by the slight tightness to his eyes that it's borne out of concern for my giant, Macy-sized secret getting out. Underneath all of the assholery, he really does have my best interest at heart. Unfortunately for him, I don't tend to heed his warnings as often as I should.

Honestly, he's not wrong, given how often Leopold Fucking Regis likes to pick on the infamous Harper Bloom. I'm no saint, that's for sure, but it would be nice if he would pick on someone else every once in a while. I mean, there *are* other celebrities in the world after all. As much as I love the spotlight, it doesn't *always* have to be the Harper show, right?

"Oh come *on*, Chase! It was just a joke. You know? Like 'if you can't laugh at 'em, laugh with 'em' or however that phrase goes. Just poking fun at myself, so they can't do it behind my back! Like Fat Amy in that old movie we used to watch all the time. Remember?" He just stares at me with a blank look that says he's simply not buying any of my bullshit today. "*Pitch Perfect?* You don't remember? Seriously?"

The blank look on his face goes nowhere, so I just roll my eyes and keep making my way toward the dressing room. If he's going to keep riding my ass, then I can at least multi-task and get ready for the meet and greet while he does it.

"You really need to loosen up. Right, Stella?" I cast a hopeful glance at my best friend in hopes that she will have my back, but she is mysteriously nowhere to be found. Damn her. She's always disappearing whenever I need her to step in for me. Hopefully it will be worth the abandonment issues when she regales me of whatever sexcapade she is getting into right now with one of my backup dancers. That girl seriously has a sex life the gods would envy. And maybe one that I do... just a little bit.

"Don't tell me to loosen up, Harper. You are literally the reason I am wound so fucking tight in the first place. Would it kill you to make my job easy for just *one* night?"

"I don't have the *faintest* idea what you could be referring to, Acey boy!" I bat my eyelashes at him with mock innocence. He pretends to hate that nickname, so of course, I can't resist using it during all of our arguments, which seem to be a lot more frequent lately.

Strictly speaking, I haven't been the easiest client to handle, especially in the last few months.

There was that time that Stella and I had a few too many tequila sunrises at brunch and decided to do a swimsuit photoshoot. In the MGM fountain in Las Vegas. Or that other time that I rented out basically the entire four seasons hotel in New Orleans for my 25th birthday party. Somewhere along the line, I decided that the chandelier in the ballroom would make the *perfect* swing. Needless to say, the hotel staff did *not* appreciate that stroke of genius, and I ended up paying a hefty fine for the damages done. Or, most recently, when Stella convinced me that I could most definitely play the role of flag bearer at a car race, to which she was totally right. I was *amazing* waving that checkered flag while hanging from the window of the most recent cup winner's car as he zipped around the track. I seriously thought I saw Chase's life flash before his eyes when he realized I could have lost my wig somewhere around the 75 mph mark. Thank God for industrial strength wig glue, though I will admit that it slipped a little. But, what Chase doesn't know won't hurt him, and it really was no big deal. You know, despite the risk to my life and all that.

In short, I make Chase's job of making sure my real identity stays hidden pretty difficult. But, what can I say? A girl still needs to have her amusement, right? Even if she is a "normal girl" by day and an international pop star by night. If I'm going to live a double life, I want to live it to the fullest.

Chase is less than impressed with my dismissal of his concerns, which he makes blatantly obvious when he throws his hands in the air and huffs a frustrated sigh that reminds me so much of our grandfather it hurts my heart just a bit. I loved that man more than I can even put into words, and knowing Chase is the spitting image of him is both a comfort and a pain I wasn't prepared to feel every day. Maybe someday it will hurt less to know that he's gone, but every once in a while, it hits me square in the chest just how much I miss him.

"Ugh, fine! You're right, I get that it's been hard managing my PR lately. But seriously, Chase, it was a fucking joke. It's not like I whipped my tits out on stage and gave my drummer a motorboat ride. It's really not a big deal."

"Macy," Oh shit, he is using my real name. "I might be taking this particular instance a little bit extreme, but I think you could stand to take your secret a little bit *more* seriously. You decided to do the double life thing for a reason. Are you really prepared to give that up just to maintain your party pop princess persona?" he asks me in a heavily exasperated tone that tells me he's rapidly reaching his limit with my laissez-faire attitude. Chase takes his job of maintaining my secret very seriously, and it does make me feel slightly bad knowing how much stress I've been putting on him lately.

"Okay, first of all, it's not a *persona.* It's the life I enjoy living when I *don't* have to worry about being 'normal.' And second of all... well, there is no second of all yet, but give me a minute, and I'm sure I will come up with something good!" I shoot back at him.

"Alright don't hurt your pretty little head trying to come up with something right this minute. I'm sure it's still ringing from bashing it against the stage elevator again anyway," he says with a chuckle and a smirk that makes me want to punch his smug face in. I settle for sticking my tongue out at him instead. You know, like a *real* grown up.

"We will talk about it more later. For now, get your ass cleaned up and smelling like a goddamn daisy again. You have fans to please and about a million and one autographs to sign. Chop to it, Ace!" He throws in our shared nickname as a reminder that despite the fact that we are at each other's throats ninety-nine percent of the time, we still love each other. Sibling love and all that jazz.

"Yeah, yeah, yeah, whatever. Hey, Chase?" I stop him before he leaves me to finish freshening up. He turns back and meets my eye with one of his eyebrows raised in question. "Would you find Stella for me please? Bonus brother points if she comes carrying a bottle of tequila, two shot glasses, and a lime! Okaythanksbye Iloveyou!" I rattle in rapid fire before slamming my dressing room door in his face, cutting off any chance of reply.

macy

COMMENCE MISSION "MACY GETS BOINKED"

"I COME BEARING GIIIIIIFTS! Of the fun alcoholic variety!" Stella sing-songs as she dances her way into my dressing room, carrying all of the necessities for our traditional post-show shots.

"Oh, thank GOD! Dealing with Chase's moody ass has given me a serious craving for something to help me forget about it. P.S. Where the hell have you been? You know it's way more fun getting under his skin when I have you to back me up!" I soften the sassiness of my words by giving her a smile as I grab the shot glasses and tequila from her hands.

"Well, you know I never kiss and tell," she says with a shrug, though her face belies just how much she actually does want to spill the beans on her most recent tryst.

"Oh, whatever. You ALWAYS kiss and tell. Spill!" I shoot back at her.

"Okay, fine, fine. The closets in this stadium are REALLY big. I'm just saying!" She remarks with a laugh. "But enough about the AMAZING sex I just had with two of your backup dancers."

"TWO? Which two?" I spin around to give her a look that should convey my shock but is more like pure envy.

She completely ignores me and keeps talking as if I didn't speak at all.

"Let's take these damn shots, and get your cute ass ready for this meet and greet already! I am making it my personal mission to find you a big ol' slab of man meat to dick you down. Lord knows you need it!"

"'Man meat?' What are you, an eighth grade boy in the phy ed locker room?" I quip at her.

"Seriously, Ace. How long has it been? I hope you're keeping up with your *self-care,* if you know what I mean. I'd hate for you to end up with cobwebs down there or something."

"Okay first of all, fuck you, Stel. It's only been a few months. It's not exactly easy getting dick around here when I have the world's biggest clam jam as an older brother. And second of all... I don't have a second of all just yet, but I'm sure I can come up with something," I finish, realizing that I *seriously* need to work on my comeback skills. It's getting embarrassing at this point that both Stella and Chase are able to outwit me in that arena.

"Hold up, wait. Did you just say 'clam jam'? What the fuck is that supposed to be? Sounds a little too close to a slang term for an STD or something. Which, I guess when we are talking about Chase, can't be far from the truth," she says with a laugh. Stella thinks she's the funniest person in the world, so of course she would laugh at her own jokes. "Next time just say cock block like everyone else, Ace. But regardless, we WILL be getting you laid tonight. Chase doesn't even have to know about it, and if I find the right person to send you to orgasm bliss, maybe you two won't be at each other's throats as much. It's a win-win!"

She does have a point. I definitely tend to turn into the bitchy version of Macy when it's been too long without actually getting off with another person. My fingers and sparkly pink dildo can only take me so far. It might sound cheesy, but I really enjoy the connection that comes from getting absolutely railed by another person and having them whisper sweet nothings and filthy declarations in my ear. Even if they are almost always a total stranger that I don't even bother to learn the name of. What's the point, when I am always getting ready to skip town for the next show? Maybe someday the right person will come along and force me to learn their name, but for now, I'm content with the occasional "wham bam, thank you ma'am," if you know what I mean.

"Okay, fine, you're right. I could use a little connection with someone before we take off on the next phase of the tour," I cave to her, and she wraps me in a huge hug with an ear-splitting squeal.

Stella may enjoy getting it on her own, but I swear she gets extra satisfaction out of managing my sex life. Who am I to deny my best friend her sexy matchmaking fantasies?

"But seriously, Stel, Chase can NOT find out about this. He's made it clear that I am on thin ice when it comes to shenanigans. Add in a mid-tour one night stand, and he might just pop the last remaining blood vessel in his forehead. We just don't have the time to deal with that level of clean up."

"Yeah, yeah, yeah, I get it. Operation 'Macy Gets Boinked' is totally under the radar!" She says with a mock zip of her lips, but a beaming smile still breaks across her face.

"Ew, don't say boinked. It makes me think of a pig, and those are decidedly unsexy in my mind." I give her the most disgusted face I can manage. "Okay, now turn the damn music up, and let's finish getting ready. I have places to go, people to see, and someone to fuck or whatever."

She laughs and connects her phone to the bluetooth speaker in my room, blasting the music as loud as she can. Pouring two shots, we clink our glasses and throw them back, biting on a lime to dull the flavor just enough, and work on getting ready to go.

* * *

We finished getting ready in record time and even had time for an extra shot before rushing to the room where the meet and greet is taking place. With the extra liquid courage, I am actually starting to look forward to the rest of my evening. I always enjoy getting to hang out with my fans, but the added excitement of knowing how my evening is going to end (preferably with multiple orgasms) means I am extra smiley and energetic. I even spotted my chosen dick for the evening about two minutes into the event.

Most of my fans are pretty stereotypical for my brand of pop-star, being teenaged girls who eat up the party-girl lifestyle and the sugary sweet lyrics about falling in love, so it wasn't hard to pick out the six and a half foot blonde giant with bulging muscles covered in tattoos that just screamed "I can totally throw you around in the bedroom but will still whisper sweet nothings while I do it." Definitely my cup of tea.

"Stella," I whisper, pulling my best friend's attention away from her latest backup dancer conquest, Phoebe. They've been seeing each other for a few months, so it's nothing new to see them flirting, but I am more than a little curious which of my dancers was chosen to mix things up in their relationship tonight. I make a mental note to ask her about it again later. "Turns out, I don't need you to find me someone after all. Got that part covered. Check out the blonde hulk about ten people down in line." I nod in the direction I'm looking before the next fan steps up and we snag a photo together.

I give what seems like my millionth hug of the night before the 14-year-old looking girl bops her way back to the other girls in her squad. They all squeal, looking over the photos on their phone, and head out of the room so more can filter in.

"Oooh, you picked a good one, Ace!" Stella nearly shouts, and I fight the urge to clap my hand over her mouth from the embarrassment. I love my best friend, but she definitely doesn't always realize the level of her voice volume, especially after a couple of shots of tequila. "I'm a little mad I didn't scope him out for myself. Think you might want to add a third for the night?" She licks her lips and looks at me hopefully, but the next fan steps up to snag a photo before I can respond. She always gets a little extra flirty when she's buzzed, so I don't take her seriously, especially since Phoebe is still right there. They're in a pretty open relationship, so I'm sure she wouldn't mind, but I'm a one at a time kind of girl. At least, most of the time.

Still sporting a megawatt smile, I look at her. "Sorry, not tonight, babe. I am way too single-minded tonight to allow his focus to be on anyone but me. Besides, I would think Phoebe has you covered for the night. We have about ten more minutes of this meet and greet, so you have that much time to get him to my dressing room. Ready, set, go, boo."

Never one to shirk her duties as my sex matchmaker, Stella jumps into motion, making a beeline for Blonde Hulk. As she chats him up briefly, he glances my direction with a gleam in his eye and a smirk on his full lips. God, it's enough to make my mouth water. I seriously can't wait to wrap myself around this particular tree. He steps out of line and follows Stella out of the room.

As predicted, the rest of the meet and greet goes quickly,

and I wave goodbye to everyone before heading toward my dressing room. As I step up to the door labeled "Harper Bloom" in calligraphy style gold lettering, I take a deep breath and get my game face on before stepping through the door.

Blonde Hulk is lounging on the white leather sofa as I step in and close the door. Deciding to play aloof for a minute, I ignore him completely and walk over to my vanity to start taking off my jewelry. I mean, clearly I wanted him here, but he doesn't need to feel my desperation for him just yet. I'm the catch here, right?

I start taking off my earrings before addressing him through the mirror. "You know breaking and entering is generally frowned upon in most states." My words might sound aggressive, but the husk in my voice must be enough to convince him that I am flirting. He smirks and smoothly stands up before moving toward me.

"Ah yes, but I was under the impression you *wanted* me here," he quips, his voice dripping with innuendo. He crowds behind me, brushing my wine red hair off of my shoulder and running his nose up the column of my throat. "In fact, the little dark haired pixie girl kind of insisted on it. So feel free to call security, but I can't imagine they will offer you the same kind of fun that I can."

He ends his statement with a whisper directly into my ear before gently nipping at my now earring-less lobe. My heart starts racing, and I squeeze my thighs together to relieve the ache that is starting to build there from his words and proximity alone. God, it really has been a while. He's barely touched me and I am practically melting into a puddle on the floor.

I lean my head more toward the left to give him more access to my neck before meeting his eyes in the mirror and playing along with his teasing, "So sure of yourself. Care to test that theory?"

With that, he gives me one last smirk before fully kissing along where my neck meets my shoulder and reaching down the front of my thighs to slowly lift the hem of my black leather and sequin dress.

"Wait," I say, meeting his eyes again in the mirror, and he instantly pauses. "In front. Now." He gives me a huge, toothy smile before following my order and getting on his knees in front of me in the chair. Good boy. Follows directions.

I run my fingers through his thick blonde curls, shooting him a seductive smile before guiding his face where I want it most, getting absolutely zero resistance from him.

Oh, yes. This is going to be a fun night.

macy

FUTURE AUTOBIOGRAPHY IDEA: HOW TO MANAGE WHEN YOU ACCIDENTALLY CREATE A SEX TAPE

AFTER SUCH AN AMAZING ending to my night, you'd think I would have slept like a goddamn goddess. Multiple orgasms usually leads to a great night's sleep, feeling like I'm floating on cloud nine.

To be fair, I *was* sleeping well, until I was so rudely awoken by some asshole.

As my eyes flutter open, I realize that the aggressive pounding of a headboard in my rather passionate wet dream starring Blonde Hulk is actually Chase pounding on the door of my hotel suite like his life depends on it.

"Macy, I swear to God, if you don't open this damn door right now, I am burning the fucking thing to the ground before tossing you into the flames alongside it!" He screams loudly enough that I am sure the rest of the hotel must hear him. Thank God we booked the entire floor for me and the rest of my entourage, or we'd be in deep shit if someone heard him using my given name. He must be *really* pissed at me if he doesn't give a shit about maintaining the ruse.

I toss the blankets off of my head and rush toward the door before swinging it open as Chase keeps banging away. He almost nails me with his fist in his state of rage, stopping his fist only centimeters from my face.

"Jesus Christ, Ace. What the fuck? You do know it's like... five in the morning, right? What could *possibly* have you in such a rage this early in the morning? Can't your tantrum wait until I've at least had my morning coffee?"

He brushes past me angrily with a glare and opens up my laptop sitting on the living room coffee table. "Don't fucking test me right now, Macy. Get over here. Now. Sit." He barks at me as he types away like my laptop killed his favorite pet or something. It's really been a long time since I have seen him this worked up, so I heave a heavy sigh and go sit by him on the sofa where I notice the headline splashed on Leopold Regis' celebrity gossip blog, *The Regis Report*.

Party Pop Princess with a Praise Kink? Harper Bloom's Wild Night with Personal Trainer

What. The. Fuck?

I have to reread the headline three times before I am able to register what it's really saying. In my shock and panic, I'm not able to focus on the words of the article much, but that's not really where the meat of the article lies. About a paragraph into the scathing article denouncing me as a sex-crazed party girl, there's an audio clip with a play button. As soon as I click on it, I really wish I hadn't, as I hear my breathy voice ring out from the clip alongside a deep masculine one I recognize instantly.

*"Oh my God, YES! That feels so *bleep* good. Say it again. Tell me again how much you love it." "Your *bleep* is the best *bleep* I've ever had. So *bleep* tight and--"* I click the pause button and jump up from the sofa wringing my hands out as I fight to keep the nausea at bay.

"Oh my God. Oh fuck. Oh my God." A fucking sex tape? Okay, sex audio, but is that *really* any better? No wonder Chase is basically the human version of a volcano eruption right now.

This is, objectively, a PR disaster of epic proportions. Every other mishap I've had in the last month definitely pales in comparison to this catastrophe.

"How did this happen? Where did Leopold get that audio? I did *not* consent to being recorded!" I turn toward Chase to see him sitting with his elbows leaning on his knees and his hands clasped in front of him staring at the floor. Usually my antics just slightly irritate him, but I can tell from his posture and expression that he's far beyond the typical frustration. He's pissed, and I am about to really be in hot water. It takes him a minute of deep breathing through his nose before he addresses my question.

"Consent? *That's* what you're worried about right now?" He asks calmly, still not looking at me, keeping his eyes glued to the floor as if it will hold all of the answers to the current predicament we are in. "Macy, I think it's more than clear that you were into whatever else was happening in that fucking dressing room last night. You may not have consented to that clip being recorded, but it was, and now it's out there. The entire *fucking* continental U.S. has probably heard it at this point, not to mention the rest of the world. What were you *thinking?* We vet the people we interact with for a reason. This *exact* reason, actually. So I ask you again... What. Were. You. Thinking. Bringing a total stranger into your dressing room after I explicitly told you no more goddamn scandals?"

I just stand there trying to formulate my thoughts, my mouth kind of opening and closing like a fish as he stares me down, waiting for an answer. After a minute or so of me practicing my best Nemo impression, I feel myself getting angry and snap my teeth together before glaring at Chase with my fists balled at my sides. I'm definitely defaulting into defense territory, but with all of the emotions running through me right now, I am beyond the point of caring.

"I was *thinking* that maybe I just wanted to feel good for a fucking night! I was *thinking* that I am not a goddamn robot who can do show after show, night after night, without having some kind of connection with another person! I was *thinking* that I am a 25-year-old adult woman with adult needs that a handsome man was able to fulfill last night! So you can keep your judgmental bullshit to yourself, Chase! I'm not a child that needs to be saved by my older brother on the playground. Fuck off!"

With that, I stomp out of the living room area and make my way toward the kitchenette to start brewing some coffee to alleviate the stress headache that has started to set in. I mean, I know this isn't good, obviously. But honestly, it's not like I am the first pop star to accidentally release a sex tape, right? It's not like my brand is squeaky clean anyway, so it can't really be that shocking, can it?

Of course, Chase doesn't let me just storm out of the room without following me like he's my goddamn shadow.

"I'm not fucking judging you, Macy. I know that it's been a minute since you've had any sort of romantic connection with somebody. Believe me, I get it. But I don't think you understand how serious this is. You've been able to get away with all of your other bullshit up to this point because it was relatively harmless. Just some party girl nonsense that we can write off as you enjoying the perks of life as a pop star. But this? This is the label looking into your morality clause level of serious. This is people digging more into your personal life, level of serious. This is saying goodbye to the anonymity that Macy White gives you, level of serious! It's a big deal, and I think it's time that you stop for a minute to think about the consequences of your actions."

"Okay, I get it! It's serious. But come *on*. You really think the label would try to drop me over this? We totally operate as a sex-positive brand! It can't be that bad, right?" I may have gone with my label as a naive 17-year-old, but I didn't go into it blindly. I chose them for a reason, and being a more forward thinking company was one of them. At least, I thought they were on the same page as me when it came to this sort of stuff, but maybe I was wrong.

He chuckles with absolutely no humor at all. "Oh my God, you have absolutely no idea how much of your bullshit I have had to smooth over with the record execs, do you? Yes, Macy. I do think they might be wondering just how much more their brand can handle when it comes to keeping you as a client. Your voice is beautiful, and you have more talent on the stage than anyone I've ever seen, but that might not be enough when it comes to what image the label wants to project."

Well, fuck. I can write songs about making passionate love and getting shit-faced in Vegas, but the execs draw the line at *actually* engaging in any of those activities? Hypocritical assholes. If I were a man, I guarantee I'd be getting a slap on the back and a congratulatory bonus in my bank account. I guess maybe the label isn't as progressive when it comes to sex as I would have hoped. Something to think about for future deals, I guess.

Chase is looking at me expectantly, as if I am all of a sudden going to miraculously come up with the solution to fix this, while I just blow on my coffee to cool it down knowing full well a single sip of this will totally sour my already roiling stomach. It's not like they handed me a manual titled "How to Handle It When You Accidentally Create a Sex Tape" when I signed the record deal, and the anxiety coursing through my body right now is making me feel extra nauseous.

He taps his right pointer finger on the countertop before slamming his palm against it with a deep breath. "Okay, here's what we are going to do. You are going to give me the name of the dipshit you brought back to the dressing room, and I am going to sue to the fuck out of him for releasing that audio clip without your explicit consent. While I do that, you're going to go take a shower and a nap and we will assess what kind of statement you're going to make after that. Deal?"

His plan makes total sense to me, except for one little detail.

"Um... I kind of... don't really... know... his name," I say, making an "oopsy daisy" kind of face pulling on the ends of my natural black hair nervously. I hope my sheepish look is enough to dissuade Chase from totally ripping me a new asshole. Unfortunately, I am out of luck in that respect.

"Y-you didn't get his name? You're fucking joking, right?" Chase asks, pinching the bridge of his nose like he's the CEO of a fortune 500 company and I'm the college intern who brought him a 2% latte when he specifically asked for skim.

"I thought I was never going to see him again. One track mind and all that. It just didn't come up. I'm sure it's some-where in that article anyway. I mean... they knew he was a personal trainer, right? They must also know his name," I say in a hopeful tone. I will admit, I didn't fully read the article, but it stands to reason that they would have done some digging. Leopold Fucking Regis is nothing if not thorough.

He heaves a heavy sigh and mutters something under his breath that I can't quite make out, but I am sure sounds a lot like "Lord, what did I do to deserve this?"

"Okay, I will figure it out. Just go take a nap and... leave the rest to me. As per usual, you fucking nuisance." The words are rude, but I can tell he's starting to cool down and soften himself to me again. Despite my craziness, my brother really does love me and loves his job, just as I love him for always taking care of me. He can only stay mad for so long, and then he goes into full blown problem-solving mode.

"I love you, Chase. I'm sorry. I don't know if I even said that, but I am. The dick was good, but honestly if I knew this was how it would end, I probably would have at least gotten his name," I say with a smirk, shoving his shoulder as I head toward the bedroom.

"Good God, Ace. Please stop talking. I've heard more than I ever wanted to about your sex life, and I do not need a repeat of that," he says with a shudder and a gagging noise. Rude. "Now seriously. Go take a shower and get some beauty rest. Lord knows you need it."

"Hey!" I shout at him, but he's already walking out of the door of my suite, laughing at me under his breath. I hop into the shower and try to wash the shame of the morning off my skin before jumping into my California king size hotel bed. The really fucked up thing is, I didn't feel ashamed until they turned it into a shameful thing. Leave it to Leopold Fucking Regis to turn a really fun and pleasure-filled night into something dirty and wrong. I'm sure even that little toad boy gets it in every once in a while, as disgusting as that image is in my head.

And the worst part is, this could turn out just like Chase said and end up blowing my secret identity sky high. If that happens, I'd have to totally give into the pop-star lifestyle and would never have a day to myself ever again. At least, not out in public.

Then again, I do really love being a pop star. Getting to live out my dreams as Harper Bloom for the last eight years has been a dream come true. Literally. I think I still have my second grade dream journal where I wrote "become a worldwide superstar by the time my boobs grow in" on page one. Thank heavens I was blessed by the titty gods and was an early bloomer in that regard. I may not have hit my childhood goal, but I came damn close, starting my singing career before I even graduated high school.

As I drift off to sleep, I think about what could happen if I really did have to open up my entire life to the world and hang up the Macy White hat forever. Would it really be so bad to only have to worry about being one person and never having to wear a wig again unless I really wanted to? Sure, I'd have to give up some anonymity when I go out in public, but that's what hats and sunglasses are for, right? Like, ninety-nine percent of Hollywood's A-listers do that, so how hard can it really be? Maybe it's time to make the secret part of my identity less... secret.

With that thought rattling around in my brain, I drift back to sleep to forget the stress, if even for just a minute.

* * *

I wake up to a tornado in the form of my best friend blowing around my suite blasting old school Taylor Swift while she sings along. Seriously, what the fuck is going on today? Is everyone making it their mission to wake me up in the most disruptive way possible?

"Stella, what the fuck?" I prop myself up on my elbows and watch her buzzing around like a hummingbird on steroids. She completely ignores me, singing the lyrics of "Our Song" extremely off-key and pulling all of the clothes down from my closet and tossing them haphazardly on the bed, flinging sequins and glitter everywhere.

I drop back onto my pillow with a groan, pulling the blanket up to cover my head, just as Chase strolls into my bedroom.

"Enough beauty rest, Ace. Time to go. We leave in fifteen minutes, and anything you don't pack gets shipped to Malibu until *we* get back. Chop, chop!" He emphasizes with a clap of his hands.

"Excuse me? Get back? Back from where? I have a show in Dallas tonight, so none of this stuff should be going back to Malibu. It should be coming with us!" I spring out of bed and follow him out into the living room area of my suite. I grab him by the elbow to stop him from ignoring me, swinging him around to face me.

"Seriously Chase, what is going on? Is it more stuff about the... sex tape?" I whisper, knowing full well both Chase and Stella already know about it, just like the rest of the freaking world, but not wanting to completely voice it back into existence. I was living in blissful ignorance in my sleep, and it honestly brings me physical pain to remind myself of my current predicament.

"Ah, I'm glad you asked!" He says with a huge smile. He's pretty chipper for a guy who just this morning had to do damage control on his sister's sex tape. In fact, he's too chipper, and my internal alarm bells are playing a damn symphony.

"I got to thinking about it, Ace, and I think I came up with a pretty solid solution to our problem. You've been playing the role of party princess for too long, and it's time you get some perspective. Plus, in light of your most recent transgression, I think it's probably best for us to lay low for a while, anyway."

"Perspective? What perspective? Chase, stop with the fucking theatrics and just tell me why Hurricane Stella is currently ravaging my toiletries?" I snap at him, not having slept long enough to handle his crypticness.

"I *mean* you need to take a step back and remember who you really are. I spoke with the label, and they agreed with me that you need a break. We are temporarily suspending your tour dates and making a trip back home."

"To Malibu? I don't think–"

He cuts me off, holding his hand up in a gesture to indicate I should stop talking.

"No, Macy. I mean we are going *home*." He grins at me as if he didn't just blow up my entire life with one decision.

Oh. My. Fucking. God.

Home.

brody

THE DEATH OF A LEGACY

"FUCK," I whisper, leaning back in my desk chair and staring up at the ceiling. I grind my teeth in frustration, trying to keep my cool so I don't completely trash the office in my fit of irritation.

"What's the matter?" my secretary and co-editor Josie asks, peering up at me from her position on the leather couch I keep in my office for potential meetings. That is, if we were actually having any meetings lately, which we definitely are not. Over the last few weeks, I swear that the couch has seen even less action than I have, which is saying a lot.

I purposefully avoid her gaze, closing my eyes and letting out an irritated sigh.

"Brody, seriously," she starts, her own frustration bleeding through her words. I haven't been the easiest guy to be around lately, and her patience must be starting to wear thin. "You should know by now that I am here to help you figure it out, even if you've been a grumpy fuck lately who doesn't deserve my help."

I bark out a short humorless laugh, shaking my head at her boldness. I may be her boss, but Josie is never one to hold back, especially with me. It's one of the things that I love about having her as my secretary. She gets to the heart of things, which makes her a damn shark at the paper. I wish it were enough to keep things afloat around here, but unfortunately, that's not the case.

I lean forward on my desk, my elbows pressing into the wood, and meet her gaze.

"I just," I pause, unsure of exactly where I'm going with my thoughts. Trying to bottle in the emotions rolling through me is only serving to piss me off even more, but she doesn't deserve my ire, so I do my best, clearing my throat before speaking again. "I'm just getting tired of scrambling to figure out a worthwhile story for this fucking paper, Jos. I was never meant to do this, and everyone damn well knows it."

Her face softens at my moment of vulnerability, and I curse myself for letting even that much of my true feelings slip. I have become a master of hiding my emotions behind a mask of animosity, but sometimes I let them out when I don't mean to. Now is one of those moments, and I regret it instantly, taking in the look on Josie's face. Her pity matches every one else in town that I've encountered over the last six months, and I've hit my fucking limit.

"Jesus, Josie. Don't fucking look at me like that. I didn't want your pity the day they died, and I sure as fuck don't want it now. Save your sympathy for someone who gives a shit about it."

Instantly, her face turns to anger, and I know I succeeded in placing space between her and the truth behind my mask. It doesn't bring me the relief I was hoping it would, but at least we can stave off the heart to heart conversation. For now.

"God, Brody, you really can be such a prick sometimes. I am not pitying you. I am trying to *help* you, but I'm losing the desire more and more every day," she says, frustration lacing every word. She stares me down, and I roll my eyes sheepishly in hopes that it will soften her disdain.

She pinches the bridge of her nose before continuing to speak. "Look. I get it, okay? Your parents are gone, and you had to step into a role you weren't prepared for. That's tough, and your parents left you with some seriously large shoes to fill. They were larger than life, and I don't blame you for feeling overwhelmed."

My heart aches with her words, knowing they're true but desperately wanting them not to be. It's been nearly six months, and I still haven't really dealt with all of the emotions running through me over my parents' absence. We were always very close, and not having them here feels like I am missing part of myself. I clench my teeth, trying to fight off the lingering grief, and recenter myself in this conversation.

"But Brody," Josie says, forcing me to refocus my attention onto her. "You *can* do this. I believe in you, and I believe in this paper. We will figure it out, okay?"

I am unable to answer her question with words, still struggling to work through the unexpected knot in my throat, so I just nod at her, closing my eyes and releasing a long breath. I don't have her level of confidence in myself, but I know I need to do something. If not for myself, then for her and everyone else that works here.

"Alright then," Josie says, nodding in confirmation like we settled something between the two of us. "Now, go home and take a fucking shower. You look disgusting. I can practically smell your feet from here."

That does bring a genuine laugh from me, and I roll my eyes at her.

"Never one to sugar coat anything, Jos," I say, shaking my head while she just shoots me a satisfied smirk. "Fine. I'll see you tomorrow. Don't forget to grab a copy of *The Daily Gazette* on your way in."

She rolls her eyes at me. "As if I could forget. I do it every damn day, Brody. Give me a little credit." She mutters something under her breath about how frustrating men can be and stands up to leave.

She grabs the few things she had on the coffee table and heads out of my office. I sigh, finishing up a couple of things on my laptop before closing it to head home for the day. I'm not doing much good moping around here, and Josie is right. I really do need a shower. I gather my jacket and make my way out to my car.

* * *

I finish rinsing my face at the double vanity sink after taking my shower, glancing up in the mirror to take note of my appearance. The first thing I notice is how tired I look and how dull my eyes are. They're that level of dead looking that makes them appear almost gray, rather than the normal striking blue that melts the panties off all of the women in the office. The dark circles underneath them are doing nothing to help, and I run my hands through my dark brown curls while breathing a heavy sigh. I could probably be the poster-child for grieving orphans right now, which only makes me feel angrier.

Grumpy asshole is my usual state of being, but ever since my parents died a few months ago, I have been even worse, much to the chagrin of all of my employees. As if losing both of my parents in a fatal car accident wasn't bad enough, they had to go ahead and leave behind a legacy I can never live up to in their wake.

My parents were the co-owners and editors-in-chief of the local newspaper, *The Oaken Tribune*, and rather than let the paper get sold to the highest bidder if something happened to them, they graciously left it to me. Unfortunately for both the paper itself and their legacy, I don't possess anywhere near the level of dedication to a story that my parents did. They could find a story in the middle of nowhere that could sell papers faster than we could print them. Me? Not so much, which is leading to the slow and incredibly painful death of my parents' second child. It's a level of stress I wouldn't wish on my own worst enemy, which seems to be everyone these days.

I shake my head, trying to dispel the lingering feelings of animosity and sadness I feel at the loss of my parents, and head back out to my bedroom to grab a clean pair of shorts. I forgo a shirt, being that I am in my own home, and head into the kitchen to snag a box of cereal from the cabinet. Pulling a fistful of Cap'N crunch out of the box, my four-year-old Corgi, Allie, waits at my feet for me to drop some pieces. Fortunately for her, I do just that as I reach into the box again, and she gets nearly half a handful of cereal for herself. I probably shouldn't be feeding her human food like this, but fuck it. Someone deserves a small piece of happiness in this house.

Watching her sniffing around the floor for anything she may have missed, I let my thoughts return to the paper and how I am continually letting my parents down. I may have wanted to work there when I was a kid, and even studied journalism in college knowing I'd end up there when I finished, but I never expected to be running the whole damn thing. My parents never mentioned that it was a possibility, and I never expressed that it was something I wanted. While I may love reporting on amateur sports in our local area, the level of journalistic skill needed to manage every story in every section is something I was not prepared for, and everybody knows it. I'm sure when I leave the room at our office downtown, the heavy sighs and disappointed head shakes start up immediately. Add in the fact that most people get their news from Google, and it's basically the perfect storm for this paper to fail.

Putting the box of cereal back in the cabinet, I snag an IPA from the fridge and toss myself over the back of my sofa, settling in to stare at the ceiling. Allie jumps up near my legs and settles herself on my feet. I take a few sips of my beer, allowing the alcohol to somewhat dull the panic I can feel settling into my chest. I just wish I could find one good story that would change the tides and keep the paper afloat long enough to help me get my head on straight. I mean, Jesus, I haven't even really had the time to totally grieve the loss of my parents.

Grabbing my laptop off of the coffee table, I pull up Google and am immediately greeted with a clickbait headline: *Party Pop Princess with a Praise Kink? Harper Bloom's Wild Night with Personal Trainer.* Jesus Christ, Harper Bloom again? Normally I skip this kind of bullshit, but knowing this is the stuff that sells, my curiosity wins, and I click on the link. Call it research for future articles.

I can't say I am overly surprised by what greets me, knowing the infamous pop star's antics and how they have graced the cover of every major tabloid and gossip column over the last few years. Her accidentally creating a sex tape is not nearly as shocking to me as it probably is to her PR team or whoever's in charge of making sure she doesn't totally fall from grace. I will even admit that hearing her muffled cries gets me semi-hard as I listen to the audio clip accompanying the article. While I find her general bubblegum pink outlook on life irritating, I am still a man, and hearing a beautiful woman moaning from my screen is bound to initiate a reaction. Sue me.

Pinching the bridge of my nose to recenter my less than holy thoughts, I continue skimming down the article. The first thing I note is how ridiculous the writing is. This is seriously what people want to read about? My soul must be much older than my thirty years, because this is seriously melting my brain. The next thing I notice, at the very bottom of the article, is the number of views, shares, and comments. Holy fuck. Twelve thousand comments, nearly as many shares, and two million views in less than twenty-four hours? I guess this really is what people want to read about.

If only something this interesting would happen in my tiny corner of the world. Maybe then I could keep the paper going and put food on all of my employees' tables. With that thought adding fuel to my already festering terrible mood, I slam my laptop shut and abruptly shift forward to sit with my elbows balanced on my knees, clenching my jaw tightly.

Short of a pop star skydiving her way into the town square naked, there doesn't seem to be a story worth finding in Oaken, which means both myself and the paper are royally fucked. Great.

FIVE

macy

JUST CALL ME "MINNESOTA
MACY"

I CAN'T FUCKING BELIEVE that I am sitting in the passenger seat of this beat up piece of shit truck driving down a dirt road in the middle of nowhere Minnesota. After living in the spotlight for so long as Harper, riding in nothing but private jets and limos, this comes as much more than a small shock. This is Chase's personal form of torture. What I wouldn't give for a bottle of tequila right now.

Chase is sitting in the driver's side barely containing a smug smirk on his stupid older brother face while I stare out the window pouting. I know I haven't been on my A-game when it comes to publicity stunts, and a sex tape for sure didn't help smooth things over with my brother, but did he really have to drag me back here? *Here*, of all places? Where the only thing to look at for miles is never-ending corn fields, broken up only by the occasional creek named after The Millers, or something equally as generic, and a few tree barriers? Not only that, but I don't think anything could have prepared me for the overwhelming cow manure smell. While I may be a reformed farm girl, I haven't had the displeasure of being so up close and personal with the black and white beasts of the plains in years.

I wrinkle my nose as we barrel along toward my parents' old farmhouse. I seriously can't wait to get back to Malibu. I may even throw a rager at my mansion and invite Leopold Regis himself just to spite Chase for this stunt. I nearly smirk at the thought.

Noticing the brief reprieve from total disgust on my face, Chase glances over at me with a huge grin on his face. "Aww, come on, Ace! I know it's been a few years, but can't you at least appreciate the subtle beauty of this place? You used to love getting your hands dirty and putting on concerts for the cows!" He pokes me in the side as I desperately try to scoot out of his reach. Spoiler alert: It's impossible in this damn truck, and he gets in a few good ribs before I push him away.

"I can't believe you're making me spend an entire month here, Chase! A month?! I know the sex tape was bad, but does it really look good to run away like I did something totally horrible? I should make a quick statement and then go kiss some puppies at the humane society or something to smooth things over. Then we can get right back to normal, and I can get back on my tour!" I give him my best puppy dog hopeful face to try and trigger his softer side. I should have known he wouldn't take the bait. He just rolls his eyes and chuckles at me like I just told the world's funniest joke.

"Macy. We aren't just getting away from Malibu to get away from the story, though admittedly I think it's good to lay low for a bit after that. We are back here because, if we're being honest, you've been playing the role of party girl a little too hard lately, and it has to stop. You made the decision to keep your life as Macy White separate for a reason, and it's about damn time you start living it again," he chastises in his best impression of a dad voice. Unfortunately for him, I am not so easily influenced, so I just scoff and roll my eyes at him.

"Besides, Nana has been missing you lately. You know it hasn't been easy for her since Pop Pop died."

This makes me pause for just a minute in my pouting, my heart clenching painfully. My Nana and Pop Pop basically raised Chase and I after our parents died when we were kids. I hardly remember mom and dad, but Nana and Pop Pop? They were my entire world when I was growing up. Even in the first few years of me pursuing stardom as Harper, I would come home and visit just to get away and to keep myself grounded in my roots. After Pop Pop died from pneumonia complications a few years ago, I stayed away because setting foot in that house without him there felt like it would shatter the last remaining shreds of my already bleeding heart. Since then, I've fully leaned into my role as Harper and haven't thought much about the life I was missing as Macy.

I shake off the thought and turn my head back to glare at Chase.

"Fine. But I'm warning you right now, Chase, I will never give up my life as Harper, party girl and all. In fact, I've been thinking maybe it's time to give up the double life craziness and just... be Harper full time," I say in a quick breath. I expect Chase to totally freak out and crash the truck or something, but he just gives me a quick side eye and stays silent. He's quiet for so long, I start to wonder if he might be plotting my murder as we rumble along the road.

Heaving a weighted sigh, Chase finally speaks. "Give it the month, Ace. I know you feel like the best parts of you are in Harper, but I don't think that's the case. You are so much more than a party girl with a killer voice. Getting back to your roots for a while might be just what you need to reset. Give it a chance, okay?"

"Awww, Chase. You think my voice sounds like an angel? You're going to make me blush," I tease him with a lighthearted punch to his shoulder. He probably thinks he won this round, but after this month is up, it's back to the spotlight I go.

Chase gives me a lopsided grin, just as we pull into my parents old, white farmhouse. My heart gives another painful squeeze as I glance up at the black roof, navy blue shutters, and wraparound porch. Nana is at her usual spot on the porch swing, but she jumps up, tossing her old school Fabio style romance novel aside, and bounds down the stairs with a shriek.

"My babies are home!" Nana continues shrieking, skipping steps on the stairs as she goes.

Chase barely has the truck in park before Nana is wrenching open the passenger side door and tearing me out of it to embrace me in one of her signature Nana bear hugs. She lets out a few more shrieks as she pets my hair before abruptly releasing me to hold me at arm's length.

"Oh my God, I can't believe you're finally home! And look at how fancy you are. I swear those lashes could pick up a stiff wind. With the way they make your eyes pop, I can see what caught you that hunky fella back in Texas, huh?" She pats my cheek as she speaks, looking me directly in the eyes with some mischief in hers.

I roll my eyes and groan, dropping my head into my hands to hide the embarrassment creeping onto my cheeks.

"Can we please pretend like that guy doesn't even exist? As much fun as the night was, I don't think I'm really in a place to discuss it. Especially not with you, Nana. No offense."

"Yes, offense! Macy, you're a grown ass woman now, and I've been one for longer than you've been alive. I'm not afraid of a little sex talk. Besides, since your Pop Pop passed, it's not like I'm getting any action anymore. I gotta live vicariously through my glamorous baby girl," she says, making my flaming cheeks even hotter with her candidness.

"Nana!" I exclaim, laughing at how she's managed to shock me within the first five minutes of my arrival.

"What? All women have an itch, Macy, and mine hasn't been scratched in quite some time. Humor me, will ya?"

I chuckle and wrap her in another hug.

"I've missed you, Nana."

She smacks a kiss onto the side of my head and says, "Missed you too, Ace. Now, where's my grandson at? He's got some hugs to make up for, too."

She heads around the other side of the truck to snuggle up to Chase, grabbing his cheeks as she does. My heart squeezes at their encounter, and I try not to feel guilt over the fact that my work also means that Chase doesn't make it home as often as we used to.

Shaking off the feelings for now, I make my way around to the bed of the truck and shudder at just how many bags are waiting to be unloaded. Unfortunately, there isn't a valet here, and I once again lament the downgrade in my current situation. I really thought I had packed light, knowing most of my Harper clothes probably wouldn't be the most appropriate for rural Minnesota, but seeing the four giant suitcases, I feel like maybe I overdid it. Well, at least I will be the best dressed filly at the hoedown.

"Macy, let Chase grab those suitcases. You and I have years worth of catching up to do. I want to hear all about your fancy shmancy life out in New York," Nana shouts back at me as she makes her way back up to the porch.

"It's California, Nana. Other side of the country."

Swinging the screen door open, she tosses over her shoulder, "Yes, well... that, too. I'm going to grab us some cookies and some lemonade, and we are going to chat on the porch, goddamn it. It's family time!"

I look over at where Chase is standing with his hands on

his hips, glaring at my extensive luggage collection, and give him a halfhearted shrug.

"You heard her, Ace. You've got this, right?"

I jog away before he can stop me and launch myself up the few steps of the porch, planting myself in the swing before crossing my legs and batting my eyelashes at him with mock innocence. Regardless of being back in the role of Macy White, I still revel in the star treatment. He gives a disgruntled sound but grabs the suitcases two at a time and hauls them inside.

Nana makes her way back out to the porch and plops down beside me with her promised goodies.

"Now, what's it like being America's 'Pop Party Princess' anyway?" she asks, running one of her hands down my black tresses. I settle back into the routine of letting my Nana mother me like she always used to when I was a kid. It might not be Malibu, but it is nice to feel genuine familial love again. Maybe this won't be so bad.

A few hours later, after thoroughly interrogating me on all things stardom, Nana excused herself to go to bed, despite the fact that it was only eight o'clock on a Friday night. I suppose, though, at 72 years old, there probably isn't a whole lot to stay up for. Chase and I are watching some old sitcom on the TV in the living room, but I'm not really paying much attention. I have been texting Stella off and on to give her an update on things back home, but she's off to some party tonight before she makes her way here later in the month. To say I am jealous of her right now is a massive understatement, and I am practically crawling out of my skin to jump on the first flight out of here to surprise her.

"Jesus Christ, Ace. What are you being so dramatic about

over there?" Chase abruptly asks me, startling me out of my wallowing. I must have been sighing out loud instead of just in my head if he noticed.

"I'm bored, Chase! Stella's going out to some celebrity's 'getting out of rehab' party tonight, and all I'm doing is sitting here watching you watch something on TV. I wasn't meant to be stuck inside on a Friday night. Don't you know that people can literally die from lack of movement? If we sit here any longer, that could be us."

Chase just looks over at me with a deadpan face that tells me he isn't buying into my antics. I drop my head to the back of the sofa and give a loud groan that I hope doesn't wake Nana. Though, if we are being honest, that woman could sleep through a hurricane, so I probably don't need to be that worried.

Rolling my head to the left to look at Chase again, I say, "Come on, Ace! Just because you're sentencing me to a forced Harper Bloom detox doesn't mean that we have to stay cooped up in this old house all day, every day. We should go hit the bars and see if there's some karaoke or something. Maybe even an old flame of yours still in town that can cure the insufferable dry spell you're in that's causing you to be such an ass."

By this point, I have made my way over to the armchair and am legitimately pleading up at him from the floor, while he pointedly ignores me. But if the clench of his jaw and the slight twitch to his mouth is any indication, I am starting to wear him down a little bit. Progress.

"Puh-lease Chase! Please! Please, please, please, please, please, please, pl–"

"Fuck! Fine. You are seriously the most annoying person on the planet sometimes," he says while pushing my head away from him, a slight chuckle in his voice. "But I'm laying down some ground rules before we go. No alcohol. No karaoke. Just a quick walk downtown, maybe pop into a bar to say hey to anyone we might recognize, and then straight home. I'm serious, Macy. You're going to stay drier than the Sahara the entire time we are here. Got it?"

I give him a mock salute, "Yes, sir. I'm going to go get ready. Thank you, Chase! Love you!"

With that, I jump up, smack a kiss to the side of his head, and head out of the living room in a rush.

"Yeah, yeah, I love you, too, menace. Remember, nothing too over the top. We are trying to not stand out, remember? Mild Macy tonight."

"Don't worry Chase. I got this. I can *totally* rock a muted vibe tonight. Wait and see." I bound up the stairs already formulating the perfect outfit. Despite what I said to Chase, he doesn't get to dictate my fashion choices, and while I may not have every Gucci dress or Louboutin shoe I own with me on this trip, I definitely never leave the house feeling less than spectacular. I will wear what I want to wear, and Chase can deal with it.

I am bound and determined to have some fun in this small ass town even if it kills me.

brody

LUSTING AFTER MY HIGH SCHOOL BEST FRIEND'S NOT-SO-LITTLE SISTER

"ALRIGHT, boss, I'm headed out. Need anything else before I go?" Josie asks from the doorway into my office. She looks stunning with her brown skin glowing and her dark hair cascading over one shoulder. Once upon a time, I was totally into Josie and would have gladly tried something with her, but that ship sailed a long time ago. As soon as we started working together, it became clear that we make really great work friends, and that's all we'll ever be. But I can appreciate knowing someday, she's going to make some guy really happy. I can't exactly say the same for me in the women department, but who knows? Maybe there is the perfect one out there that will be able to handle my attitude and obvious parent issues.

"Nah, I'm good. Have a good weekend," I say in a monotone voice before turning back to my computer and the fifty thousand tabs I have open on potential stories, all of which amount to a huge pile of nothing. I don't even notice her leave as I keep scrolling trying to find *something* worthy of a front page spread. I keep coming up with nothing, so I give up, slamming my laptop closed and leaning back in my chair with my hands on the back of my neck and my eyes on the ceiling.

For the life of me, I can't stop thinking about that fucking story about Harper Goddamn Bloom and her fucking husky voice that has kept me semi-hard for three days now. Not only that, but that story is still all any of the news outlets can talk about, especially after she pulled her disappearing act, canceling a month's worth of shows and fleeing to God only knows where. I would absolutely kill to know where she went and hold a story like that in my hands.

Unfortunately for me, I doubt she's running around Oaken, Minnesota as we speak. If fucking only.

Deciding I can't do anything about the lack of interesting things happening here, I grab my stuff and head out of the office, locking up behind me as I go. I almost head straight for my car to go home for the night but decide I am in serious need of a drink to numb my irritation before I can focus on trying to relax and getting a few hours of sleep. I make a pit stop to drop my things in the car, and head back to the bar, Main Street Tavern, across the street from my office.

As I head up to the giant, rectangular bar in the center of the room to order my rum and coke, I notice a copper headed woman chatting up a man I haven't seen in years. Not since he moved away to Los Angeles to pursue a booming career in PR for some of the hottest celebrities. I do a good job of telling myself I'm only mildly envious of his success.

"Holy shit. Chase White? Is that you?" I step up to him, distracting him from whoever he was talking to. The redhead glares at me for interrupting them, but I ignore her. She huffs an irritated sound and then turns to walk away. I almost feel bad for fucking up Chase's game, but my need to see how my high school buddy is doing overrides the guilt.

"Oh my God, Brody McAllister? Man, I haven't seen you in ages! Not since... when was that, anyway?" He asks, standing up to give me the classic bro hug.

"Not since high school graduation, but who's counting?" I say, attempting to hide my bitterness at him not having kept in touch since then. We used to be best buddies after all, but I suppose he's not the only one to blame. A phone goes two ways, and after a few months of being out of high school, we just kind of stopped texting altogether. I'd be lying if I said it didn't sting a little, but I guess that's how life goes sometimes.

I shake off my lingering feelings of hurt and focus on just being happy to see him again. We had some of the best times in high school, and I can admit that sometimes I relive them on days when the stress gets to be too much.

"What brings you back? Aren't you supposed to be out rubbing elbows with the people we townies only ever see on magazine covers?" I ask him, genuinely curious about his life that is significantly more successful than my own. I try not to sound too envious, but I'm sure I come off sounding like a jealous asshole. I almost care enough to add in a smile to soften the sarcasm. Almost.

He laughs, and punches my shoulder. "Yeah, well. Sometimes you gotta get back to your roots to remember what all of the hard work was for in the first place. Plus, spending some quality time with Nana and Macy hasn't been easy to come by since Pop Pop passed. So back to Minnesota it is, even if it means I run into your cranky ass while I'm here."

At hearing his little sister's name, a memory of a mouthy 13 year old with black hair and pigtails bouncing around the living room singing into a hairbrush flashes through my brain. When I used to hang out with Chase, Macy would usually insert herself into whatever we were doing, no matter if we wanted her there or not. Always the little shadow that we both pretended to hate but secretly loved dragging along on our shenanigans. When she wasn't chasing us around, she would be doing crazy shit and getting herself into trouble. I wonder if she ever grew out of that phase. Despite being closer to her brother than I was to her, I had always thought of Macy as a little sister of sorts. The annoying kind, but a little sister nonetheless.

"Yeah, man, I'm sorry about your grandpa. My parents passed not too long ago, too, so I get how tough it can be. How are Macy and your Nana doing?" I surprise myself by bringing up my parents, but I guess it's hard to forget the comfort of having a true friend, even though years have passed.

"Well Nana seems to be doing okay, though being alone in that giant house probably isn't great for her mental health. She plays bridge with the old ladies from her knitting club, so she's got that going for her," he adds with a laugh. "And as for Macy, well... see for yourself." He nods behind me with an eye roll and points the neck of his IPA in the same direction. I detect frustration in his tone but don't think much of it, chalking it up to the brother-sister dynamic. Those two were always on each other's last nerve, despite the deep love they clearly have for one another.

Turning to follow his motion, I blink in confusion. I didn't realize that it was karaoke night, so I just figured the music I was hearing was the old jukebox that the bar owner, Max, has had since the dawn of time. Man, was I wrong, and holy shit can this girl sing. She's currently belting out an incredible rendition of "Fantasy" by Mariah Carey and hitting every note like she is the 90s star herself. It's enough to make my jaw drop, just a little.

I am distracted so much by the sound of her voice, that it takes a good minute of her bopping around the small stage for me to take note of her appearance.

Jesus. Fucking. Christ.

She's my favorite wet dream come to life. Black hair that cascades in waves down her back, glowing green eyes, plump rosy lips, bronzed legs that seem to glow in the bar light, an ass that makes me wonder what it might look like bent over my desk, paired nicely with tits that would fit perfectly in my hands as I rail into her. Everything about this girl has me immediately turned on, and I'm sure I'm sporting a semi just watching her. It's damn near enough to make me forget about the terrible mood I was in earlier, especially as she sways and sashays across the stage like she was made to be up there in tiny black sequin shorts, a backless halter crop top, and gold wedge high heels. I'm surprised she can be as graceful as she is in those fucking things.

After a good thirty seconds of gawking at her, I force myself to remember who she is. The little sister of my high school best friend, and definitely not someone who I should be lusting after, especially since I don't even know her anymore.

Trying to distract myself from thoughts of Macy, I look away from the stage and glance around the room. I'm definitely not the only one who has noticed her performance, as I take note of just how many of the dudes in here are adjusting their junk as they hoot and holler at her. I feel a rush of anger burn its way through my blood, and clench my jaw, grabbing for my drink to stop myself from going all rage monster on these guys over a chick I have zero claim over. She's not mine, so I have no right to be as frustrated as I am. I turn away, putting my back to the stage, and tip my now empty glass to the bartender, indicating I am in need of a refill.

The song ends, and Chase spins in his chair to watch his little sister, who really doesn't seem to be so little anymore to me, bounce her way toward us with a huge grin on her face. As she passes by me to sit on Chase's other side, I am forced to inhale her lavender and vaguely spicy scent that is laced with an undercurrent of tequila. It's distracting, and I'm immediately irritated by her for stirring emotions within me when I came here to numb myself.

"Ah, that was fun! Don't you think so, Ace? I mean, *I* had fun, that's for sure!" She chirps in a bubbly yet husky voice that sounds vaguely familiar to me. It makes me wonder how she might sound in other settings, namely with her hands tied to my headboard. Jesus.

I force myself to relive her more irritating moments from my childhood, just to remind myself again that she is not someone I should be interested in.

Chase clenches his jaw in irritation before responding, "Damn it, Macy. I thought you promised me you were going to keep it low key tonight? That was the furthest thing from low key." The growl in his tone immediately sparks my interest, but I don't get involved, just allowing them to work through whatever issues they have going on right now.

Macy huffs at Chase, "Ugh, you're *such* a buzz kill. Isn't he a buzz kill, beautiful blue-eyed stranger?" She asks, turning toward me, like I'm going to play the role of knight in shining armor tonight and save her from her brother's scrutiny. Too bad for her, knight in shining armor isn't really my speciality.

"Sorry, Songbird, I'm with Chase. You were definitely drawing all kinds of attention up there. If your goal was to be incognito, I'd say you failed," I say to her, unintentionally reminding myself of all the attention she was garnering from the other men in this bar and pissing myself off all over again. I clench my hand on my drink at the reminder.

She gives me an incredulous look like she simply can't believe I wouldn't take her side before quipping at me, "Oh yeah? Some of that attention you're speaking about couldn't have been yours, could it?" She bats her eyelashes at me, leaning over the bar in just the right way that I get a nice flash of her cleavage. My eyes dip for a moment, which she definitely notices, as her eyes flash with heat. I glare at her, pursing my lips before looking away and shrugging my shoulders noncommittally.

Chase cuts into our weird moment, reminding me that he's still here.

"Okay, well, I'm not going to stick around and babysit you if you're determined to cause a scene tonight. Macy, get yourself home. Brody? Keep an eye on her for me, would you?" Chase asks, not bothering to wait for an answer, as he gets up and walks toward the redhead he was chatting with earlier, whispering something in her ear that has her dragging him out of the bar.

Good for him, I guess. Though, I'm still slightly irritated that he leaves me here to babysit Macy.

I look over at her, and she is grinning that stunning smile that stirs a memory within me while simultaneously reminding my dick that it's interested in getting more acquainted with that mouth in other ways. Fucking hell.

She bites her lip, running her eyes down my frame before flicking them back up to mine and saying, "Looks like you're stuck taking care of me tonight, handsome. Think you can handle it?"

I'm not sure if she's intentionally trying to piss me off by not recognizing me, or if it's the tequila blocking her memory. Either way, it pisses me off that my mind has already run through a million and one memories of our childhood while she is acting like she hasn't even met me.

Letting go of my frustration for now, I lean in toward her. I am near enough now to notice her pupils dilate at my proximity, and I lick my lips before whispering in her ear. "Do your worst, Macy."

Feeling her fidget in her seat as my words register in her tequila addled mind, I think I've won this round of verbal sparring. She, however, is not to be outdone and turns her head to whisper right back in mine. "Be careful what you wish for, Brody."

Damn if I don't love the sound of my name rolling out of her lips in that husky tone, and it takes me a minute to register that she used my name. So, either she does remember who I am and is trying to get under my skin, or the conversation I was having with her brother is catching up to her.

She lightly nips at my earlobe, sending a jolt of adrenaline through me, and then she jumps off of her chair, shouting to some guys at the end of the bar. "Who wants to do a shot-ski with me!?"

She downs the rest of her drink in one go, drawing my attention to her throat as she swallows, and then beams a smug grin at me as all of the guys eagerly agree to do shots with her. She bounces over to them, leaving me in the dust.

Jesus fucking Christ, what did I get myself into with this one?

macy

WHEN YOUR CHILDHOOD CRUSH
IS EVEN HOTTER THAN YOU
REMEMBER

ONE OF THE serious downsides of being a tequila girl is the massive hangover that happens the next day. I mean, would it kill the makers of Patrón to add some pain killers in the recipe for those of us who like to down shots like they're water and dance on tables?

I groan as I roll over in my bed to grab the bottle of ibuprofen that is a staple on my nightstand for mornings such as these. Squeezing my eyes closed, I sweep my hand across the top of the table, and accidentally knock over a picture frame in my pursuit of sweet relief. Which would be fine, except that I don't have a picture frame on my nightstand in my Nana's house. My eyes fly open, and I immediately realize this is definitely *not* my old room, and this for sure isn't my matching pajama set. Where the fuck am I?

I only get about five seconds to take in my surroundings before I am viciously attacked by an energetic ball of fur.

"What the fuck?" I exclaim, shooting my hands up to block my face from the slobbering kisses I am currently receiving from said furball. After a few seconds, I start laughing.

"Okay, okay. That's enough," I chuckle out, trying to push

the little dog off of my chest to sit more on my lap. It continues trying to lap at my face, but I manage to keep it down long enough to take in that it's a corgi. I pet along its head, making a note of the name on their collar.

"Allie," I say, reading the tag. "Well, Allie. Do you happen to have any idea where I am?"

She just looks at me, her tongue lagging out, and I shake my head with a laugh.

Just as I am about to set Allie aside and stand up to figure out where I am, a towering frame walks into the bedroom carrying two cups of coffee. A very, very shirtless towering frame of six pack muscles and that perfect V shape that just begs for me to run my tongue along it. I momentarily forget my hangover as I take in the man in front of me.

"Oh good, you're finally awake. I was worried your snoring was going to bring the walls down in my apartment," Brody fucking McAllister quips in my direction. "I see you've met Allie. You're lucky she didn't kick you out of the bed, as that is usually where she sleeps."

He places one of the coffee cups on the table next to the bed, and then reaches over to grab my chin before gently closing my mouth for me. It must have been hanging open in shock like I'm a cartoon character with her tongue lagging out.

"Careful. Wouldn't want you to start drooling. Again," he smirks, nodding at the so-not-sexy drool spot on the pillow I was using, and then moves to sit in the armchair five feet away. My face burns with embarrassment. Definitely not because my childhood crush is in the same room as me without his shirt on. No, it's definitely just because of the drool thing.

Collecting myself with a shake of my head, I muster as much of my chill as I can before speaking.

"For your information, I don't snore. And furthermore... what am I even doing here? We didn't... you know, did we?" I ask, not really sure if I want the answer to be a yes or a no. Definitely a no, right? Though if we did, I imagine I would still be feeling it this morning if the bulge in his sweatpants is any indication.

He lifts one of his eyebrows at me and takes a sip of his coffee before giving me a look that I can't even begin to decipher. He stares at me with whatever that look is for so long I start to wonder if I may have asked the question in my head instead of out loud. Either that, or this guy has "broody asshole" down to a T.

Just as I open my mouth to ask him again, he breaks his apparent vow of silence.

"I'm trying not to be offended here, Songbird. Not only am I not the kind of guy to take advantage of a woman who clearly wouldn't have been able to give me a coherent yes, much less scream my name the way I'd like, but if we had fucked, I can assure you, there's no way you'd forget." He leans back in his chair, his words dripping with confidence.

Damn, if that doesn't immediately make my non-existent panties wet. Say what you want about him being arrogant, but there's something about a man being totally confident in not just his appearance but in his ability to satisfy a woman that gets me all sorts of hot and bothered.

Despite knowing that about myself, I simply can't help but snark back at him. "Are you sure about that? Maybe you're not as unforgettable as you think you are."

Narrowing his eyes slightly, he lifts himself out of his chair, stalking toward me before caging me in toward the headboard and leaning down to look me directly in the eye. "Maybe if you're lucky, Songbird, you'll find out just how unforgettable I can be."

I take a sharp inhale, breathing in his whiskey and cedar scent, flicking my eyes to his full mouth. His eyes do the same before he abruptly moves back to his chair and I nearly topple forward. I hadn't realized I was unconsciously leaning in. Damn him.

"Okay, fine. So we didn't rattle the headboard last night. Do you mind explaining to me exactly how I managed to end up in your bed, and wearing one of your old high school t-shirts?" I look down at myself, noticing the faded logo from our high school on the front.

The smirk that graces his face has me simultaneously wanting to smack the fuck out of him and wipe it off of his mouth with a hot and heavy make out session. I thought I had it bad in high school, but the teenage version of Brody McAllister has nothing on the adult version.

"Oh, you mean you don't remember doing shot-skis with your brother's old baseball bros and then climbing up on the bar to sing a rendition of 'I Will Always Love You' before kissing the floor?"

I groan and drop my head into my hands, noticing the slight twinge of pain on the right side of my head where I must have hit it on something when I fell.

As if that wasn't bad enough, Brody continues speaking.

"No? How about when you tried to grab the sheriff's radio and make a public service announcement about how boring this town is? You're lucky he didn't slap you in handcuffs right there for the comments alone."

It wouldn't be the first time I've managed to snag a ride in a cop car, but Brody doesn't need to know about my Harper shenanigans right now.

I open my mouth to say something, but he cuts me off as he continues talking.

"Or how about the, really terrible I might add, strip tease you insisted I needed in order to show me your gratitude for taking you somewhere safe? Or how about –"

"Stop! Okay, I get it. I was out of control last night." I hold up both of my hands to get him to stop. Clearly, I didn't follow Chase's rules of "No Fun Times for Macy." In fact, I'm surprised that he let it get that far in the first place.

Confused, I ask, "What happened to Chase?"

"Ah, Mr. Straight-Laced himself ended up leaving early with someone. I didn't get to see who it was, but he left you in my care so he could no doubt bore the mystery girl with missionary sex all night long. Lucky me," he adds with an eye roll and heavy sarcasm. Rude.

"Wow, so chivalrous of you," I deadpan in his direction. I mean, Jesus. I know I probably wasn't on my best behavior last night, but does he have to act like it was such a freaking task taking care of me? I am a goddamn delight, even three sheets to the wind. This guy really needs to lighten up.

Letting the conversation die for a minute, I grab the coffee he brought me earlier off of the bedside table and take a look around his bedroom. His room is rather messy, considering he seems to be a minimalist kind of guy, at least judging by his attitude and general crankiness. I don't remember him being such a grump when he was hanging with my brother, but then again I was a 13 year old kid last time they spent any significant time together.

His room lacks any touch of character, with very minimal furniture to help make it feel homey. There's a bookshelf with a few random classics and some sports biographies, a couple of photos hanging on the wall, an armchair that the grump is still occupying, and clothes and old newspapers scattered every-where. The blanket I am currently still covered in to hide my naked legs is gray, and soft in the way that blankets get when they've been used and washed for a few years. Despite the clutter everywhere, it smells just like Brody, which is making me all kinds of crazy.

Trying to distract myself from getting too turned on thinking about how good he smells and how he is still staring at me with those damn blue eyes, I nod at the piles of papers on the floor. "What's with all of the old papers? You know there is something called the internet now, right?"

He narrows his eyes at me, pursuing his lips before answering. "Not that it's any of your damn business, but I happen to have inherited *The Oaken Tribune* from my parents when they died."

He doesn't offer more information, clearly upset by the turn in conversation. I battle with indecision on whether or not to press him to explain further. I don't remember hearing that his parents died, so this hits me as a bit of a shock. I guess if anyone would know how jaded a person can get when their parents unexpectedly pass, it should be me. Maybe I should cut him some slack on his attitude.

"Brody, I'm so sorry. I didn't know. What happened?" I say, softer, so he understands how sorry I am for his loss.

"Car accident. Six months ago," he answers tersely, lowering his eyes to the floor, effectively making it known that he doesn't want to talk about it anymore. I guess I probably wouldn't either with someone who's basically a stranger.

"And the paper? Do you run it by yourself?"

"Again, none of your business," he barks, flicking his eye back to me with a glare. I've definitely hit a nerve with my line of questioning, but he doesn't have to be such a prick about it. I immediately jump on the defense and narrow my gaze at him.

"Fine, I was just trying to make this morning a little less awkward since I'm sitting here, sans panties in your t-shirt after a night I barely remember half of. But if you want to be a total dick and make it weird for both of us, I will just go," I snark, before whipping the blanket off of myself and throwing myself off the bed in a flurry.

Hopefully he doesn't get a flash of my cooch as I throw my legs over the side. Locating my shorts on the floor, I crouch down and slip them on as quickly as possible so he can't get much of a glimpse of my naked ass. With his bad fucking attitude, he doesn't deserve to see the golden, round perfection of it anyway. Asshole.

As I continue huffing and puffing around his room, trying to gather all of my things that I clearly tossed every which way in my attempt to "show my gratitude" as he said before, he grabs me by the bicep, sending an unexpected zing through me. Despite the thrill of his hand on me, I snap my head around to glare at him.

"Stop, okay? I'm sorry. I didn't mean to be so short, I'm just... the paper is a sore subject for me right now," he says so earnestly, I almost believe him.

"Why?"

Huffing a sardonic laugh, he says, "Because, as you said before, there is such a thing as the internet, and people just aren't interested in buying papers anymore. Add in the fact that I used to be a sports journalist, now turned editor that can't find a good story to save my fucking life, and the legacy my parents spent years building is dying a slow and painful death right alongside them."

My eyes search his, noticing the pain he's trying to hide under layers of bitterness. He clearly wants the paper to be successful to honor his parents and their years of hard work, and the fact that he's struggling is hurting him. My heart clenches and hurts for him, not knowing exactly what to say to comfort him at this moment.

He's still holding my arm, so I reach up and squeeze his hand in what I hope is a reassuring way. He glances down at our locked hands before flicking his eyes up to meet mine again. The anger in his gaze shifts to one of confusion before becoming something I can't quite decipher. It's intense in a way I can't describe, and I feel our shared irritation change to something much more charged.

I flick my eyes down to his lips, noting how close we are to one another. My body flushes with awareness, and I return my gaze to his. He lifts his hand to cup my cheek, glancing at my lips as he does. I close my eyes, savoring the simple touch on my skin.

Abruptly, he clears his throat and steps away, removing his hand. I nearly stumble forward, realizing that I was leaning into his touch.

My eyes fly open to see him running one of the hands that was just caressing my cheek on the back of his neck awkwardly. He clears his throat again and shakes his head slightly before speaking.

"You don't want to hear my sob story. I need to get going anyway. Need a ride back to your place?" He grabs a shirt off of the pile of clothes closest to him and throws it on before heading out of his bedroom into the living room, leaving me behind to deal with his weird mood swing. What the hell was that?

I shake my head quickly, grabbing the last of my things and trying to let some of the heat of our interaction fade away. I'm confused and slightly embarrassed that our conversation moved so swiftly from irritation to sexually tense. Couple that with his obvious rejection, and I am feeling some serious whiplash.

"Um... yeah. I guess a ride would be nice."

I'm not sure what else to say, so I awkwardly follow him out of his house and out to his car. I spend the majority of the ride brooding over our strange moment. He *wanted* to kiss me, I know he did. Did my breath smell bad or something? What stopped him?

I am so stuck in my own head about it, I don't even notice when we make it back to Nana's place until he pointedly clears his throat, shaking me out of my reverie. I look over to him with a quick shake of my head, and ask, "What?"

"We're here," he says with a nod at the windshield toward the house.

"Ah, I guess I must have dozed off," I say trying to mask that I was really just in my own head over this guy. "Okay, well... see you around, I guess. Best of luck with the paper and all that. If you ever want to run some ideas, Chase would be a great resource, being a publicist and all. I know you guys haven't kept in touch much or anything, but he might have some ideas on ways to boost sales or maybe some stories you could look into."

"Thanks, but I don't need charity. I'll figure it out," he snaps at me with a huff. "Try not to hit the tequila so hard next time. I'm not really into babysitting drunk party girls."

I am taken aback by his rudeness, especially given our brief encounter into friendlier territory, and I feel a rush of anger flood through my body.

"Whatever, asshole. See you never." I hop out of the car and slam the door as I stomp toward the porch. I quickly glance back at him to notice him smirking before he throws it in reverse and speeds out of the driveway. God, what a prick.

Forcing myself to forget his moodiness for now, I head back inside and up to my room to freshen up before I'm able to accidentally run into Chase. I am too rattled to deal with his judgment right now.

Hopping in the shower, I do my damndest to think about anything other than that set of full lips, striking baby blue eyes, and bronzed abs. After about five minutes of trying to write a new song in my head and just ending up with a bunch of incoherent nonsense about a sexy, brooding asshole, I give up.

Apparently, my brain is choosing to only remember just how in love with Brody I was back then, despite how much of a dick he was to me today. Not only that, but my body doesn't care either way and is focused solely on just how sexy he has become as a man.

Setting my logic aside for the moment, I give into my body's desire and remove the detachable shower head off of the wall. I switch it over from the waterfall to the power setting and run it over my shoulders and down my torso. I circle the water over my peaked nipples, groaning at the sensitivity. Spending some time there, I run my left fingertips down my stomach, toward the juncture of my hips, before circling my clit and letting out a quiet whimper.

Closing my eyes, I lean into the sensations and draw up the image of Brody's chiseled jawline and icy blue eyes. In my mind, he is the one running his tongue along my heaving breasts and sensitive nipples, as he adds pressure with his fingertips and slowly massages my throbbing clit. I bring the shower head down my body, picturing Brody kissing his way down toward my pussy.

One of Brody's fingers moves to dip inside of me while his tongue takes its place on my clit. He curls his finger inward and up hitting my G spot. I continue this fantasy, increasing the pace, adding two more fingers like I know Brody would, stretching and massaging my inner walls while the pressure from the water hits my clit in just the right way.

I continue building and building, as the sensation curls through my lower belly in the most delicious way. I explode, suddenly, tossing my head up and back with his name on my lips.

Just as I do, my head cracks against the tile of the shower, and I let out a loud shriek. My feet slip out from under me, and I fall on my ass, still clutching the shower head to my body.

As I struggle to reconcile the high of my orgasm with the low of my fall and head injury, I hear a knock on the bathroom door.

"Macy, are you alright in there? I thought I heard you scream?" Nana asks on the other side of the door, concern lacing her voice.

It takes me a minute to compose myself, and I yell out a quick "I'm fine" before resting my head back on the floor of the shower in embarrassment. Thank God that's all she heard, since I'm still rocking some aftershocks from my orgasm. My fantasy is still playing in my head, and I can almost hear him whisper "songbird" in my ear as I come down.

Before I can fall into the fantasy again, I force myself to remember his earlier rejection and general assholery. It's enough to yank me back into the present and force myself up off of the floor.

Exiting the shower, I wipe down the mirror and stare at my reflection. I make peace with my past self and her crush and vow to keep my Brody fixation as a one time shower fantasy.

Besides, I probably won't see him again before I head back to Malibu. For some reason, though, the thought doesn't give me the relief I was hoping for, but I disregard the lingering pang of loss and move on with my day.

brody

TIME TO PUSSY UP

DESPITE THE DISTRACTION of events over the weekend, Monday rolls around too soon for my liking. I tap my pen in a rhythm against my notebook as Jackson, one of my junior employees, gives me a report on potential stories we could run in this week's Tuesday paper. So far, nothing of note has caught my attention, not that I'm surprised with how little happens around here. If I am being honest, not much has been able to capture my attention for long enough to make me forget about a certain dark-haired woman.

It's incredibly irrational for me to be so enamored with her already, but my brain can't seem to stop obsessing over our "moment" from Saturday morning. I barely even touched her, but my palm still feels like it's been shocked by an electrical wire from the small moment of contact.

My rational brain is trying to chalk it up to the ease that I felt with her when we were talking about my parents and the stress from the paper. I usually make it a point to never let my emotions get the better of me when I'm feeling particularly upset or stressed out. But when it comes to Macy White, there's just something about her that makes me want to open up and let her distract me from the never-ending frustration that is my current predicament. Not only is she no longer the annoying little kid that I remember, but she's a full fledged woman who knows exactly who she is. The confidence she displayed at the bar followed her into the next morning, and I'll be damned if it isn't intoxicating. Combine all of that with how sexy she is, and my body is basically begging to lose myself in her until I forget everything except the sound of her voice and the feel of her skin on mine.

God, how she would scream as I whispered filthy secrets in her ear, my front to her back and my hand winding underneath her arm to wrap around her throat. My cock throbs painfully at the thought, and I almost palm myself through my dark wash jeans before someone clears their throat loudly.

I jolt out of my thoughts that are definitely not on the story of a long lost family dog being found two towns over, and my eyes meet Josie's across the table as she raises one of her eyebrows in question. I mentally shake myself for getting lost in the fantasy of all of the dirty things I want to do with Macy. I mouth a "sorry" to Josie, and do my best to give my full attention back to the meeting. No more letting my high school best friend's little sister distract me. At least for now.

After another grueling thirty minutes, and settling on another boring story that won't capture anybody's attention long enough to actually spend money on a paper, I grab my stack of papers and head back toward my office. Josie follows me out of the conference room, her lingering disapproval for my lack of attentiveness in the meeting palpable. As we both get to my office, she follows me in and closes the door behind her.

"What the hell was that? You looked like a total zombie in there. Care to explain what the fuck is going on with you today?" She asks me with sincere concern in her voice.

"I'm fine, Josie. Just stressed. None of these stories are good enough to turn us around. We need to find something truly interesting, or our sales are going to continue to plummet," I huff as I plop down at my desk and lean back with my head resting on the back of my chair. "I just don't know where we are going to find a story to break that will get people buying papers again."

Josie purses her lips, knowing the predicament we are all in. Not only will I fail if I can't pick up the pieces, but everyone else who depends on me will be left with nowhere to go. I'm truly fucked if I can't figure this out.

After a couple seconds of pondering, she snaps her fingers quickly and points at me before shouting emphatically, "I got it! What about Chase White?"

Creasing my eyebrows in confusion, I wait for her to elaborate. When she doesn't, I ask, "What about him?"

"Well isn't he a hot shot Hollywood publicist or something fancy like that? I saw him in town this weekend. Maybe he has a good idea or a lead on something that we could pursue. Or maybe he has some crazy connections that we could leverage to get someone interesting to come to town. Who is he working with these days anyway?"

I rub my forehead in annoyance, "How should I know, Josie? I ran into him for all of five minutes on Friday and didn't get his entire life story or anything. We aren't exactly buddy-buddy anymore."

God, what is it about the fucking White family coming back to town that's throwing me off? As if I didn't have enough to worry about, now my secretary wants me to actively seek out one of its members, which might just bring me back into the presence of a certain someone I'm trying not to lust over at the moment. The second I think of her, my earlier fantasy comes roaring back to life, and I have to lean forward in my chair to hide the interest my cock is currently showing. Goddamn it.

"And what would you have me do anyway? Just show up on his Nana's front doorstep and beg him to help me?" I ask, sarcasm lacing every word. I even add a sardonic laugh to emphasize just how insane I find the prospect.

"Yes," she says matter of factly, as if I am the one being ridiculous. "It's the eleventh hour, Brody. We don't really have the luxury of waiting for the perfect story to drop from the sky. We need to look at using our connections wherever we can get them, and right now, Chase White might be your only option. You guys used to be buddies in high school, and I am not above abusing that nostalgia so I can keep my fucking job. So I suggest you pussy up and get your ass over there to shmooze something out of him before I quit and leave you without a secretary."

I heave a heavy sigh, and roll my eyes. She's right, I don't really have many options right now. Chase White and his connections might be my only option to save the paper, and subsequently, everybody else's jobs alongside my own.

"Fine. I will reach out and see if he has any ideas. But don't be surprised if he can't help us. Small town papers probably aren't his specialty," I say, knowing full well I don't actually know a damn thing about what Chase does for work now. Who knows, maybe he really does have a passion for small town papers.

Honestly, I'm not as opposed to the idea of reaching out to him as I am making it seem to Josie, but I am doing my best to avoid Macy. I've been doing fine at avoiding my feelings until she blew into town, and I am not ready to confront just how quickly she's able to knock down my defenses.

"Good, so that's settled. So we're good? Head in the game and all that?" She questions, no doubt remembering my earlier space out session. I love her, but Josie never lets anything go and she never forgets, much to my chagrin.

"Yeah. We're good. I will touch base with Chase later this afternoon and see what he has to say."

She claps her hands together, and stands to leave. "Great. I expect to hear that you talked to Chase by the end of the week and that we have at least one lead going for us. Let me know if you need anything, otherwise I am heading on my break," Josie says before she heads out of my office. As usual, she doesn't give me the chance to argue with her any further, leaving me with my roiling thoughts.

I take a deep breath to center myself before making a game plan to find Chase. I'm confident he won't have much of an idea on how to help me, but for everyone else's sake, I have to try. My best bet is at his Nana's house, so I gather my things and head out the door.

* * *

Making my way up the winding dirt driveway for the second time in forty-eight hours, I am reminded of the last time I was coming this way and the raven-haired beauty that was sitting in my passenger seat. God, she smelled so fucking good, and I couldn't help but clench my fists on the steering wheel to keep from reaching over and running my palm along her inner thigh. I can almost feel how smooth she would have been.

What is it about her that drives me so crazy? It's not like I really know anything about her or her life as an adult. The girl I remember was still a kid, so I am baffled at how quickly I am becoming attached to the idea of knowing her as a woman.

I bark out a groan of frustration, knowing I once again lost myself in the fantasy of her. Good thing my general lack of social skills and grumpy attitude will likely keep her far away from me. If I'm lucky, she won't even be here when I knock on the door, and I can keep my distance. Honestly, I can't decide if that's truly something I want or not.

Putting my car in park, I hop out and make my way up to the wrap-around porch, and knock on the front door. I hear a distinctly feminine voice shout down that they are coming, along with footsteps jogging down a set of creaky steps, before the door whips open and Macy's bright green eyes and flushed cheeks come face to face with me.

She looks at me with a spark of surprise in her eyes before her eyebrows pull together in confusion. Clearly, she wasn't expecting to see me again so soon after our last encounter. That makes two of us, and I clench my jaw to keep my emotions in check.

"Brody? What are you doing here? Did I forget something?" She crosses her arms, giving me a once over. The expression is so cute and reminds me of just how much fire this woman harbors inside of her. It's intoxicating, and I find myself being drawn into her again.

I clear my throat, and try to focus on her words, rather than the feelings she is stirring within me.

"Actually, I'm here to see Chase. Is he around?"

"Chase? Um... no. He went into town to get some groceries. What do you need to see him about?" She questions, sounding suspicious. God, she's just as irritating as she is sexy. She's clearly still annoyed over our last interaction, and it gives me a small amount of satisfaction to know that I can rattle her, even days later.

"What is it with you and asking questions that don't concern you?" I ask, more teasing in my tone than anything. While I can't deny that I am not much of a sharer, her questions don't bother me nearly as much as I let on. I simply enjoy getting under her skin. Call it payback for her digging her way under mine.

As expected, she doesn't appreciate my attitude, and closes her mouth with a click of her teeth, narrowing her eyes at me. "Always a pleasure, asshole." She moves to close the door in my face, but I catch it before it can slam.

"Wait. I just need to talk to him okay? I need his help." She pauses in her pursuit to shut me out, and confusion crosses her beautiful features once more. Every expression she gives me only serves to make her even more irresistible and makes me want to learn all of the different ways I can get her to show me each one.

"His help? With what?"

Sighing and giving into her demands, I say, "I wanted to pick his brain about a few things regarding the paper. Leads and things like that."

Macy looks me up and down, glaring at me in silence. Feeling her eyes touch every part of my body, I fidget, a little bit uncomfortable and more than slightly aroused to be under her scrutiny. She drags her gaze back to mine, before seeming to make a decision.

"Fine. He should be back soon. You can wait outside," she says quickly, shooting me a conniving smile.

"Wait a minute –" I try to say, but before I can even get it fully out of my mouth, she slams the door in my face and locks it for good measure, as if I would burst through the door regardless. To be honest, I probably would. If only to bend her over my knee and give her the spanking she deserves.

I bang my fist angrily against the door. "Fuck!" I shout before taking a seat on the porch swing.

Frustrating, provocative, fucking woman.

macy

SOMEBODY NEEDS MORE
IMPROMPTU DANCE PARTIES IN
HIS LIFE

BOUNCING on the balls of my feet away from the front door, I beam with a huge grin on my face hearing Brody scream and bang his fist against the door. Annoying him might just be more entertaining than it is annoying Chase. I can just picture the way Brody's muscles must bulge out of his t-shirt as he clenches his fists and the way the small muscles in his jaw flex as he grinds his teeth in irritation. God, such a sexy mental picture that makes. I may have to pull that one out in the shower later.

I make my way into the farmhouse style kitchen and blast some pop music, so I can dance around while I make myself some lunch. I'll be damned if I let Mr. Broody outside mess with my good vibes today. Plus, I'm sure he can hear the music, and it brings me that much more joy to know he probably is a pop music hater. I wonder if he ever listens to my music. Somehow, I doubt it.

Just as I'm belting out the chorus of "Break Free" by Ariana Grande, the music abruptly cuts out of the bluetooth speaker with an incoming phone call, leaving me singing alone in the silence before I cut myself off with a curse. Seeing who it is, I roll my eyes and huff out a sigh of irritation before answering.

"Damn it, Ace. You should know not to call a girl when she's vibing to the queen of pop herself!" I chirp at him in lieu of an actual greeting. He really should have just texted. Who calls these days anyway?

"The queen of pop? Isn't that supposed to be you?" He snarks back at me through the phone. I can practically hear the smirk in his tone, and I roll my eyes despite the fact that he can't see it.

"Well, duh, but I'm supposed to be keeping a low profile, remember? And I don't think belting the lyrics to my own songs while Brody McAllister sits on our front porch is exactly what you had in mind. Unless you're cool with me moving ahead with my plan to kiss the whole secret identity thing goodbye?" I add in, hopefully. I haven't had a ton of time to chat with him about this plan, and he's been pretty adamant that he doesn't want me to make any decisions until we head back to Malibu.

Ignoring my question altogether, he speaks again, "Brody? Why is he sitting on our front porch?" I hear shuffling through the line as he speaks, which leads me to believe he's pressing the phone against his shoulder.

"He's actually here to see you. Something about wanting to ask for your help finding some leads on potential stories or something. I didn't get all of the details before I locked him out to wait for you to get home. Speaking of which, when *will* you be back? I'm not sure when he'll decide to go all caveman on our front door again, but I'm sure the clock is ticking on that particular time bomb."

"Well that's what I called to tell you, actually," He says. "Nana needs me to drive her to Rochester for something, so I won't be back for a while. Can you just help him with whatever he wants? You probably have just as much knowledge as me when it comes to ideas on stories he could run or other publicity things. You are the center of half of the stories these days after all." His tone tells me he's still irritated with that tidbit of information. Clearly he's not over the whole sex tape nonsense. So boring.

"So you *are* giving me permission to feed him the story of Harper Bloom secretly being a Minnesota Country Bumpkin?"

"Don't start with me, Ace. You know that's not what I said, and we are *not* talking about that right now. You're supposed to be focusing on being normal while we are home, not worrying about when you'll be free to get back to stardom," He snaps at me through the phone. I can hear Nana in the background telling him to calm down before he drives them off of the road in his anger. He takes a deep breath before speaking again. "Just point him in the direction of some people who might be good resources for him. And definitely don't tell him anything about Harper Bloom."

"God, fine! You know, I see why you two were such good friends in high school. The two of you could probably build a skyscraper with the amount of poles you have up your asses at any given moment. I'll see you back at home later. If you happen to make a pit stop at the liquor store, Nana's out of tequila. Okaythanksiloveyoubyeeeee!" I rush out in a sing-songy voice and hang up on him before he can yell at me again. I really am getting sick of the men around here thinking they can rain on my parade all the time. Frankly, they all could use a little more spice in their lives, and I am just giving enough to take on that particular charity case.

I turn the music back on, turning the volume up for good measure and start my dance routine over again.

Impromptu dance parties in the kitchen are always a good idea when you need a good serotonin boost. That's just a fact.

After my conversation with Chase, I need all of the happy vibes I can get. I love him, but sometimes I wish he would take off his publicist hat and just be my brother for a little while. I miss when we would just mess around and get into trouble together.

I finish making myself a sandwich, plus an extra one for Brody, and head out to the porch with a grin on my face.

Brody is sitting on the rickety old swing, leaning forward with his elbows on his knees and scrolling on his phone. The soft squeal of the old chains hums as he moves it slightly back and forth. His head snaps over toward me as I swing the door open. And holy fuck, it should be actually illegal for a man to be this fucking hot. My body flushes, and my cheerful grin drops as his eyes meet mine. His jaw is clenching in a way that reminds me he's probably still pissed at me, but it does absolutely nothing to detract from his sex appeal. In fact, it's having the opposite effect, and my breathing becomes shallow seeing the muscles quiver along his jawline. I wonder what it would be like to press my lips against it.

His irritation turns smug as he notices the effect he's having on me. He blinks, breaking our stare off, and slowly allows his gaze to travel down my frame, lingering on my bare legs in the shorts I'm wearing. I can almost feel where his eyes touch as he drags his gaze back up mine, his pupils blown out, enhancing just how fuckable this man is. He puts up a good fight, but I can tell that he's just as attracted to me as I am to him. The problem is, I don't know if we will ever get passed arguing long enough to do anything about it.

I blow out a breath, shaking my head to break the tension and make my way over to him offering him the extra sandwich I made. He takes it, but doesn't move to take a bite yet, setting the plate next to him on the swing.

"So Chase isn't going to be back for a while, but he thought

I might be able to help you, since I've been around him when he does his PR stuff."

Not a total lie, but not exactly the truth either.

"You? Nah, I don't think so. I figured it was a long shot anyway, so tell Chase I said hey, and I will see him next time he's in town."

He moves to stand, but I quickly grab his forearm, much like he did to me when I tried to storm out of his place over the weekend. He glances down at my hand that doesn't even come near wrapping all the way around his arm. I mean, seriously, how can a person's arm even have that many muscles? I am a major sucker for arm porn, and this guy could probably make a living from just one photo.

Before I can get lost in my thoughts again, I roll my eyes and speak, "Oh come on, Brody. I know just as much as Chase does. I have been in the middle of every one of his PR disasters." Definitely not a lie. "So I know a thing or two about how to break a story and which ones are truly interesting. Could you please just set aside your piss-poor attitude for a minute and let me help you?"

He locks eyes with mine again, doing absolutely nothing to tame my libido, and he bites his bottom lip in contemplation. Goddamn it, what I wouldn't give to feel those teeth biting into mine instead. My panties must be absolutely soaked at this point. That is, if I was wearing any. I take a deep breath and remind myself that he's been nothing but a total dick to me since he saw me at the bar.

After a minute of contemplation, he finally speaks. "Fine. But if I have to hang out with your peppy attitude, I'm gonna need a drink." He steps out of my reach, forcing me to drop my hand, which is probably a good thing because one more minute of direct skin to skin contact, and I would probably have jumped his bones right there on the porch. I try not to be disappointed by the loss, even as my hand buzzes with the memory of his skin on mine.

"Ah, that I can do. Though, we don't have any tequila," I say with a pout. I move to head into the house, and he follows me into the kitchen. "I hope you're good with beer."

I reach into the fridge, bending so my ass is sticking straight in the air. I might be teasing him, just a little. I hear him inhale behind me, and smirk to myself as I grab a bottle of beer to hand to him. As I do, our fingers brush, and that spark of heat runs through me again.

I clear my throat, and move to the other side of the kitchen island from where he is sitting and lean forward. His eyes drop to my cleavage, and he quickly closes them, taking a sip of his beer.

I beam at him with a huge grin on my face. "So... where should we start?"

brody

PLAY NICE, BRODY

I'M ABSOLUTELY CONVINCED this woman is trying to kill me. As if her ass in the air in those tiny shorts wasn't bad enough, she's still beaming at me with a grin only a person who un-ironically refers to themselves as an optimist could manage. She leans against the countertop, showcasing her perfectly bronzed tits, and it's just about enough to snap my last thread of composure. They seem to have some sort of shimmer to them, as if she applied something that is meant to draw a person's eyes down. It's working, and I find myself increasingly frustrated, both sexually and emotionally. I'm supposed to be tamping down this attraction, but for some reason, she's doing her best to entice it out of me.

Palming the beer she gave me earlier hard enough that I am sure it will shatter, I close my eyes and take a sip before refocusing them on her beautiful face. Not totally sure that it's any less distracting than her body, as I realize for the first time that she's wearing a vibrant shade of lipstick that catches my attention. I can't help but conjure up all of the ways in which I could go about smearing that color. Goddamn it.

It takes me a minute to collect my thoughts enough to

realize she asked me a question. She's looking at me expectantly, with those wide green eyes that hold enough mischief to inform me that she knows exactly the path my thoughts have taken. Well, maybe not exactly, but paired with the smirk her lips have curved into, she has a pretty good idea. Is she thinking the same thing?

Clearing my throat, I take another sip of my beer before I address her question. "Where do we start? Aren't you the one that basically told me you knew just as much as Chase? You should be the one starting this conversation, songbird. Not me." My voice is a bit huskier than I would have liked, dulling the irritation I was trying to portray. Damn it. What is it about this woman that has me leaning toward her instead of away? It's distracting, and it's definitely not going to get me anywhere closer to saving the paper.

She rolls her eyes anyway, making an annoyed sound in the back of her throat before responding. "Fine, no asking questions around you, I guess. And you're right. I may not be the publicist, but being around Chase has had its perks, especially when he's had to deal with crises of the pop star variety. I could probably spin a story about a priest falling in love with a stripper and make it sound like a fucking fairytale!" She laughs a little at her own joke, and damn it if the sound of her laughter doesn't do something weird to my stomach. I clench my jaw again to ground myself in the conversation instead of getting lost in how much this fucking woman gets to me.

Focus, Brody.

"Great," I say. "So let's use some of that knowledge in your pretty head and get a story going. No chance you've met any stars that just might happen to be wandering around Oaken while you've been rubbing elbows with the one percenters?" I say with as much sarcasm as I can muster. Something like shock flashes across her face briefly, before she realizes I am teasing her and sticks her tongue out at me, her eyes narrowing.

"Jesus, Macy, what are you? Five years old?" I reach out and grab onto her tongue before she can pull it back into her mouth. Instead of reacting in outrage like I figured she would, her eyes heat and she quickly nips at my fingers, forcing me to let go. I snap my hand back, my face heating unexpectedly. How is she able to always turn the fucking tables on me like that? Wicked woman. I'm honestly not even mad about the bite she just gave my finger. It stings slightly, so I bring it to my mouth to ease the pain. I can almost taste her on my skin.

She smirks, knowing she's flustered me again, and starts talking. "You know, Brody, I know you're being a total asshole, but you're also not wrong. I *do* get to rub elbows with some of the coolest celebrities, and that is exactly why you need me. So stop being a dick for two seconds and let's do some brainstorming. I might even be able to find one of my super famous Hollywood friends who could do some sort of an exclusive interview with your paper or something. If, and only if, you can manage to be nice to me for the rest of the night."

She flashes another one of those smiles that has started to burrow its way under my skin, and something in me fucking snaps.

I want her.

Despite knowing that she's my best friend's little sister. Despite the fact that we haven't gotten one shred of anything accomplished tonight. Despite the fact that I have given her absolutely no reason to like me.

I want her so intensely, it's rapidly becoming a need, and I'm not sure how much longer I can pretend like she doesn't affect me.

I find myself out of my chair and stalking toward her before I realize it. I know it's a bad idea, and that I should stay away from her. I know that she deserves more than the emotionally unavailable man I've become.

Even so, I need to feel her skin under my hands, and I need it now. She wants me to play nice? She's going to find out just how goddamn nice I can be.

macy

CAUGHT WITH HIS HAND UP MY SHIRT

HE PROWLS TOWARD ME, and I instinctively take a step back that places me with my back to the kitchen island and nowhere to go. He continues toward me with a predatory look in his eye, boxing me into the counter with his arms on both sides of me. Our chests are so close together that each of our heavy breaths brings the tips of my peaked nipples to brush against his pecs in the most delicious way. His eyes rake down my frame before they lock with my own, the heat between us nearly buckling my knees.

For several moments, we just stand there and stare at each other, neither one of us willing to make the first move. He's given me very little reason to believe he would ever make a move or that he even liked me, so I am surprised by his actions now. Though, I can't say that I am complaining.

He breaks the stalemate by smirking at me, and says, "You want me to be nice, songbird? I can be nice."

He reaches up with one hand to feather his fingertips along my collarbone, making me close my eyes and exhale a shaky breath.

"Though, I'm not sure it's fair for you to demand cordiality from me, when you're the one making it impossible for me to focus. Do you think you were playing nice when you bent over for me earlier, showing off that luscious ass of yours that is just begging to be slapped? Seems only fair that if you get to play dirty, then I get to play dirty, too."

My eyes fly open at his statement, and the lingering tension that has been brewing between us finally snaps. He takes the hand that was giving me such a gentle caress before and wraps it around the back of my head, drawing my lips to his in a demanding kiss. I let out a whimper as he nibbles on my lower lip until I open for him fully and finally, *finally*, get to taste this broody god of a man. He tastes even better than I imagined, like a strange combination of whiskey and spearmint gum that shouldn't make sense but somehow works because it's him.

He pulls away from my mouth and trails open-mouthed kisses along my jawline and down my neck, taking small bites along the way that are just strong enough to sting but not enough to break the skin. Absolutely, infuriatingly perfect. I pull at his hair roughly as he continues his descent, dropping his mouth to gently tug at my peaked nipples through my top. Thank God I'm not wearing a bra.

"Jesus, songbird, you drive me fucking crazy," he whispers along my skin. His hands are running along my sides, feeling the exposed skin underneath my tank top, driving me crazy. I want those hands so much lower than they are. He lifts his head and crashes his mouth down on mine again before his hands reach under my knees and lift me up onto the countertop in one swift motion, somehow managing not to break our savage kiss.

My God, this man can kiss. I feel nearly feral for him at this point, and in my frenzy, I reach down to tug his shirt off of him. Before I can manage to get it even halfway up, he gruffly grabs my wrist, pinning my hand on the counter. I make a sound of protest, but he quickly devours it with his mouth.

He pulls me gruffly to the edge of the counter top, and I can feel that he is just as affected by our sensual moment as I am. One of his hands roams up my arms and tangles in my hair as his tongue plunges in and explores my mouth. His other hand snakes its way up my shirt to caress just under my breast. I resist the urge to reach down and force his hands to cover my breasts entirely, and instead reach down to try removing his shirt again.

I'm almost successful in my endeavor when I hear a loud screech from behind me, causing me to break the kiss and whip my head around.

"Oh my God! Macy, what in God's name is your behind doing on my kitchen counter? And who the hell are you trying to ravage where I cook you breakfast?" Nana yells in a high pitched tone, covering her eyes. I quickly jump down from the counter and push Brody away from me, my face flaming with embarrassment at very nearly being caught in a much more compromising position.

"Nana! What are you doing here? I thought Chase said he was taking you to Rochester?"

I don't hear her answer as she rushes out of the kitchen muttering under her breath something about how she needed to stop home first and how deeply she regrets that choice. I bring my hands up to cover my mouth and glance over to Brody, mouthing an "oh my God" in his direction.

We both stare at each other for a second before bursting out laughing. And God, what I wouldn't give to hear that man laugh every day of my life.

macy

OH MAN, I'M IN TROUBLE

AFTER NANA LEAVES, and our giggles subside, we just kind of look at each other for a minute without saying anything. I expect it to be awkward, considering we were just playing some serious tonsil hockey a minute ago, but we seem to have successfully broken the tension between us. I don't think I will ever be able to kiss another man again without being reminded of his mouth, and that thought scares me a little bit.

I mean, I know we used to hang out sometimes when we were younger, and sure, my massive crush on him was borderline obsessive, but we barely know each other now. Is it weird that we went from basically strangers to making out on my kitchen counter within a few days?

A spark of insecurity floods through me, and I turn away from him to avoid the feelings. I make my way over to the fridge and grab out two beers this time. I hand him one and take note of his expression.

His already luscious lips are swollen from the intensity of our kiss, but that's not what draws me in. He looks actually content, which is something I haven't seen from him since I've been back in Oaken. It dissolves my fear that he would already have regrets about kissing me, and I beam at him.

He matches my smile, and I swear I die a little just looking at him. I think it's safe to say my childhood crush is back with a raging vengeance, and those baby blues and that five o'clock shadow are doing nothing to stop me from diving headfirst into it. Dismissing the rising feelings in my chest, I finally speak.

"So... that was fun. Not sure Nana would agree, but I had a good time," I add with a wink. "But we probably should do a little bit of brainstorming, don't you think?"

At the mention of the paper, I instantly see his demeanor shift, and he's all business again. I heave a sigh and roll my eyes. Seeing Brody smile and hearing his laugh was great while it lasted I suppose. The more sullen side of him was bound to come back sooner or later, and I guess sooner has won out.

"Look, I know talking about the paper turns you into a Sour Sally and everything—"

"It does *not* turn me into a Sour Sally."

I continue as if he didn't say anything. "But I really do want to help you. I'm stuck here for another few weeks, and I am already bored out of my mind. I could use a project, and this seems like a good use of my extensive knowledge and talents."

I give him a smug smile hoping to get one in return, but this time, all he does is give me an exasperated look. His jawline quivers as he is no doubt gritting his teeth together in frustration. I can't believe he still manages to have such perfectly pearly white teeth with all of the grinding those babies must have to endure.

His chest expands as he drags in a deep breath before slowly releasing it. I can tell he's fighting the urge to lash out at me, which he tends to do when he's stressed. I may not know everything about the adult version of Brody McAllister, but I do know that was always his way of dealing with things as a teenager, and it doesn't seem like much has changed since then in that regard.

To his credit, he succeeds in managing his emotions, and he addresses me with a much calmer tone than normal.

"You're right. So, where do we start? Clearly, I don't know a fucking thing about where to find a story. Where would you start if you were me?"

I expect his question to be riddled with sarcasm and irritation, but he seems more defeated than anything. It makes me feel sad that he doubts his ability this much, and I am actually looking forward to helping him out and boosting his confidence a little bit. He sees himself as a failure, and that won't stand with me. As if *the* Brody McAllister could ever fail at anything.

"Okay, first of all, what we are *not* going to do is allow you to feel sorry for yourself and make yourself feel bad. You're struggling right now, but that doesn't mean you can't do this."

He rolls his eyes at me, huffing out a sardonic sound, but I continue. "Secondly, I would start with seeing what connections you have to something you find intriguing or something that could potentially spark interest. For me, I'd probably reach out to some of my celebrity friends and see what they've got going on and if I could cover something exclusive."

His eyes snap up to mine. "Celebrity friends? You're telling me you are actually *friends* with some of the people that work with your brother?" His eyebrows raise as if he simply can't believe that anyone famous would want to be friends with Macy White. In a way, I guess he's right, since none of them have actually *met* Macy White, save for Stella.

"Of course I am," I toss at him indignantly, with my hands on my hips and a scowl on my face. "I am a fucking delight,

Brody. In fact, Harper Bloom and I are basically connected at the hip, so don't act like I'm some nobody!"

Shit, I wasn't actually intending on mentioning anything about Harper to him, but of course my obsessive need to be right gets in the way again. Chase would literally murder me if he knew I just casually brought her up essentially unprovoked. I hope Brody is one of those broody types that only listens to hardcore metal and doesn't even know who Harper Bloom is. Judging by the astonished look on his face, though, it's clear I am not going to be so lucky.

Trying to swerve the conversation away from any questions Brody might have about my relationship with Harper, aka myself, I rush out, "Moving on. What are some connections that you could work with? Any hot shots you know that are doing something really special in the area that you could cover?"

He rubs his large hands – that I am trying really hard not to remember were just running all over my skin not even twenty minutes ago – down his face and along the stubble on his jawline. That single motion is enough to cause my stomach to flutter. Him and his magic hands. I push the thought aside so I can focus on actually getting something accomplished today.

Just as I am getting a little bit lost in the thought of him again, Brody speaks. "Before I took over the whole thing, I was covering sports for the paper. My knowledge of important high to-dos is limited to the local high school football coach, and a guy who almost made it to minor league baseball. I suppose I could reach out to them, but other than that, I've got nothing." He takes a long pull from his beer, pulling my attention to the lips that were crushed against mine not too long ago.

Clearing my throat, I say, "Okay, well you're not the only one that works at the paper, right? Is there anyone else who might know someone?"

"My secretary, Josie, might know a few people. I guess I can ask her if she has any ideas." He chews over that thought for a minute, but then his head snaps up to me, his eyes going wide as he snaps his fingers and points at me. "Wait a damn minute. Weren't you just going on about how you have all of these crazy connections and fancy people in your social circle?"

I narrow my eyes suspiciously, hoping he's not going in the direction that I think he's going. "Um... yes?"

He gives me a look like it should be totally obvious the direction his thoughts are taking. "Well... what if you reached out to someone and set up something here in town that I could cover? Weren't you just saying your twin is the pop princess herself, Harper Bloom, or something like that?"

Damn it, he did catch that little slip up of mine. But honestly, isn't this what I wanted in the first place? To bring Macy out of hiding and totally embrace the double life thing? The secrets really are starting to get old. I consider just telling Brody straight out that the reason I know Harper is because I *am* her. To be honest, he probably wouldn't believe me, even if I did tell him, so what's the harm, right? Just as I open my mouth to blurt it out, Chase's voice runs through my head and stops me. He would be absolutely furious if I didn't run something like this by him.

Deciding I should definitely not make any rash decisions about telling Brody my little secret, I look him in the eye and say, "I said we were friends. Sort of. And where are you going with this anyway?"

"You're the one who told me to use my connections. So this is me using my connection, and that just happens to be you. Come on, Macy. It wouldn't kill you to reach out and see if she'd do some charity thing like kissing babies or some shit. I'm sure she needs the good publicity after pulling her little disappearing act post-sex tape debacle." He chuckles under his breath, shaking his head like it's just more celebrity nonsense he's discussing and not my actual life.

I turn away from him so he can't see the way my cheeks are burning with embarrassment. Even Brody fucking McAllister has heard of Harper's wild night with what's his name. I seriously won't ever live this one down. What would he think of me if he knew it was my voice on that audio clip? Did he recognize it when he kissed me just now? There's no way, right?

My heart starts racing and I am about to go into full panic mode. I am breathing rapidly, when all of a sudden I feel strong arms wrap around my middle from behind and a chin rest on my shoulder. I am surprised by his sudden affection, but I lean back once the brief shock wears off. Apparently, we are on the snuggling level now, and I can't say that I'm mad about it.

"Hey. Macy, it's okay. You don't have to call her, I just thought it was a good idea. I don't want you to feel like I am using you or that you owe me anything. We can come up with something else, alright?" I nod my head, not looking at him and just allowing myself to revel in the fact that his hands are on me again.

Just him being wrapped around me is enough to calm me down. He doesn't need to know that I am not at all worried about him using me and more worried about him hating me if he ever finds out who I really am. I hope he would be understanding, but honestly, I don't know enough about how he handles things now to know if he would be. He may brand me with a scarlet letter for all I know. One earth shattering make-out session isn't enough to know if he would judge me or not.

Sighing deeply, I turn in his arms and look up into his piercing eyes. My heart starts racing again for an entirely different reason, but I tamp that down and say, "I will talk to Chase about it later. Maybe he has some ideas or knows some people who might be willing to stop in town. Okay?"

He nods his head and gives me a quirky half smile that does weird things to my insides. God, I am slowly but surely becoming obsessed with this man, and that's a problem. I am so not here to get attached to anybody, and the first opportunity I get I am hopping on a plane back to Malibu. Unfortunately, or fortunately, depending on how you look at it, Brody McAllister has other ideas, and he lowers his lips to mine for a tender but demanding kiss. This is exactly the type of kiss that has the power to fuck up all of my plans to get back to the spotlight, and I hate him a little bit for it, even as I lean into his touch even more, tangling my tongue with his own.

After a minute into our make-out session, he pulls back and leans his forehead against mine and says softly, "Thanks for your help, songbird. I don't know how I can ever make it up to you."

"Hmm," I tap my lip and pretend to think for a moment. "I have a few ideas."

"Absolutely not," Chase cuts me off. He came home shortly after Brody left, and I immediately mentioned how I was trying to help him come up with ideas and how he happened to bring up that Harper Bloom could really use a positive PR moment. After having another panic attack about the possibility of Brody finding out who I am, I settled down enough to realize that, while it might not be the safest option, bringing Harper into town might not actually be the worst idea. Brody might really be onto something.

"You won't even think about it? Come on, Ace! This could actually be a really good thing if you'd stop being a dick about it for five seconds," I shout at him, exasperated that he won't even consider it. "I mean, really. Harper could do a story reading or something at the local library for six year olds, and it would look totally wholesome and definitely not sex-tape level scandalous. It's actually a good idea from a PR standpoint. Stella thinks so, too."

"Oh, I'm the one being a dick in this situation? You're way out of line, Macy. You're the one who almost blew the fucking secret we've been keeping for damn near a decade because a pair of shiny blue eyes got under your skin. I told you to give him some ideas! Not let him seduce your biggest secret out of you!" His eyes flash with fury and indignation at me. I may like to irritate him, but it's no fun when his serious glare levels you like that.

"And Stella thinking it's a good idea isn't exactly a selling point, considering she's your partner in crime in literally everything."

"I didn't tell him that I *am* Harper. I just sort of... insinuated that we might be close," I say innocently, with a shrug like it's no big deal. It is, objectively, kind of a big deal, and we both know it. Chase scoffs at me and rolls his eyes like I am being the biggest dumbass in the entire world.

"Ace, seriously, just think about it for a minute. It's not like I'm saying I should come right out and admit it to the world that Harper Bloom is actually Macy White in disguise. It would just be one day of doing something that would put Harper back in the good graces of the tabloids. You're the one who said that my record label isn't too pleased about my recent exploits. Maybe something like this could help ease their minds. Plus, then I can get back to being Harper and we can get back to our normal lives."

He looks at me again, with something like sorrow flashing across his features, before speaking. "Macy, this *is* your normal life. You've just forgotten that somewhere along the way between becoming a superstar and swinging from chandeliers."

It sounds like a joke when he says it like that, but he's being totally serious.

Shaking his head and sighing, he continues. "I will think about it, alright? Maybe there is a way for us to spin this to get Brody the help he needs and to boost the Harper Bloom image again."

I run up to him and give him a hug, squealing in his ear. "Thank you, Ace! I can't wait to tell Brody the good news!" I give him a swift kiss on the cheek and bounce away from him.

He recovers quickly. "Yeah, yeah, yeah. I'm the best big brother in the world. I know."

I just scoff at him and make my way toward the stairs.

"Macy?" Chase says quietly, and I turn around to look at him again.

"Yeah?"

"Do you maybe want to hang out tonight? We could start a fire in the back, roast some marshmallows, and just chill out or something. I feel like I haven't seen you much since we've been home, and I've..." He cuts off with a cough, looking slightly embarrassed, before finishing his sentence. "I've really missed you. I miss getting to just be your brother. Could we do that tonight?"

I rush right up to him and wrap him in a bear hug.

"I'd love that, Chase," I say, and smack another kiss on his head. "I've missed you, too."

brody

ACTIONS SPEAK LOUDER THAN WORDS

TWO DAYS LATER, and I still have the lingering taste of Macy's lips on my tongue. Kissing her felt like being bathed in sunshine, and though I should have exercised more restraint, I can't bring myself to regret it. I already miss the feel of her skin on my palms, and it's making it hard for me to focus on anything but her. I could lose myself in her every day and never be satisfied, even knowing I am a little pissed at her at the same time.

She said she would talk to Chase about some potential leads, and then there's nothing but radio silence for two days straight. I can't tell if I am more irritated that she isn't pulling through the way I need her to, or if I am just frustrated because I haven't seen her face or heard her voice in that amount of time. She's digging her way under my skin, and I'm honestly not sure that I care to stop her anymore. I'm amazed at how quickly this siren has enraptured me.

A knock at my office door pulls me from my thoughts, which is probably good. I'm sure Josie wouldn't want to walk in on me in a compromising position with my hand, lusting over a certain brunette and wondering when I might see her again.

"Hey! Just wanted to check in and see how those stories are coming along?" Josie asks, nodding toward the papers I should have been looking over instead of lingering over thoughts of Macy White and her husky voice murmuring my name as I make her fall apart.

I clear my throat, bringing myself to the room again. "Um, yeah. I have been looking through a few of them, and they seem good." I haven't been looking through them at all, but I am trying not to put her on high alert right away. Something tells me she doesn't believe my bullshit at this moment.

"Oh yeah? Which one do you think we should run tomorrow?" She asks, raising her brows at me, sensing my lie.

"How about this one?" I grab one of the papers off of the stack, and hand it over to her, not knowing at all which story I just handed over. Hopefully it's a good one.

Josie's brow wrinkles, and she gives me an incredulous look. "'Local woman claims marijuana made her hallucinate a 10 foot sphinx in her front yard?' This is the story you want to run on the front page?"

I sigh and toss my head back, looking at the ceiling. "Okay, fine. I don't have a fucking clue what any of these stories are, and it doesn't matter anyway because we just don't have anything interesting enough happening in this goddamn town worth covering. Not even a whiff of the school superintendent abusing his privileges to steal from the basketball concession stand or anything." I clench my jaw so hard I think I hear it pop. I should probably invest in a mouth guard to protect my teeth at this point.

"Well, what happened when you went to talk to Chase? You're telling me he didn't have a single good idea of something we could pursue?" Josie asks, skeptical that I would have met with him and still not had any leads worth writing about.

I snap my head back up and smack my hands down on my desk in frustration. "Chase wasn't home, so Macy was helping me out. She had a few ideas about inviting a famous person into town to do some charity or something, but I haven't heard from her in two fucking days, so I think it's safe to assume it was another dead end."

"Wow, if I had known you missed me so much, I would have come by a hell of a lot sooner!" A bubbly voice chirps from my doorway. I snap my head toward it and see my songbird swirling her way into my office.

God, she looks fucking delicious, and my heart instantly starts racing taking her in. Her waist-length black hair is tied back in a ponytail on the crown of her head, bouncing along with her as she walks toward me. What I wouldn't give to reach out and snatch her around the waist, quickly bend her over my desk, and wrap that damn pony around my fist as I pound into her from behind. I can even envision exactly how her pouty pink lips would part as she moans my name, giving herself over to me entirely. One kiss, and I can't help but want everything that she has to give.

My eyes meet hers, and she smirks as her eyes droop and fill with heat. I'm not sure what my face looks like right now, but if hers is any indication, I'm doing exactly nothing to hide where my thoughts have traveled. She must be thinking the same, and I feel the room fill with tension.

"Um, hello? Who are you?" Josie asks, turning Macy's attention away from me. I really do like Josie, but I hate her a little bit at this moment for breaking our moment.

"Oh, right! Sorry, I'm Macy White! What's your name?"

"Macy? Oh my God, I totally didn't realize that was you. It's Josie! We used to do choir together in high school, though I'm not surprised you don't remember me. You were always the star, that's for sure," Josie gushes at Macy, a slight laugh in her tone as she reminisces.

"Oh my god, Josie! Of course I remember you! You sat in the front row, four seats from the left, right? Your style was to die for. I could never forget you. How have you been?" Macy moves over to Josie and wraps her in an embrace. She's one of those people that makes best friends with every person she meets, and it's endearing to watch, despite my usually prickly demeanor. Something about her thaws my general anger for the world. However, right now, we have other things we need to be focusing on.

"Okay, okay. You two can catch up on your own damn time. Songbird, what are you doing here?" I ask Macy, redirecting her attention back where it belongs. On me.

She flashes a conspiratorial look with Josie, and they both fight smiles before she says anything.

"So I see you're back to being a prick again, huh? And I had hoped we had made it past that." She winks at me. I chew on my lower lip to stop myself from smirking at her insinuation and reminder of the last time we were together. I'm still annoyed with her for not reaching out for two days.

"Don't mind him. He's just pissy that you haven't stopped by to give him an update on some story leads. Which is why, I assume, you're here now?" Josie asks hopefully.

Macy squeals suddenly, clapping her hands together and jumping up and down excitedly.

"Eeeeek, yes! That is exactly why I am here! Brody, remember when I told you I am sort of, kind of friends with Harper Bloom?" Her eyes are shining as she looks at me, imploring me to remember, as if I could forget such a thing as her being besties with one of the most infamous party girls on the planet.

I eye her suspiciously, and respond, "Uh... yeah?"

"Well, after you took off the other day, I talked to Chase, and he agreed with me that she could use some positive PR right now!" She beams at me, as if her statement wasn't leaving out some crucial information, and I should just understand where she's going with this.

I wait to see if she will explain further, but when she doesn't I ask, "Okay... so what does that mean for me and the paper?"

"Don't you see? Harper's going to come! Here! And do a few publicity things, like we talked about. Maybe even a small concert in the park. Isn't that amazing? And because I'm freaking incredible, I will have Chase give you the inside scoop on everything for the paper," she says, her emerald eyes glittering with her elation over the news.

I am, however, stunned into silence.

I eye her warily and flick my gaze over to Josie. "Could you give us a minute?"

Her brows furrow once again, confused at my gruff tone and general lack of enthusiasm over the news.

"Uh, sure." She shakes her head, and then heads out of my office, with me on her heels. I lock the door behind her as she leaves and turn to face my songbird.

Noticing my look and domineering stance, her face falls, losing some of the spark she was just displaying. I bite back my disappointment, seeing it leave her eyes, but I know it will return tenfold soon. I stalk toward her, and she backs up, her lush ass bumping into my desk forcing her to stop.

When she realizes that she has nowhere else to go, she steels herself and lifts her chin in defiance, leveling me with a glare. "What is your problem, Brody? I thought you'd be excited about this, not bite my freaking head off! You asked for my help, and—"

I cut her off as I reach for her and quickly spin her around so that her ass is perfectly lined up against my cock. She gasps at the sudden change of position, and I run my hands up her arms in a featherlight touch, noticing how she shudders underneath my fingertips. I drag my nose up the column of her neck, breathing in her lavender scent that drives me wild. I feel her pulse quickening as my lips brush along her skin.

As I reach her ear, I growl, "You've got me wrong, Songbird. I'm not going to do any biting that you're not going to beg me for."

To punctuate my point, I gently tug on her earlobe, eliciting a hiss from her mouth that sends blood rushing straight for my already painfully hard cock. Feeling her supple ass rubbing against it is enough to drive me insane. I hear a small whimper come from the back of her throat as she feels just how hard I am behind her.

"I am going to show you just how excited I am. I'm going to brandish my gratitude all over this gorgeous body so many times you'll never be able to forget how indebted to you I am. But you have to promise me you'll be quiet. Wouldn't want Josie to hear you screaming for me and get the wrong idea, now would we? Think you can do that for me, songbird?" I flick my tongue out, and press open mouthed kisses along her neck, and bite down on the curve of her shoulder, causing her to moan, throwing her head back with closed eyes.

I reach back and swat at her backside. "Use your words, Macy. I can't show you if you don't tell me."

She nods enthusiastically before whispering, almost too quietly to be heard, "Yes. God, yes."

A smirk tugs at my lips. "That's my girl, but just to be sure..." I slap one of my hands over her mouth, and dive the other one into her pants, dragging a fingertip through her pussy. She shivers and drags in a shuddering breath through her nose. I feel her whimper against my hand, the vibration of her plea running straight down to my rock solid cock rubbing against her lush ass.

I run two of my fingers along her slit again, gathering the wetness there before dragging it up to her clit, pulling in a deep breath of my own feeling just how drenched she is for me.

"Jesus Christ, songbird. You're absolutely soaked. Is it all for me? Please, tell me it's all for me."

Unable to speak with my hand still firmly clamped over her mouth, she just nods along, with an accompanying moan that only I can hear. I have already gotten the affirmation I asked for, but just for good measure I draw my name with my fingers across her clit, silently marking her as mine. She frantically bucks her hips against my hand, seeking the exact pressure that will push her over the edge.

I run my nose along the column of her neck again, before whispering in her ear, "Ah, ah, ah. I know what you're trying to do, Macy, but it's not time yet. I haven't even begun to show you my appreciation, and you'll ruin all of my grand plans if you come too soon. You made me wait for you to come around. Now it's your turn to exercise some patience."

I remove my fingers from her clit, and run them along her pussy again, denying her the orgasm she was so determined to chase. She huffs a frustrated noise behind my hand, and I chuckle against her skin. I run my fingers along her a few more times as she continues to try and force them closer to where she wants them.

I bite along her neck again and finally give into what she wants as I plunge two of my fingers inside of her. Fuck, I almost forgot how tight she is, and with this angle and the desk between her and my hand, it's almost a struggle to fit both of them inside of her.

"Look at my good girl and her tight fucking pussy taking

my fingers so well. Just imagine how full you'll feel when you take my cock in it."

Her answering moan against my hand and the way she is pushing against my fingers is enough of a confirmation for me. Keeping my fingers inside of her, I bring my thumb up to continue drawing circles along her clit, hard enough to make her moan, but not enough to send her over the edge.

Her breathing has picked up even harder, sawing in and out of her nose at such a frantic pace, I am almost worried she's going to pass out. Both of her hands have a death grip on my desk so strong her knuckles are white as she rides my fingers chasing her orgasm.

"That's it, Macy. Ride my fucking fingers. God, baby, you feel so fucking good on my hand while your ass rubs against my dick. So fucking hard, and all for you."

Punctuating my point, I push against her ass, which causes her to ram against the edge of my desk and shoves my fingers even further inside of her. I feel her moan against my hand, almost loud enough that I am sure Josie will have heard, and her eyes roll to the back of her head. She's so fucking close, if the small flutters of her pussy on my fingers are any indication.

"Are you ready, songbird? Are you ready to come all over my hand, marking it so I'll feel you on my fingers for the next week?"

She mumbles something against my hand, and I take it as a yes, curling my fingers inside of her, hitting her G-spot at the same time I press my thumb down with enough pressure to push her over the edge.

Her pussy clamps down on my two fingers, and I hold her against me as she comes so hard her knees give out. She reaches her hands up to claw along my arms, leaving marks in their wake. I watch her with reverence, and I swear I've never seen anything so fucking beautiful in my life. Seeing her fall apart because of me might just be my new favorite pastime.

After a minute, I release my hand from her mouth, noting how my fingerprints linger on her skin for a moment. The possessive part of me likes knowing that I marked her in this way, if only temporarily. She breathes deeply through her open lips and leans against my desk as I draw my hand out of her pants and draw my fingers into my own mouth, savoring the taste of her yet again. Her pupils dilate slightly as she watches the motion of me sucking her pleasure from my fingertips.

"Delicious. Want a taste?" I offer it as a question, but I don't give her any time to protest before I spin her around, popping her ass onto my desk, and press my mouth to hers. She makes a surprised sound in the back of her throat, before immediately giving herself over to the kiss. Our tongues mingle together, and she moans at the taste of herself, making me impossibly harder for her.

I pull away from her after a few minutes and stare down at her, admiring just how stunning she is as she keeps her eyes closed with satisfaction written across her face. She opens her eyes slowly, and I smirk down at her.

She smiles back at me and gives me a quick peck on the lips before hopping off of the desk, bringing our chests together again. She reaches her hand up and pats me on the chest and offers me a cheeky "you're welcome" before sidling out from between me and the desk.

I huff out a breath, turning to see her plop herself down on the sofa I keep in my office.

"Now, ready to make a plan for what we do next?" She says with a wink.

I chuckle and nod my head. Yeah, I'm ready to make a plan alright. And every single of them involves making her mine.

macy

THE BEST LAID PLANS

GODDAMN, my heart is still racing after accepting Brody's "thank you gift." I will have to make it a point to do more nice things for him if that's the way I get rewarded. I thought his kisses were explosive, but being fucked by his fingers? I swear, they should be given an award and plated in gold or something equally as deserving.

Interrupting my thoughts, Brody clears his throat, recapturing my attention. I shake my head vigorously and blink a few times before looking up at him. He's still sporting a cocky smirk on his beautiful face as if he knows exactly where my thoughts just wandered. I glance down briefly to see the outline of his still hard cock pressing against the seam of his black jeans. I really should repay the favor.

Just as I am about to drop to my knees and take care of him, he snaps his fingers in my face.

"Focus, Macy. I can practically feel your gaze roving over my dick, and as much as I can't wait until you make good on those dirty thoughts running through your pretty head, now's not the time. You were just about to tell me your grand plans to bring Harper Bloom to Oaken, were you not?" His surly, no-

nonsense, attitude is back, and I fight the urge to roll my eyes at him. Okay, I fail at fighting the urge and actually follow through, eliciting a clench of that gorgeous jawline from him.

"You know, you might be worse than Chase with your one-track mind. And he really takes the cake for laser focus." He shoots me a sardonic look. "But fine, you're right. I should probably give you the scoop on what Chase thinks Harper will agree to."

He takes a seat at his desk and pulls open his laptop, I assume to take some notes. His seriousness in this moment takes me by surprise, especially given that he just had his fingers knuckle deep in my pussy not even five minutes ago.

"Okay, so like I said before, you were totally right. Harper definitely could use some good press these days, especially after that sex tape got leaked. But really, why is it even an issue for people? Everybody has sex, right? Half the shit in her songs is about it. Why does society have such a huge issue with women who are confident sexually? It's such bullshit!"

"Macy!" Brody snaps at me with a clap of his large hands that reverberates around the room. I jump from the sudden noise. "Focus, please. While I agree with you, we really don't have the time to discuss your stance on sex-positivity right now."

I take a deep breath. I hadn't even realized that I was getting myself worked up over it again. Clearly, I'm still not over how every major news outlet is ripping me apart for this, in my opinion, minor slip up. I am probably lucky that Brody stopped me when he did since I was spiraling into dropping the Harper Bloom sized bomb on him. If it weren't for Chase, I think I would just say "fuck it" and tell him right now.

I square my shoulders, refocusing myself in the conversation, and continue. "I'm just saying, women have sex, and we enjoy it, too. Most of the time, anyway. I wish people would stop slut shaming her. However, I realize that's not the reality at the moment, so she needs to do something to get her some better press. Chase even mentioned that she could get dropped from her label if she doesn't clean it up a bit."

"Damn, I can't believe Chase really just goes around sharing that information with you. Doesn't he have to worry about client/employee confidentiality or something?" Brody questions me, still taking notes on his computer.

Shit, he's right. Chase definitely *wouldn't* share that with just anybody, and I may have revealed more than I intended with that little slip up. For a second time, I consider just telling him, and letting the chips fall where they may.

I shrug like it's no big deal. "Well, I kind of work for Harper, too, so I guess he didn't really think anything of it since we are all so close." The lie rolls easily off of my tongue, and I feel my stomach knot with guilt. I don't want to lie to him, but it's a necessary evil at this point.

"I thought you were just friends with her? You work for Harper, too?" He raises his eyes to look at me. Fuck me, I need to stop giving away information like this. All of these little white lies are going to get me in trouble. I drop my gaze to the floor and shrug again.

"I'm kind of her stylist. I don't like to publicize it much, but that's besides the point. Weren't you the one who said we shouldn't get distracted? Let's get back to the plan."

This time, he's the one who rolls his eyes at me, and thankfully flicks his gaze back down to his computer, letting it go for the moment.

"So, Chase and I were thinking that for Harper to get some really good PR again, she could do a reading for some kids at the elementary school and do a meet and greet with them. Then, maybe do a small benefit concert and donate all of the profits to a local charity. And, of course, you'd get the exclusive on the story and all of that jazz. We'd have to pull Chase in to really discuss all of the details, but for preliminary plans, I think it's a good start. Harper has already agreed, so it's just hammering everything out at this point!"

He doesn't say anything, as he keeps typing on his laptop. After a few minutes, he finishes whatever he was typing, and closes the laptop to look at me. His gaze drops down my frame again, heating slowly before he draws his eye back up to my own. He really needs to stop looking at me like that if we are ever going to make these plans a reality.

"So, what do you think? Will it work?" I press after another minute of him just staring at me.

He taps his fingers on his desk and runs a hand over his jawline before answering. "I have a few logistics questions I'd like to talk to Chase about, but all in all, I think it sounds like a good place to start. Bringing a major celebrity to our little corner of the world will be pretty challenging though, don't you think? How do we go about making sure that my paper really gets the inside scoop? I can't have anyone getting the drop on us, or it won't boost sales of the paper like I need it to."

"Like I said, we need to talk to Chase about it and figure all of it out, but I'm sure we can write up a contract that will work for you for an interview or something. We really want to help you out, Brody, so we will make something work. I promise. I don't want you going all pessimist on this yet. Just be excited!" I beam at him and bat my eyelashes with my best "pretty please" face on.

He looks like he still wants to fight me on some of the logistics, as he runs his tongue over his front teeth, before nodding his head.

"You're right, I am happy this seems like it's going to work out." He opens his laptop again, and does some scrolling quickly before turning the screen toward me. He has a summer calendar pulled up with a few key dates marked on it. "See this week? This is the week of our town festival. It's about two and a half months away."

He's pointing to a week in the middle of August, way past when Chase and I had agreed I could go back to Malibu. I flick my gaze up to him, questioningly.

"Okay?" I ask warily, drawing out the end of the word to emphasize that I am not quite following his line of thinking.

"So, this would be the perfect weekend to host a concert, as most people are in town to celebrate. We could make Harper's events part of the week leading up to the concert, and publicize all of it through the paper. She'd have to agree to be here for the entire week, but I think the extra excitement around the festival could be mutually beneficial for her and the paper. Seeing her buzzing around a small town will humble her."

I purse my lips and consider what he is saying. It makes sense from a PR standpoint, but that's two more months that I don't get to go back to my life. That's two more months of hiding out while the tabloids speculate about where Harper is. That's two more months of, well... being just Macy White, and I'm not sure that's something I want right now. Is it?

I must show the indecision on my face because after a minute, Brody speaks up again. "Do you think that will be a problem? I figured the great Harper Bloom and her team would want an extra couple of months to figure everything out, but if not, we can make something else work."

I hate the tone of trepidation in his tone, as if he's doubting himself and the idea that he came up with. So, instead of voicing my hesitation, I say, "No, you're right. It's a big deal whipping together an impromptu concert. I will talk to Chase about it, but I'm sure he will agree."

He shoots me one of his oh so rare grins, and says, "Cool. I will start looking at my calendar and get something on the books for Chase and I to chat." He goes back to his laptop, and I chew on my lower lip, contemplating what I just agreed to.

I know Chase said that the hiatus from my life as Harper would be a good thing for me, but did he really mean for us to spend an entire summer away from the spotlight? I agreed to a few weeks at most until I could step back on the stage. I haven't spent this much time at home since I was a child. I don't even know who Macy White is anymore, and I'm not sure I want to be her without Harper, anyway. I love my life as a pop star, and to not be one for three whole months feels like I've lost a piece of myself.

But, looking over at Brody, I feel myself getting slightly excited about the possibility of us spending more time together. I didn't come here intending to find a fling, but I'm not sorry that we have hit it off. It's only been a couple of days, but it's been a long time since I've really felt a connection with someone in the way that I feel it with him. It's almost like my childhood self is fulfilling yet another one of her dreams.

"Penny for your thoughts, songbird."

Brody's smooth baritone voice cuts through my reverie that is rapidly turning into panic.

"Um… just thinking about what I'm going to have for dinner later. Speaking of, I should go, you know… talk to Chase or whatever. Um… bye." I quickly jump up from the sofa and try to rush through the door. Just as I'm unlocking it to pull it open, Brody's hand slams it shut, and I feel his chest press against my back.

"Before you go…" he rumbles in my ear before quickly spinning me around and pinning me to the door, crashing his mouth down on mine. I let out a surprised whimper, before sinking into the kiss. He smiles against my lips and seizes the opportunity to run his tongue along my own, turning the kiss feral. Just as I am about to reach up to remove his t-shirt, he pulls back, leaving me stunned. I flutter my eyes open to find him just a centimeter from me still, his baby blues twinkling with mischief.

"Couldn't let you leave without giving you a proper goodbye. Let me know if you're up for dessert later." He smirks at me with a wink and drops one last quick kiss to my lips before returning to his desk and leaving me turned on all over again.

I shake my head to clear it of the lust he just instilled and mutter a breathy goodbye before turning to leave his office. I wave goodbye to Josie before running out of the building and jumping into Chase's truck that he may or may not have let me borrow without his knowledge. I take a deep breath and press my fingers on my mouth. Brody Fucking McAllister and his sinful lips and magic fingers will definitely be starring in my wet dreams later tonight if my drenched panties are any indication.

Before my mind can sink even further down that line of thinking, I throw the truck into drive and head back toward Nana's house. I should probably break the news to Chase that we will be here for another couple of months. Something tells me he's probably not going to be that upset by it, and I will be stuck playing the role of regular old Macy White for an indefinite amount of time. Somehow, the idea of that isn't as upsetting as I thought it would be.

macy

LEOPOLD FUCKING REGIS...AGAIN

"FUCK ME! Are you serious right now?" I hear a shout from Chase's room in Nana's house.

"What the hell are you yelling about, Ace?" I ask bolting into the room, feeling both confused and disheveled at his sudden outburst. "I was trying to take a nap, you know. You and your dramatics are making that kind of hard. What is going on?"

"Have you seen this?"

He spins the laptop toward me and jumps out of the chair allowing me to read the latest Harper Bloom scandal that just hit *The Regis Report* website. Apparently, my silence following the postponing of my tour, accompanied by my lack of sightings by the public eye have yielded some scrutiny and speculation. Namely, Leopold Fucking Regis prattling on in some online article about how I could potentially be pregnant with the personal trainer's baby. Either that, or my recent antics indicate a drug addiction that has landed me in rehab.

"This is what you're so worked up about? We knew there would be some backlash when we decided to extend our stay here, Ace. They're grasping at straws trying to drum up a story.

Nothing I haven't dealt with before, right?" I dismiss him, closing the laptop as if this isn't a big deal. Regis is just trying to drum up a story out of nothing, and it's not like I haven't had crazy rumors running around about me before.

After leaving Brody's office, I came home to talk to Chase about our idea for the town festival. Not surprisingly, he agreed that spending some extra time away from stardom would do me some good and give us some time to really spin the story in our favor while also helping Brody and his paper. I tried to convince him that I could head back to Malibu and make some appearances in the interim, but he said it would be better to "keep myself grounded" here instead.

So, it appears that I am staying here for the next couple of months. At least I have a certain broody editor to keep me company in the meantime. Unfortunately, the decision to stay has clearly caused the tabloids to start sniffing out for a story. Super.

"You're supposed to be laying low right now, Macy. Not making people curious about where you actually are. The sex tape was bad enough, but these rumors? The label isn't going to be happy about this, and I am the one who's going to have smooth everything over. Goddamn it!" He runs his fingers through his hair, pulling on it in frustration.

I try to contain my sigh at Chase's antics. For someone who's constantly dealing with crises, he struggles to maintain his composure in the face of a new issue. After he gets the initial frustration out of the way, he'll calm down and will be much easier to talk to.

Unfortunately for him, and me, my patience with this conversation is running thin at the moment.

"Jesus, the fucking label again? Those pricks seriously need to lighten up. It's getting kind of old having to dim myself to manage their antiquated ways of looking at the world. Maybe we should be looking for another label if they're going to get their panties in a twist over some false rumors," I shout, unable to keep my disdain for the label execs at bay any longer.

I thought when we signed with them, they knew who they were signing on, but apparently not. I'm not so sure I want to be part of a company that would believe rumors so easily and threaten to drop me as quickly as this. Fucking assholes.

Chase shoots me a look and drops his hands to his sides. He heads out of the room, and I follow him down the stairs to the kitchen, where he grabs two beers out of the fridge and passes one to me. Normally, I'd turn him down in favor of something just a bit stronger, but I accept, knowing that he is waving the metaphorical white flag at me right now.

After downing half of his beer in one go, he places it down on the counter and runs one hand along his jawline before addressing me again.

"Okay, here's what we are going to do. We can't let these rumors go unanswered for the next two months or they will keep getting out of hand. So, I will reach out to Regis and see if we can set up a very brief interview with him over Skype."

"But–" I try to protest, but he cuts me off with a hand in the air before continuing. I glare at him, scrunching my face up so he understands just how annoying it is when he does that.

"Not negotiable, Ace. I had hoped that we could take the next few weeks to really be here with family, but clearly, we are going to have to make some sort of a statement. I will prepare everything, get you some quotes out there, and then we can focus on prepping for the festival. Deal?"

I groan out loud and throw my head back in annoyance.

"Does it seriously have to be with that limp-dick fuckwit? I hate that guy! All he's ever done is write trash stories about me that make me look like a brainless party girl. Why doesn't he ever write stories like that about the men in music? I know for a fact that half of the dudes I've done collaborations with have done way worse things than me."

"I'm not disagreeing with you, Macy. He's a sexist fuck who gets all of his money by making women feel like shit, and I would rather eat my own shoe than work with him," Chase says. "But the reality is, he's the one that's shouting the loudest right now, so we need to shut him the fuck up or he's just going to keep spewing his bullshit."

I make a face, knowing that Chase is right. Leaving Regis unanswered has never gone well for me, and I know I have to make some sort of a statement to get him to back the fuck off.

"Fine. But I'm not happy about it, and I refuse to be nice to that fuck. He doesn't deserve even a smile from Harper Goddamn Bloom," I say, caving to his logic.

He claps his hands together, definitively, and says, "So, it's settled then. We make our statement, and then move the fuck on."

I lean forward against the kitchen counter, dropping my forehead onto its cool surface with a frustrated sigh. Chase better spin a good fucking story, or I am going to shave his hair off in his sleep and plaster the photos on his hinge profile for good measure.

"Don't worry, Ace. I promise to only let him ask you a few questions about your recent sex-capades and tabletop dancing days."

He smirks at me, coming around the island to wrap me up in a headlock and giving me a noogie with his fist. Prick.

"Stop it! You're going to fuck up my hair! I'm serious, Chase, you have no idea how long this effortless wavy look took me to achieve!" I scold him, trying to get out of his grasp but chuckle along with him, lightening the mood.

Just as I am about to punch him in the side to get him to let me go, the doorbell rings. He releases me, and I attempt to smooth my hair back into place.

"I'll go see who that is," he says before exiting the kitchen, leaving me to continue fixing my now heavily knotted locks. How he managed to do this much damage in such a short period of time is truly a skill. One that I am going to pay him back for later.

"Brody! What's up, man? Can I grab you a beer?" I hear Chase say from the other room, and I freeze with my fingers still in my dark hair. Of course he would show up while I am rocking post-nap and post-brotherly harassment hair.

I mutter a curse under my breath, and try to sneak back upstairs before he can see me, but unfortunately, I'm not so fortunate. As I rush out of the room, I smack straight into his rock solid chest. He wraps his huge hands around my biceps, saving me from what would have surely been an embarrassing face plant at his feet.

I flick my eyes up to meet ocean blue irises that hold a hint of humor in them as he smirks down at me, well and truly knocking whatever breath I had left in my lungs straight out. I don't think I will ever get over how this man affects me, and I can't say that I want to.

"Careful, songbird," he says before lowering his mouth to whisper in my ear. "While I'd love to see you on your knees, I hardly think now's the time."

I shiver at his words and release a shuddering breath as his teeth graze my earlobe before he releases me, tossing a lopsided grin my way and heading into the kitchen to take Chase up on his offer of a beer from earlier. Great, now not only is my hair a mess, but my panties are too.

I shake my head and huff out a breath to clear my thoughts, following him into the kitchen. I admit, I spend an extra couple of seconds while his back is turned to check out his sculpted ass. Seriously, you could bounce a quarter off of that thing, and I feel my pussy clench just thinking of how it would look from behind as he pounds–

"Alright, ready to talk some details?" The sound of Chase's voice halts my less than holy thoughts and forces me to remember the fact that Brody came over here for a reason other than turning me on. Unfortunately.

No worries. Once we get this out of the way, I can make good on my nasty thoughts and work on repaying my mounting sexual debt.

The thought has me smiling, and Brody looks at me quizzically before he turns back to Chase and they start making plans. In the meantime, I start making plans of my own.

brody

LET'S GET DIRTY

I AM DOING my damndest to focus on the conversation with Chase, but fuck, is it hard with Macy stealing heated glances at me every two minutes. This girl is begging for a repeat of our last encounter, and I'd be lying if I said I wasn't waiting for this to wrap up so I can make good on that glimpse of mischief in her eyes.

"So far we have dinner with the mayor, a reading at the elementary school, and the concert. Does that sound right?" Chase types away on his laptop, writing down everything we've been chatting about for the last half an hour.

We only have a couple of months to make all of this happen, so we have had to scale down some of the more grand ideas I had brewing in my head. Add in the fact that Harper will only be here for the week of the festival, and our options are somewhat limited. Regardless, it's a lot more than I had a week ago, so I am grateful for whatever they can make happen. It just might be enough to skyrocket the paper again, and make my parents proud of me, wherever they are.

"Yeah, I think that all sounds doable, right?" I ask, redirecting my attention to Chase, rather than the siren trying to catch my eye with a sashay of her luscious hips. I swear my cock jumps against my gray sweatpants at that small glance out of the corner of my eye. Apparently he doesn't give a fuck about the fact that I'm currently in conversation with her brother. "And I have the exclusive rights to all of the publicity for the week, right?"

"Of course. I can't promise that word won't get around, though. With Harper being such a huge name, it's bound to cause some whispers, but we will yield all official PR to you and the paper," Chase confirms. I wasn't really doubting him, but I had to be sure that I didn't miss out on the story that would likely make or break the future of my parents' legacy. He's right, though. He can't really guarantee others won't come sniffing around, and it causes me more anxiety than I care to admit.

"Great. Thanks a lot, man. You can't even begin to imagine how much this means to me," I say earnestly. "You're really doing me a solid, and I don't know that I can ever repay the favor."

"Don't thank me. Thank Ace. It was her idea after all, and she really did have to convince me. Chalk it up to right place, right time with all of the bad press Harper's been getting recently. We might need this more than you do."

He cuts a sharp glare in Macy's direction, and I swear I see embarrassment creep up her neck for some unknown reason. Either way, the blush that paints along her skin reminds me that my dick is interested in being the cause of it in the near future.

"Wonderful, so can we please go do something fun now? All of this shop talk is seriously boring me to tears," Macy says, hopping up on the counter with a nonchalance that feels slightly forced. It's obvious that she is changing the subject, and my brows pull together as I wonder why she would feel so embarrassed that she needs to redirect our focus.

"Don't you think you've been having enough fun lately, Ace? The bar from last weekend is still on my ass to replace the table you broke in your tequila haze," Chase glowers at his sister and reaches out to swat her on the leg with his fingers.

She just makes a face at him and flips him off while he opens up his phone and starts scrolling on something. I swear I hear her mutter something along the lines of "stick in the mud" before she returns her gaze to mine. This girl really does know how to get under her brother's skin. And mine, if I am being honest. Lucky for her, it turns me on when she tries to piss me off.

"What about you, Brody? Do *you* think I've had enough... *fun* lately?" She emphasizes the word enough for me to pick up on the fact that she's trying to draw attention to just how much fun we've been having together.

I shift my position on the island chair to hide my rapidly thickening cock. I purse my lips at her and narrow my eyes so as not to give anything away in front of her brother. She's making it difficult, but I give her nothing to work with, other than an impassive look.

"I don't know," I say, shrugging. "But I'll never say no to a drink. What do you think, songbird? Ready to finally repay the favor from the other night?"

I purposely don't elaborate on which favor I am referring to, and my omission has the intended effect. I watch her intently as her thighs clench together and a scarlet blush creeps along her cheeks, enhancing her already vivid green eyes. My heart fucking thuds in my chest seeing her so beautiful. She is stunning, and I can feel myself becoming more obsessed with her as time goes on. Something tells me that regardless of what I try to do, it will always be me who ends up being starstruck by her instead of the other way around.

"Oh? And what favor might that be?" She finally finds her voice, breathy with her clear arousal. I hope Chase is preoccupied enough with his phone not to catch it. At the very least, I hope that he intentionally ignores it if he does. No need to alert him just yet that I'm crushing hard on my former best friend's younger sister.

"Don't tell me you've forgotten all about me playing knight in shining armor for you after the bar last weekend. You'll forever break my heart if you tell me my heroics meant nothing to you," I say, only half joking. I bring one of my hands up to my chest as if the aforementioned organ is physically crumbling at her lapse in memory.

"Right. That," she says, shaking her head as if she needs to clear her mind from other, decidedly more dirty favors I have been bestowing upon her as of late. "Well, need I remind you, Brody, that I actually have already done you a huge favor by, you know, bringing a certain pop star to our esteemed hometown? Did you forget about that, huh?"

I open my mouth to snap back at her, but she cuts me off before I can say anything snarky in her direction. I know she's just teasing, but part of me wonders if she really wants to help me with this, or if she just feels like she owes me something.

"Relax, Brody, I'm just fucking with you. I would have helped you either way. You just had to ask." Her words clear the lingering anxiety of her motives behind helping me. The party girl persona that she likes to put out into the world is more of a mask to hide just how incredible and caring she is. "Regardless, I think we should go do something more exciting than this, but I'm not in the mood for the bar scene tonight."

"Really? *You're* not in the mood to get some drinks? I

thought you were the self-proclaimed queen of tequila herself?"

"Hush. What I meant was, I can think of a few more things that sound a lot more... thrilling than hitting the bottle tonight," she says suggestively, adding a wink and a slow perusal of my frame that has my mind conjuring up some ideas on its own.

I clear my throat loudly, readjusting on my seat yet again. Apparently my dick hasn't yet realized there's a third person in the room with us and won't be making an appearance just yet. "And what did you have in mind?"

She hops off of the counter and stalks toward me with a wicked grin splitting her gorgeous features. She stops just to my right side and reaches out to run one of her perfectly manicured fingers down my tattooed bicep, dropping her gaze down my frame as she does and dragging it back up to meet my eyes with lust sparking in hers.

"How do you feel about getting a little dirty with me?"

brody

NOTE TO SELF: NEVER LET MACY DRIVE AGAIN

"JESUS FUCK, Macy! I can't hold on any longer! Fuck, fuck, FUCK!" I shout out as my knuckles turn white on the "oh shit" handle in the passengers' seat of her brother's truck. Her peeling laughter rings out emphatically as she whips the steering wheel sharply left again and slams her tiny foot on the gas pedal. The truck lurches to the left slightly while the back tires spin out, causing the back end to whip about uncontrollably as mud flies, completely drenching the entire lower half of the vehicle.

Macy somehow convinced me that playing teenager for the day would be fun, and the best way to do it was to snatch her brother's old pickup and take advantage of the recent summer storm by mudding out on the old four-wheeling trails in the woods on the south side of town.

I haven't done anything this reckless in years, and I admit the idea sounded just nostalgic enough to get my heart pumping. Though in my head, I would be the one driving the truck, and I am definitely starting to regret my choice to go through with her insane plan. Who gave this woman a driver's license? Come to think of it, I'm not even sure she *does* have one. I should have asked before I agreed to this.

The truck lurches viciously again as she wrenches the steering wheel in the opposite direction as before.

"Goddamn it, Macy! This is not what I was envisioning when you suggested getting dirty with you! Are you trying to get the two of us fucking killed?" I scream at her, my fear shining through on all of my words. I wouldn't say I'm exactly Mr. Safety by any means, but even this is a bit much for me. It's not even me that I'm worried about either. All I can picture when I squeeze my eyes shut is us hitting a wayward pothole and Macy wrapping herself around a tree.

She chuckles again before flashing her gaze sideways at me and saying, "Oh yeah? Not the version of dirt you were hoping for, huh? What did you have in mind?"

I open my mouth to quip back at her, but at that moment, we hit another large dip in the trail, and a huge spray of mud rushes up the windshield. My stomach drops right along with the road, but I laugh despite myself, momentarily forgetting my anxiety.

Macy grins outright at me now, hearing the sound of my unabashed laughter, and hits the windshield wipers to clear a small break in the dark color enough for us to see the trail. The sight of her smile takes my breath away. Well, it would have, if it wasn't already gone from this ride from hell.

"Aww, see? You're having fun, right? Besides, we can always explore your other filthy avenues later," she says with a wink and a chuckle. I can't tell if the rapid beating of my heart is from her playful tone and laughter or if it's from her truly terrifying driving. Probably a combination of both.

"Oh, trust me, we will *definitely* be revisiting– Macy, look out!" I shout at her, bracing my hand on the dashboard for the inevitable as my gaze snags on the giant hole that we are headed directly for at top speed. Unfortunately, I didn't catch it with enough time, and her side of the windshield was too caked with mud for her to notice.

We crash headlong into the pit, with a huge rush of beige, muddy water splashing high enough to spray through our open windows and soak our pants. We both jolt forward, and I quickly reach my left arm out to wrap it in front of Macy's chest, so she doesn't go face first into the steering wheel, while bracing my other hand on the dashboard to prevent myself from a similar fate. Macy's hands white knuckle the wheel and her head whips forward with the impact.

All of my anxieties from earlier come rushing back, and I whip my head around to make sure she's okay. Her breathing is rapid, and she seems to be in a little bit of shock, but she, otherwise, seems fine. Thank God. I force myself to calm down and just take in the fact that we are both unharmed.

"Well... that happened," Macy says with feigned nonchalance that betrays just how rattled she is by the crash. She shakes her head quickly and goes to step on the gas to try moving forward again. The tires spin, and spin, and spin. As she continues pressing on the pedal, steam starts to roll out from under the hood of the truck, and she starts muttering a curse under her breath.

"Um... I think we're stuck," she states, meeting my gaze.

I stare deadpan at her. "You think?"

I open my door and hop out to go inspect the damage. If this were my truck, I'd be shitting a brick right about now. I round the back of the truck and realize just how stuck we actually are. We are going to have to push this fucking thing out.

"Damn it!" I shout, kicking the tire in my frustration. As I do, Macy hops out of the driver's side and comes to inspect as well.

"Oh, relax. It can't be that bad."

"No, you're right, songbird. We are just stuck in the middle of fucking nowhere, drenched in mud, with a stolen truck engulfed in two feet of straight mud. And not only that, but you could have seriously gotten hurt, and I could never live with myself if I allowed that to happen," I snap back at her, bringing my hands up to rest on my hips. I grind my teeth in irritation at this situation, unable to fully process just how much the idea of her being harmed is affecting me.

Her face softens as she takes in my words, and she breathes out a light sigh.

"I'm fine, Brody. You don't have to worry about me. Let's just focus on getting this thing unstuck, okay? We can dig around the front tires and then I will jump back in to press on the gas while you push from the back. Sound like a plan?" She blinks at me, waiting for my confirmation of her plan.

After a minute of worrying my jaw, I huff out a mumbled "fine," and we both get to work digging some of the offending mud out from behind the front tires. After a few minutes, we have enough cleared to start on the next phase of getting the truck out.

I hustle around to the back, while Macy hops into the front seat. I holler at her to press on the gas, and put all of my muscle into pushing from the back. It moves a few inches, but doesn't quite make it out of the giant pit.

"Come on, Macy! All the way down! Now!" I shout at her, knowing her window is still down and she can hear me. As she presses on the throttle again, I get a better grip on the truck and push with everything I've got. I feel it starting to budge, so I yell back at her again to keep the pressure on. After another thirty seconds or so, I finally feel the truck catch some traction and lurch completely out of the hole. Macy drives it forward a few more feet before throwing it in park and jumping out, running straight for me.

"Oh my God, we did it!" she screams before launching herself straight into my arms and wrapping her thighs around my middle. I wrap my hands under her ass to keep her aloft as her laughter twinkles in my ears, bringing a grin to my own face.

Just as I start to chuckle alongside her, she rears back and looks down into my smiling face with a stunning expression of her own. I feel her legs tighten even further around my waist, and my eyes flick down to her lush mouth. I adjust her slightly, so I can reach one of my muddy hands up and cup her cheek. I'm not worried about leaving muck on her face as she's already coated in it. She inhales a sharp breath at my touch, noting the change in my expression as my smile dissipates under her gaze.

"Songbird," I breathe out, my voice catching slightly with my emotion. "I'm glad we are spending time together, but could we maybe do something a little less risky next time? I can't bear to think of you getting hurt, especially doing something I shouldn't be encouraging."

Her eyes soften again, and she says, "It's okay, Brody. I'm okay."

I breathe out, relief running through my entire body as I hold onto her, realizing that she's right. She didn't get hurt, and up until then, we were having fun just getting to be silly with each other for a little while. I lock eyes with her again, noticing that hers have filled with heat once more. I glance down to her mouth, sure she can read my intention.

My eyes never leave her lips as her face gets closer and closer to my own. I feel my jaw tick as I anticipate the kiss I know is coming. A hair's distance away, I hear her softly whisper my name, and I mutter a quick curse before grabbing her loosely by the throat and dragging our lips together.

God, her fucking mouth. I taste a mixture of the cherry

chapstick she put on before we left the house and the grit of muddy residue that coats both of our skin. The blend should be too much for either of us to handle, but somehow it works for this gritty moment between us. I make a gravelly sound at the back of my throat before I use my tongue to pry her lips open. It takes almost no effort as she yields herself to me completely, whimpering and running her dirty fingers through my hair, coating the strands even further with muck.

I continue rolling my tongue with hers as I make my way up and out of the muddy divot in the road and toward the truck. I break away briefly to suckle on her neck in just the right spot to make her squirm against me. She breathes my name again before using her leverage on my hair to pull my mouth back to hers.

I finally make it to the truck, and push her against it, forcing her to feel every inch of my stiff cock pressing against her plush center. My lips never break hers, but I feel her moan as my cock hits her in the right spot, and I press even harder against her. After a few more rolls of my hips to her center, I pull away.

"Do you feel me, songbird? Do you feel how fucking hard I am for you?" To emphasize my point, I roll my hips again, gyrating against her pussy. I let out a low groan and repeat the motion, unable to resist the heat I feel emanating from her even through our layers of clothing and grime. She rolls her head back against the side of the truck and releases a moan.

"Brody... oh my God, yes," she whispers, unable to add any more force behind her words. She pulls me impossibly closer to her and pushes back against me seeking more friction against her core.

I thrust my tongue back in her mouth and give her one hard snap of my hips before I force myself to pull away from her, not wanting to get carried away out here. Despite the harsh feelings rushing through my veins, I know this isn't the way I want to take her for the first time. She deserves better than a quick fuck against the truck in the middle of the woods.

I lower her down but don't step back, leaving us pressed against one another against the side of the truck. I pull back, gazing down at her as her eyelids flutter open and her cheeks blush that crimson I love so much. My lips tilt up again, seeing her wanting beneath me, and I press a tender kiss to her lips again.

"We should stop," I say, and she whimpers in protest. Smirking, I smack another quick kiss onto her lips. "I don't want our first time together to be in the bed of your brother's truck in the middle of nowhere."

She drops her head back against the truck door, and says, "Fine, but you should know that this is the second time you've kissed me breathless and left me wanting. I'm a grudge holder, sir, and I don't appreciate you getting me all hot and bothered just to stop there."

I laugh at her pouting, and lean down to kiss her forehead.

"Alright, come on. We should probably get back and get cleaned up. So I can ruin you all over again." I punctuate by opening the door and lifting her into the passenger side.

"But this time, I'm driving."

brody

SOUNDS FAMILIAR

I PULL Chase's beat up pickup truck into the driveway of their Nana's house and throw it into park in front of the house. We didn't talk much on the way home, just allowing the sexual tension to radiate through the cab until it was damn near suffocating. I smirk as I glance at Macy out of the corner of my eye, noticing how her breathing is shallow and her nipples are peaked through her t-shirt. The anticipation of having her writhing beneath me is almost enough to have me reaching across the seat to drag her on top and bury myself inside her once and for all.

Releasing a heavy sigh, I restrain myself and go to jump out of the truck. Macy must still be lost in wherever her dirty thoughts have taken her because she remains in the truck with closed eyes and parted lips.

God, I can't wait to have them wrapped around my cock with my hands in her hair as I hit the back of her throat. I come around her side of the truck and open the door, causing her to jump enough to nearly rail her head against the top of the cab.

"Did I scare you, songbird? Care to share where your

wicked thoughts took you just now?" I bear down on her, bringing my mouth within inches of hers, and notice her sharp intake of breath. God, I am fucking gone for this girl. The flush of her cheeks, the way her eyes flick down to my mouth and fill with molten heat, her perfect bronze skin. Not to mention her playfulness, the way she attacks every problem with enthusiasm, and how much happier I am when I'm around her. Everything about her is flawless, and I am moments away from losing myself in the taste of her again.

"Wh-what? No, nothing. I wasn't thinking about anything. Taxes. I was thinking about taxes. Yeah... definitely that," she stammers out, breathlessly. I forgot to mention that she's kind of a terrible liar, particularly around me.

I lean in further, brushing my lips against hers. Not enough to be a full on kiss, but enough to bring the cherry taste of her to my mouth.

"Liar," I whisper against her. Pulling back suddenly, I make quick work of unbuckling her and swiftly wrap an arm around her to pull her out of the truck and toss her over my shoulder.

She squeals, taken by surprise, and then immediately starts squirming to get out of my hold, which only brings her succulent ass closer to my face.

"What are you doing, Brody? Put me down! I can walk, you caveman!" she shouts at me, pounding her tiny fists against my back. Even an inch lower and she'd be ramming her hands on my ass. Soon enough, she will be.

"I told you, songbird. We need to get cleaned up, and if you keep squirming like this," I swat her backside swiftly before soothing it with a squeeze of my hand, "I won't be held accountable for what happens next."

She stops squirming after that, though I can feel that part of her wants to be combative with me just to see what I'll do. She's just enough of a spitfire to want to push the boundaries in that way. For now, she complies with my request as I continue walking toward the unused horse stable on the side of her grandparents property where I know there's an outdoor shower stall for the stable hands to use.

I reward her compliance with a tender rub on her luscious ass and murmur, "Good girl," which earns me a small whimper. I almost drop her on the spot and tear her clothes off right there on the lawn. The noises this woman makes are going to drive me to the brink of fucking insanity, I swear.

I continue trekking toward the stables and make my way inside, locating the shower I remember using a time or two when Chase and I would fuck around a little too hard as teenagers and need to wash off whatever shenanigans we got into before heading back into the house to face his grandparents. I may be a grumpy fuck now, but we used to have a good time when I was younger and wasn't holding onto the grief of losing my parents coupled with the stress of potentially sinking the paper.

I shake my head to rid myself of the thought and return my attention to her. We've made it to the shower stall at this point, and I step in and drop her down inside. She slides down my front, and I don't allow even a centimeter of space between us as she does. I want her pressed against me for the rest of my fucking life.

As her feet hit the floor, it brings her eyes directly in line with my mouth that seems to be permanently frozen in a small smirk when I am around her. I can't remember the last time I smiled this much, and it doesn't bother me as much as it used to. I like getting to open up around her.

Her eyes remain glued to my lips, and I reach behind her, turning on the shower to start the process of cleaning us both off.

"Shit, fuck!" she shrieks, curling into me to avoid the offending water currently pelting both of us.

"Damn," I say in agreement, feeling goosebumps ripple across my skin from the rigid temperature. "Seems like we might have to warm things up a bit, huh?"

"Wha–?" I cut off her question by slamming my mouth to hers again. I run my hands all over her, feeling her clothes bunch in my fists, and the sluice of mud and water fall down her frame. Our tongues tangle together as I feel her shuddering against me. This time, I know the goosebumps erupting all over her arms have very little to do with the temperature of the water and everything to do with my hands on her.

I pull away for a moment, skimming my nose against hers. She presses forward, seeking my mouth in a seemingly unconscious move.

"What about now, songbird? Still feeling cold?" I whisper, running my mouth down her throat, flicking my tongue out to taste her again. She moans, and I feel the vibration everywhere. If it's possible, my dick gets impossibly harder at the sound.

"Uh... what?" She asks, gasping out quick breaths. Her fingers are twined in my hair, and she's arched against me in a way that is almost sinful.

I nip at her shoulder, pulling a whine from her, "Focus, Macy. I said, are you still feeling cold? Or are you warmed up enough?"

She doesn't miss the double meaning to my tone and quickly bobs her head in a nod, muttering a quiet "God, yes."

I stand up quickly, roughly cupping both of her cheeks in my palms and lean down to her mouth again. "Good," I whisper.

With that, all of the tension between us hits a boiling point, and we snap. We claw at each other, trying to get as close as possible as our mouths clash, all bites and teeth clicking. It happens so fast, I don't even fully register that she has both of our shirts off faster than I can blink.

"Fuuuuck," I grind out, taking in her bare tits before me. "I've never seen anything so fucking perfect in my entire life, songbird. I'm going to ruin you for every other man." I take one of those perfect breasts in my mouth and moan at the taste and feel of her nipple on my tongue while simultaneously pinching her other one with my fingers. The scream she lets out can likely be heard for miles.

"Holy fuck, Brody. Don't stop, please," she pleads, pushing her tits further into my touch while her hands glide down my bare chest, scraping her nails along my abs. She doesn't hesitate before reaching into my pants and roughly grabbing ahold of my cock.

I huff out a breath, pulling away from her chest at the sudden impact of her touch. "Fuck, Macy," I grind out through clenched teeth, and she increases her hold on me, squeezing just to the edge of pain.

Leaning into my neck, she runs her tongue up the column of my throat, making me growl, and whispers in my ear, "What's the matter? Think you're the only one who can dish it out?" She nips at my earlobe and then abruptly pulls away, dropping to her knees and reaching up to drag my pants down my legs.

"Macy..." I trail off as she releases me from my pants, my dick bobbing in the space between me and her waiting mouth. She sucks in a sharp breath, her chest expanding rapidly as she takes me in.

"Jesus, Brody! What are you, the fucking poster child for giant cocks or what? Is that a piercing?" She shoots her gaze up to mine briefly, before settling back down on my dick again with wariness in her wide eyes.

I reach down to cup her face with one hand and trace the

pointer finger of my other hand along her lips. "What's the matter, songbird? Worried you won't be able to handle it?" I tease her with a smirk, knowing it will only goad her into action.

As expected, she flicks her eyes back up to my face and angrily huffs out, "Yeah-fucking-right."

Before I'm able to snark a response back at her, she grabs ahold and pulls me all the way to the back of her throat. I involuntarily buck into her mouth and hiss out a muttered curse before roughly threading my hands through her dark locks. She moans around my dick and runs the flat of her tongue along the sensitive underside, pulling back and sucking on the head harshly. Her teeth clack against my piercing, making me feel even more sensation. I groan loudly, sure that anyone within a five mile radius will hear me and the combination of her wet mouth swallowing my cock.

"Macy, Jesus, you and your perfect fucking mouth. Holy shit, you take me so well." She hums at my praise and continues driving me insane with her tongue, alternating between taking me deep and harsh to sucking sweetly, simply enjoying the taste of my cock in her mouth.

She's so good at this, it makes me want to knock the teeth in of every man she got to hone her skills on that wasn't me. With that thought swirling through my brain, I roughly shove my dick deeper into throat, fucking her mouth with abandon.

She pushes back on my thighs as I do, resisting slightly, and for a moment I worry that I may have hurt her in my unprovoked moment of jealousy. However, just as I am about to pull out and check on her, she moans around me and digs her nails into my thighs, pulling me in deep again. Jesus fuck, this woman.

After another few minutes, I feel the telltale tingle of an impending orgasm, and I pull myself from her mouth with a pop. She whimpers and scowls up at me in protest, but I quickly grab her from the floor, lifting her back to her feet and roughly slamming her back against the wall.

"Not a fucking chance, songbird. There's no way in hell I'm coming before I get that perfect pussy wrapped around my cock." To emphasize my point, I grip her thighs, lifting her off of the ground, and wrap them around my middle as I press her against the wall, holding her in place.

I grind my solid erection along her cunt, reveling in the sounds she makes as the head of my dick passes over her sensitive clit. Something in my memory pricks at the sound of her groans, but I dismiss it for now, not wanting to think about anything else but her. I do this a few more times, only succeeding in driving us both a little crazy.

She scrapes her fingers roughly through my hair and grabs hold, snapping my head back enough to look her in the eyes. She leans close to my face, brushing her lips along mine.

Before I am able to lean into the kiss, she locks those emerald eyes with mine and whispers, "Stop fucking teasing, Brody, and fuck me already. Or are *you* afraid you can't handle it?" She smirks at me as she echoes my taunt from earlier.

I feel the corners of my own lips tilt up in a sultry grin and say, "Not a fucking chance. I'm only thinking that I should probably grab a condom. Unless..." I let the word trail off, waiting for her to take over where my thoughts are failing. I don't want her to feel pressured, but the thought of taking her bare has me feeling feral with the idea of claiming her in that way.

Her eyes meet mine, vulnerability in them as she says, "Unless, you want to fuck me bare? I'm clean, and I can promise you I'm on birth control. You?"

"I'm clean," I say, my voice husky with the realization that she's agreeing to let me fuck her without a condom. "Are you sure you're okay with this?"

"Yes. God, yes," she breathes out, kissing me deeply to emphasize just how much she wants me at this moment. I breathe a curse against her mouth and give her what she wants.

I thrust my hips forward at just the right angle, plunging deep inside of her while kissing her deeply, swallowing her scream of pleasure at my abrupt intrusion. I hold myself seated deep, savoring our lingering kiss and doing my damndest not to explode right then and there. Holy shit. I thought her mouth was perfect, but it is nothing compared to the feeling of her pussy wrapped around my cock.

She starts squirming, trying to force me to move as I continue licking my way inside of her mouth, torturing us both with my lack of movement. I pull out slowly, inch by inch, and thrust back inside of her roughly, hitting her hard and deep. She moans into my mouth and grips onto my hair tighter. I repeat the motion, over and over, driving her wild, causing her to clench around me. My fingers must be bruising her with how tightly they are gripped on her thighs, but she doesn't seem to mind. My songbird likes it a little bit rough.

I pull my mouth away, leaning my forehead against hers and look straight into those soul deep green eyes of hers. "Christ, Macy. You were fucking made for me."

I break eye contact with her to glance down, my gaze locking at where we are connected. With a groan, I say, " Look at how good you take me." She moans loudly and leans back slightly, so we can both watch my dick disappear inside of her. "Fucking perfect."

"Oh my God, Brody, harder. I need you to fuck me HARD-ER!" She nearly screams the final word, as I give her exactly what she asks for, pressing her into the wall with nearly all of my weight and slamming my cock into her. Suddenly, I pull out, dropping her back to her feet.

"Brody, what the fu– ohhhhh." She doesn't get the chance to finish her curse. I quickly turn her around and bend her forward, forcing her to rest her cheek on the wall, as I slam back into her from behind as hard as I can.

"You want it harder, songbird? I will give you harder." I smack her ass, emphasizing my point, causing her to moan loudly.

"Yes, oh my God, that feels so fucking good," she pants out, pushing back into me as I rail her from behind. She is so beautiful, bent over like this, taking my cock perfectly, pressing her beautiful ass against me.

I reach one hand up and grab onto her hair harshly, slightly adjusting the angle of my thrust inside of her. This new position helps me hit her G-spot, and I can feel her getting closer to the edge. I run my other hand sweetly down her back, caressing her spine, before reaching around to massage her clit, eliciting another loud groan from her.

"Don't fucking stop, Brody. I swear I will kill you if you stop." She's so sexy when she makes demands. As if I could stop even if I tried right now. In this moment, she's my beginning, middle, and end all rolled into one flawless, infuriating, sunlight infused woman. Mine.

"There's not a fucking thing in this God forsaken world that could stop me from fucking you until you see stars right now." I keep ramming into her, hard and fast. "But I can tell you want to come, and I can't wait to feel how perfect you feel rippling around me as I fill you with my cum. Do you want that?"

She doesn't answer me, just lets out a small laugh that quickly turns into another long moan as I hit her deep again.

"What was that?" I ask, pulling my fingers away from her

clit and smacking her ass again, eliciting a sharp inhale of breath.

"Yes, please. I want to come, Brody. Please, can I come?" She sounds like she's nearly sobbing with the force of her withheld orgasm.

"Well, since you asked so nicely. Brace yourself, Macy. Hands on the wall."

She does as I ask, and I return to my ministrations on her clit while simultaneously ramming into her hard and fast from behind. With her hands on the wall, she's able to push back even harder into me, causing my cock to hit even deeper, as we both chase our orgasms.

She pushes back one last time before exploding with a sharp cry. Her pussy flutters around me, gushing with the force of her orgasm. She clamps down on me like a vice, drawing my own orgasm out right along with her.

I grab onto her waist, my massive hands nearly circling all of the way around her, as I pump into her a few more times with a muttered, unintelligible curse on my lips. Blackness and stars dot along the periphery of my vision as I come hard inside of her. Despite my earlier taunts, it seems that I am going to be the one who has been branded with the haunting memory of her and how utterly perfect she is for me.

Both of us are breathing heavily, the sound echoing all around us. I am still inside of her, so I lean down and kiss her back before pulling out of her and spinning her around so she doesn't fall on her face. Her legs are barely holding her up at this point, and I need to make sure she's safe. I rest her back against the wall again and cage her in with my arms, running my nose up her neck and inhaling her scent.

I pull back and smirk at her while she raises her gaze to mine, her eyes glittering with pleasure and unadulterated satisfaction. She grins back at me, her cheeks pink, and breathes out, "Holy shit, Brody. That was–"

"Hot. Like, melt the panties off of a Catholic nun, hot. Any chance you two are looking to mix it up with a third person next time?" At the unexpected voice, I snap my head around, and form a naked human shield in front of Macy to hide her from the unknown visitor. My glare snags on the amused expression of a tiny, pixie-like woman.

I open my mouth to tell her to fuck off, but Macy cuts me off.

"Stella? What the fuck!" she shrieks, nearly popping my eardrum with the shrillness of it. She steps away from me and snaps back at the woman, Stella. "Get out!"

"No round two? Well damn. Next time. Meet you up at the house, Ace!" With that, Stella grins and whirls around, presumably to head up to the house. I turn and scowl back at Macy, who has her head tilted toward the sky, muttering what I can only assume is a plea to the heavens for patience. When she drops her gaze back to mine, she takes me in for all of two seconds before she busts out laughing.

"You're laughing? A fucking pixie just walked in on us, getting the show of a damn lifetime, and you're laughing? I don't get the joke."

At my grouchy tone, she just laughs harder. "I... I just don't understand... WHY... why we keep... getting caught with our pants around our ankles. Literally!"

I try to hold out, but her laughter is so infectious, I find myself chuckling right alongside her as I start to gather our clothes.

Handing hers over, I pull her in quickly, smacking a kiss to her lips, cutting off her giggles.

"Come on, then. Let's get dressed. Seems like we have a

mythical creature waiting in your Nana's kitchen." With that, we dress and head back up to the house.

As we walk, I reach down and lace my fingers through hers. She beams up at me, and my heart squeezes at the expression on her face. Looking at her, my brain remembers the twinge of a memory from earlier, and it hits me like a freight train.

I know exactly where I've heard those sounds before.

macy

OH FUCK ME SIDEWAYS

DESPITE THE FACT that hurricane Stella blew through my post-coital moment in the barn, I am still riding cloud nine after finally getting my hands – or should I say my vagina – wrapped all around tall, dark, and handsome who's walking hand in hand with me.

That is, until he stops so abruptly that I damn near get whiplash from the suddenness of his jerk on my arm.

"Ah, what the hell?" I say, whipping around to face him with a confused look plastered to my face. Brody's face holds a similar expression to mine, though his is far more accusatory than my own.

I raise my eyebrows, waiting for him to break the silence, but he just continues staring, his eyes bobbing across my face like he's searching for something and not quite finding it.

"Um, earth to Brody? Are you okay? Did you see a ghost or something?" I ask, waving one of my hands in front of him to break his trance. "Seriously, you're freaking me out. What's going on?"

"Harper?" he finally says, and I feel my heart squeeze painfully as shock rushes through my system.

I blink a few times at him, not quite sure that I heard him correctly. I mean, there's absolutely no way he just looked right at me and called me by my stage name. Right?

"Wh-What?" I say, barely more than a whisper, unable to make my voice more assertive in this moment.

"Harper. Harper Bloom. *You're* Harper Fucking Bloom?" he asks, though from the tone of his voice, it's more of a rhetorical question than actually seeking confirmation from me.

Not that he would get it anyway, as my body seems to have fully delved into shock and I'm just standing there staring at him. It's actually impressive that I am able to stay upright, since the amount of adrenaline coursing through my body right now is turning my legs into literal jelly.

He doesn't say anything else, just puts his hands on his hips and waits for me to either confirm or deny, though I'm not sure what the point is now, seeing as he's already put two and two together. Maybe it's not such a bad deal after all? Though his posture and tone suggest that I might be doing a hell of a lot of wishful thinking at the moment.

"Um..." I say, unsure what to do. I've never had anybody blatantly call me out like this in such an unexpected way. I can almost hear Chase's voice reminding me of all of the times he coached me into various denials should such an occasion arise. Unfortunately for me, my mind is a blank slate at the moment.

I scramble to come up with an excuse or some sort of an explanation that would make sense, but I ultimately give up with a sigh. I lower my head dramatically, my shoulders slumping in defeat.

"Brody, I was going to tell—" I start, but he doesn't give me the chance to finish.

"You were going to tell me? When? Before or after I had you wrapped around my cock? Jesus, Macy," he says, his frustration bleeding through all of his words like fire. His head is thrown back in exasperation as he grinds his teeth in irritation. It's either that, it's to keep his mouth closed from really laying into me. If I'm being honest, I'm not sure which is worse.

I open my mouth to speak, but he beats me to it again. His eyes blaze with anger, but behind that, I can see that he is more hurt by this realization than anything. That knowledge makes my heart squeeze painfully again knowing he's so upset.

"You lied to me, Macy. You sat there and lied to my face about everything. Did you think I was too much of a small town moron to figure it out?"

"No!" I nearly shout at him, my pleading written all over my face. "No, Brody. I could never think that—"

"Then, what? Why didn't you just tell me? Did you not trust me enough to keep your secret?" It's clear that this is what bothers him the most. The fact that I wouldn't trust him to hold my deepest secret close to his chest.

"I wanted to tell you, I swear. But this is a secret I've been holding onto my entire life, Brody. It's not something you can just blurt out and hope for the best. I was trying to find the right moment," I say, hoping my explanation is enough for him. I can't bear the thought of losing what we have already, even if I could understand why he wouldn't want to continue.

"I would have understood. I would have been surprised, but I would have understood. I wish you would have just trusted me enough to know I would never hurt you or betray your trust," he says, sighing and letting his shoulders droop. I can't tell if it's in defeat or in acceptance.

To ease my own anxiety, I say, "I'm sorry, Brody. I wanted you to know. I want you to know everything about me. I want to be able to share all of the parts of my life with you, even the parts that most of the world doesn't get to see. I know it might not mean much now, but I promise I was working up the courage to tell you everything, at least before Harper was set to arrive in town. Please tell me you believe me."

He's quiet for so long that I almost give in and tell him to just leave. I can't handle his rejection on top of this unexpected bombshell being dropped on us.

With a quivering lower lip and tears threatening to spill down my cheeks, I nod quickly in understanding and turn to head back up to the house, my broken heart throbbing in my throat. Before I can take a step, though, I feel him grab my hand to stop me.

He turns me around to face him, but I keep my gaze trained to the ground, unable to look him in the eyes at this moment. He, however, is not one to let me get away with that. He tilts my chin up to meet his eyes, and I find nothing but acceptance and affection there. A jarring opposition to the emotion that was stirring in them just moments ago.

"It's okay," he whispers out, brushing his lips along mine.

"It's—okay?" I ask, unsure that I heard him correctly.

He nods, "It's okay, songbird. I forgive you. I can't say I'm not still shocked, but I guess I can do my best to understand. But, please, trust me in the future. I can handle it. Okay?"

"Okay," I agree. One lone tear of relief breaks free and streaks down my cheek. His thumb reaches around to brush it away before he kisses me sweetly. The kiss only lasts for a few seconds, but it's enough to put all of my fears and anxieties at ease.

After he breaks away, he stares down at me again and whispers, "Harper Fucking Bloom. Jesus."

Unable to voice any words, I just let out a shaky laugh and pull him back in the direction of the house.

I guess I have more than one thing to share with my best friend.

macy

I GUESS THE CAT'S OUT OF THE BAG

"WHAT. THE. FUCK?"

I snap my gaze away from the window where I am shamelessly watching Brody's car retreat down the driveway and turn to face my bestie. I'm still slightly shaken by the fact that Brody figured out my secret so quickly, but I also feel relief. It was getting to be too exhausting and annoying trying to hide it from him, and I trust him to keep this secret.

"Earth to Macy! Am I talking to a wall right now?" Stella snaps at me again, attempting to recenter my focus solely on her.

"Hmm?" I hum out, not fully processing that she asked me a question. Sort of.

She heaves out a heavy sigh, and then repeats herself, "I *said*, 'What the fuck?' Were you really holding out on me with the details of the seriously attractive man made of muscles you were just fucking in the outdoor shower? I thought we were best friends. This is a crazy betrayal of my trust, you know!"

"Oh my God, tone down the dramatics a little bit. It wasn't like I was holding out on you, I just... got a little busy, and you were halfway across the country! Besides, that was the first time we have fully fucked, so you are really getting the real time details, especially since you were *watching,* you fucking weirdo! How long were you standing there anyway?"

She has the audacity to actually chuckle at me. "I guess you'll never know. Serves you right for not picking up your fucking phone and calling me to tell me about him. You're not off the hook just yet, Ace. I may have been neck deep in dick and pussy myself, but I could have still answered a text or two."

I roll my eyes but then drop down to my knees in front of her and crawl my way in her direction to give as little space as possible. When I reach her, I grab onto her hands and look up at her pleadingly, giving her my best puppy dog eyes, and say, "Pretty please with extra whipped cream and cherries on top will you forgive me, Stell Bell? I couldn't live with myself if I lost your friendship forever! Will you please tell me you won't shun me from your life for all eternity?" I stick my lower lip out for added effect, even trembling it slightly as if I were crying.

She rolls her eyes and shakes her head but laughs a little at my theatrics. "Jesus, now who's the dramatic one? Alright, alright! I forgive you. But you and I are sitting down right the fuck now with a bottle of tequila, and you're gonna tell me *exactly* what has been going on with you and Mr. Muscles since you've been here! Deal?"

I beam up at her. "Deal."

Hopping up from the floor, I grab her and wrap my arms around her like a snake, squeezing the ever loving shit out of her and squealing right into her ear. "Eeeeek! I am so excited you're here! I didn't think you were coming until next week, but damn am I glad to see your face. Plus, you have to tell me *everything* that's been happening in Malibu since I've been here. I am seriously in withdrawal from the glitz and the glam!"

"Can't. Breathe. Ace. Let me go!" she tries to huff out since I'm still suffocating her with my embrace. I quickly release her with a muffled apology, and she says, "Trust me, girl. Since you've been in hiding, it's all anyone can talk about. Seriously, it's annoying. But before we get into all that, get the fucking tequila and give me all of the dirty, nasty, panty-melting details about your man already! Stop trying to distract me."

"Alright, alright! Can't a girl just be excited that her bestie is in town?"

"Not when said bestie is decidedly in the dark about your sex-capades. Now move it, move it! I have been in this tiny town for almost an hour, and I haven't had one drink yet. That should be illegal." She playfully swats at my ass as I hustle toward the kitchen, grabbing the tequila and two shot glasses. We down them quickly, and she looks at me pointedly.

"Now talk."

* * *

"And that's when your nosy ass walked in. Now you're all caught up. Satisfied?" I raise my eyebrows at Stella, where she leans almost her entire top half on the bar side of the kitchen island with a dreamy look in her eyes and a sigh on her lips.

"Wow. Who would have thought that driving a beat up old truck around in the mud would be such an aphrodisiac? I might have to try that one sometime." Her eyes kind of float around the room as she thinks over that possibility for herself in the future.

She chuckles a little bit, and shakes her head before sitting up straight in her chair and reaching for the tequila and margarita mix again. We are both on our third drink of the evening, so it's safe to say we are feeling it just a bit.

Taking a long sip from her drink, she looks at me again and

gives me a somewhat confused look. Either that, or she's just drunk. Probably both.

"Okay, so I'm like, super happy you're getting dick on the regular again. I mean, besides, you know... the whole sex tape thing." I stick my tongue out at her, which only makes her laugh. "But, also, do you think it's a good idea to be fucking around with the guy when you're lying to him about who you are? I mean... doesn't that seem a little risky considering you're *also* supposed to be helping him as Harper as well? Seems like he's probably going to put two and two together when you throw on your wig and start walking around town as Harper."

"Um, about that..." I trail off, biting my lip, unsure of how to drop the bomb that Brody actually figured it out.

Stella's eyes crease in confusion, and she says, "Ace? He *doesn't* know that you're Harper, right?"

"I mean, he kind of figured it out?" I say quietly, phrasing it almost as a question as I make a face that hopefully conveys my innocence in the whole thing.

"What do you mean he 'figured it out?' How could he have done that?"

"I don't know! I didn't really ask. I was too busy panicking over the fact that he *did* put it together," I reply, throwing my hands in the air in exasperation. "All I know is that after you busted in on us outside, we were walking back to the house, and he stopped dead in his tracks and called me Harper. It all just kind of spilled out after that."

Stell just stares at me, blinking like she can't quite process my words. I almost speak up again when her face takes on an incredulous look, and she bursts out in hysterical laughter.

"Care to enlighten me on what the hell about this situation is so funny?" I ask.

She opens her mouth to answer my question, but she bursts into another fit of laughter that prevents her from speaking. After a minute more of this, and a few tears shed at whatever she has going on inside of her head, she is able to answer me.

"I think I know how he figured it out," she chokes out, holding back another giggle. I just raise my eyebrows and wait for her to elaborate further.

"Ace. You had *just* gotten done having crazy sex in the barn, and then he all of a sudden figures out you're Harper?" She raises her eyebrows at me like I should be catching her train of thought.

"Okay... and?" I say, still unsure where she's going with this.

"*And*, Harper Bloom's moans have been all over the damn internet for the last few weeks," she finishes. It takes me a minute to piece that together.

"Oh my God, he—"

"He totally recognized your sex noises! He's listened to your sex tape!" she nearly shouts, and then she breaks into another fit of laughter.

I drop my head into my hands, my cheeks heating with embarrassment. Of all of the ways I thought Brody would learn about my secret, recognizing me from my sex tape was not even on the list.

"Oh my God," I groan. "He did, didn't he? That's so embarrassing! I can't believe he didn't tell me that was how he figured it out. He's in such deep shit for that."

Stella finishes up laughing and bats at my arm with her hand.

"Oh, give the guy a break. To be fair, he is in journalism, and you are one of the most famous women in the world. Of course he would be curious."

I huff, shaking my head, but lose some of my initial embarrassment. She's right, and even though I am still shocked that he was able to recognize me from that fateful tape, it *is* pretty funny when you think about it.

"Well, at least I can stop fretting over how to tell him the big secret. No one can say the sex tape debacle was for nothing," I say, giggling along with Stella. "Now, I have an even bigger monster to tackle. Telling Chase that Brody is now a part of the inner circle."

At that, Stella's expression sobers and she gives me a sympathetic look.

"Yeah, I don't envy you that conversation, Ace. Chase is totally going to flip his lid when he finds out. I guess I should start picking out my outfit for your funeral."

I crinkle my nose at her and grab an ice cube out of my glass to fling at her. She squeals and ducks out of the way, but in her drunken state, she just ends up moving herself into the line of fire. The ice cube hits her square in the chest and drops into her ample cleavage, disappearing from sight.

"Ahh! That's fucking COLD! What is wrong with you!" she screeches at the top of her lungs, digging into her boobs, while I dissolve into a fit of laughter.

"Well, there goes the peace and quiet I *thought* we were going to have here over the next couple of months," Chase saunters into the kitchen carrying some groceries for Nana. I must have missed the front door opening in my fit of laughter. I struggle to contain myself as he makes his way toward the fridge to put his six pack of beer away. "Jesus, Stella! You're going to make my ears bleed with your shrieking!"

She glances up at Chase, still digging around in her cleavage, "Fuck off, Chase. It's Macy's fault. Yell at her."

"Oh, come on, Stella. You know you deserved it," I manage to say as my laughter dies down a little bit. She just sneers at me, but it doesn't hold any real heat. She loves me too much for that.

"Yeah, whatever. Hey, maybe now that the stick in the mud is back, we should tell him the big news," Stella says, and I snap my head toward her, giving her a motion to shut the fuck up. Of course, I'm not so lucky.

"What big news?' What happened?" Chase leans against the counter and pins me with a look. Apparently, he isn't too thrilled with the idea of there being any sort of big news to share that he is unaware of. Chase likes to be on top of the things that happen around here, especially if they involve me. It's part of what makes him such a good PR manager, and what makes him such a pain in the ass to have as an older brother.

"Um… would you believe me if I said nothing?" I say hopefully, flashing him my best smile in hopes that he will drop it. He just narrows his gaze, tapping his fingers against the counter, waiting for me to get on with telling him.

I huff out a frustrated breath. " Fine. Brody and I sort of… had a moment… or two…" I can feel my cheeks heat, embarrassed that I am being inadvertently forced to tell my brother more about my sex life. As if he hasn't already heard enough.

Stella just snorts, nearly spitting out the mouthful of margarita she just inhaled, and coughs out, "Yeah, if you call getting ruthlessly railed from behind in the outdoor shower a 'moment.'"

Chase's eyes flare wide with shock and his jaw clenches in a way that I know must be painful.

"What?" he snaps, staring at me with confusion in his gaze. I must look like a fucking tomato at this point, and I drop my head back into my hands to hide from his penetrating gaze and look over to Stella.

"Stell, I'm going to fucking kill you," I whisper to her, and she finally realizes what she just did, her eyes going big with guilt. Damn her and her stupid idea to drink tequila. It never leads to us making good decisions.

I look back over at Chase and wait for him to say something else. He's just pinching the bridge of his nose and looking slightly green around the gills. I imagine the idea of hearing that his little sister is fucking his former best friend wasn't exactly on his list of things he was hoping to hear tonight.

"Okay, so you're... *seeing* McAllister," he finally says, skirting around the more intimate details of Brody and I being an item. "Maybe that will be a good thing. He can help keep you grounded while we're here. Just make sure you're careful around him, Ace. He's a journalist, so spilling your secrets to him is dangerous, even if we are just in Oaken."

I bite my lip and cast my gaze to the floor, guiltily. He catches it right away.

"Ace..." he says, suspiciously.

"So, um... he might already know?" I squeak out quietly, hoping he isn't able to hear my words.

"Come again?" he asks, even though I know he heard me the first time.

"I said he... um... knows. All of it. He figured it out," I say more firmly, hoping my honesty will win me some points in the inevitable argument that is about to ensue with this information out in the open.

"He knows," Chase repeats, and I nod emphatically. "He knows all of it." Again, a statement, not a question, but I nod anyway.

"How? How could he possibly have figured it out that quickly?"

"Well, I'll spare you the details, but he, um... recognized me. Sort of."

Chase's eyes narrow on me again, though more in confusion than anger. He must really be in shock if he is unable to even start berating me. I thought he would be in more of a freak out state by now, but maybe it's not as big of a deal as I thought.

After a few minutes of continued silence, I say, "Well, aren't you going to say something? Yell? Tell me that I'm screwed? Something?"

Honestly, anything would be better than him sitting there like a statue that somehow also has constipation.

After another moment, he sighs and finally says, "Well, I guess there isn't much I can do about it now, can I? It's happened. He knows, and now we just need to make sure that he isn't going to tell anyone. Especially since Harper is making her debut in town in just a few weeks."

I rush toward him and wrap him in a big hug, relief flooding through me that he's not more upset about this whole thing. Maybe he's turning over a new leaf or something. Either that, or he's still in shock, and I will wake up in the middle of the night with a pillow smothering me. Hard to say at this point.

"I love you, Chase. I trust him when he says he won't tell anyone, but I will talk to him again anyway and make sure he understands how important it is to keep the secret. Promise," I say, squeezing him until he wraps his arms around me and returns the hug.

"Yeah, you better. Because not only will I kick his ass if he spills the beans, but if he breaks your heart in the process, he's a dead man," Chase says into my hair. He really does love me underneath all of his over the top concern for my reputation.

After another quick squeeze, I let him go and bound my way over to Stella so we can get back to our good vibes from earlier.

"Come on, Stella. Let's go find some other trouble to get into around here. I am just drunk enough that skinny dipping in the creek sounds like a good idea."

I grab her hand and usher her out of the kitchen before Chase can say anything to stop us.

Little does she know that the real reason I want to hustle out of there is because I don't want Chase to step back into the role of protective older brother and warn me away from Brody altogether. I don't think I could stay away from him at this point if someone told me I would win a guaranteed Grammy if I did. I am royally fucked when it comes to that man. Literally.

macy

ALL'S FAIR IN LOVE AND SEX

"PRETTY PLEASE, CHASE! PLEASE, PLEASE, PLEASE!" I beg, holding my hands in a pleading stance. Annoying Chase into doing what I want is my favorite pastime, especially when I have had a few drinks and am ready to keep the party rolling. After I successfully convinced Stella – not that it took much convincing, really – to take a brisk dip in the creek behind Nana's house, we rolled back in and took another shot of tequila. Safe to say, both of us are feeling good, and we are ready to get out of this house.

"Yeah, Chase. Pleeeeeeeease!" Stella adds to the cacophony of my own whining. We decided after our third – or fourth? – shot of the evening that we wanted to head down to the bar for karaoke again. It's been so long since I've sung in front of a crowd, and I have that itch on the back of my skull that is telling me I have to be in the spotlight soon, or I might just tear my own hair out. This is the idea that led both of us back into the living room to plead with Chase to drive us downtown. Unfortunately for us, this town is severely lacking in Ubers.

Chase is doing his damndest to ignore us in favor of whatever zombie wartime video game he is playing, but if the bunching of his shoulders and the squint of his eyes is any indication, we are doing a pretty good job of distracting him. Case and point, he gets taken down by a horde of decaying monsters and dies violently on screen. He throws the controller down, shouting out a curse word, and rounds on us.

"Fuck! Is it too much to ask that I get to enjoy my vacation, too? With the two of you lunatics here, I swear my head might just explode," he grumbles away from us, but I snag onto his arm, forcing him to stop and swing around to face me. I don't say anything, but I give him my best puppy dog eyes again, hoping it will do the trick. When he doesn't immediately concede, I open my mouth to start the nagging anew, but he cuts me off. "Fine, I will take you downtown, but for the record, I think it's a bad idea." He heads for the door, muttering under his breath something that sounds a lot like "fucking sisters."

I squeal loudly, wrapping myself around Stella like an octopus, and jump up and down. She joins me in my celebration, and soon we both descend into a fit of drunken giggles. Chase glowers at us, but he holds the door open to escort us out anyway. I think he secretly wants to get out of the house.

Before we can make it out of the door, he stops me and says, "One drink each, you got it? You're already halfway to trashed, and I don't want either of you getting put into a dangerous position." Chase might be a gruff asshole sometimes, but underneath all of that attitude, he really does want what's best for me, and even Stella, though he'd never admit it.

I roll my eyes at him but agree to his terms, knowing he's right. I have probably had more than enough tonight. I'm smart enough to know my limit, and I am definitely on my way to hitting it.

The three of us pile into the cab of Chase's pickup, with me in the passenger seat and Stella in the middle. She cranks the music loud enough to shake the windows, and we make our way to the same bar I sang karaoke at the first night I was in town. Thinking of that night reminds me of whose bed I ended up in after my not so graceful tumble from one of the bar tables.

I reach into my crossbody bag and grab my phone out, pulling up my message thread with Mr.

Broody himself.

[Macy] Hiya, handsome! What are you up to?

Immediately the three little bubbles pop up, indicating that Brody is messaging me back. I try to stifle my reaction at his quick response but am unable to contain the grin that stretches across my face. Thank God the tequila is already warming my cheeks, or I'm sure I'd be looking a lot like Mr. Krabs right about now.

[Brody] Who is this?

My brow crinkles, confused. Does this motherfucker really not have my number saved? I start to type out a scathing response, but I get another message instead.

[Brody] I can practically hear your frustrated typing, song-bird. Relax, I'm just fucking with you

I smile at that, as the three little dots appear again.

[Brody] I'm at the office finishing up some last minute things before heading into the weekend. Some of us have to actually work for a living

[Macy] Oh my God, I work for a living! I'm just on... a bit of a break. Don't you ever take a break?

[Brody] I wish I had the luxury of a break, love. Though I could make an exception for a certain dark haired songbird whose screams I'm still hearing in my dreams

My cheeks heat even further at that.

[Macy] Oh yeah? I'd like to meet this dark haired beauty. She sounds like a real goddess if you ask me. Probably has perfect tits and everything. Hopefully you manage to hang onto her

[Brody] Trust me, songbird. She's already mine. She just needs to get on board

I inhale a sharp breath, snagging the attention of Stella, who had otherwise been occupied fiddling with the radio and generally doing whatever she can to irritate my brother. She whips her head over to me, noticing for the first time that I am texting someone. She gives me a knowing look and a smirk.

"You wouldn't happen to be blushing over Mr. Perfect Dick over there, now would you, Ace?" She ribs me in the side, causing me to laugh and release a sound of agreement. She squeals in response. "Oh my God! You should totally sext him! Or better yet, convince him to meet us out and then trick him into the closet at the bar. Oh fuck, can I listen outside? Listening to you guys fucking is HOT!"

"Stella, goddamn it. Stop talking about that shit with me in the room. It's gross," Chase snaps, pressing on the brakes a little too roughly in his frustration. In his defense, I definitely have no interest in hearing about his sex life either, so I can sympathize with him at this moment.

"Oops, sorry, Chasey. I forgot you were here for a second," she jokes with him. She definitely did not forget about him; she just enjoys pissing him off a little bit too much. Normally, I'd be on her side, but in this case, I have to agree with Chase. I would rather he not hear about how I definitely do plan on getting my hands on Brody at some point tonight.

She turns her attention back to me and says, "So? Is he coming out tonight or what?"

"Oh my God, Stella, give me a minute. I was just in the middle of convincing him before you went all voyeur on me." I bring my phone back up to my face and type out another quick message.

[Macy] Hmm... seems like you might need to do some more convincing before she agrees to be yours alone. Otherwise, you never know who might come along and snatch her up. You know... her being such a gem and all!

[Brody] Is that a threat, songbird? Because I hope for the sake of whoever has the nerve to even think about touching what's mine that it wasn't

I start typing out a message, knowing he's watching on the other line, but decide to play with him a little further instead. I delete the words I was going to send to him and switch off my phone so he doesn't have the chance to reply. Messing with him might just be my favorite kind of foreplay, and I can't wait to reap the rewards of my efforts.

I turn back to Stella with a massive grin lighting up my face and say, "Alright, that's settled. Now, what song are we going to start with?"

brody

FUCK OFF, JAKE

WALKING INTO MAIN STREET TAVERN, I have the craziest sense of déjà vu. The last time I was at this bar, I ended up with a dark haired siren in my bed tempting me more than I cared to admit at the time. This time, I've already tasted that temptation, and I am being provoked in other ways.

You never know who's going to come along and snatch her up

After she sent that all too aggressive text, she abruptly stopped messaging me back, despite my attempts to get in touch with her. I even went as far as trying to call her, but it went straight to voicemail. Damn songbird threw out a text she knew would get under my skin and then shut her fucking phone off. It would piss me off to no end if I didn't already know that was her aim. Little Minx is trying to play games with me, but she's about to find out just how much better I am at these kinds of tricks.

I head straight for the bar, pointedly ignoring Macy and her friend Stella who have a crowd gathered around the stage watching them belt out a top charted pop song. Stella may not have the greatest voice in the world, but damn does my song-bird ever make up for it. If I wasn't intentionally ignoring her to get under her skin, I would be absolutely captivated by her voice.

Not to mention how fucking hot she is when she is on stage. It's easy to see how she became such a sensation for the world. I may not be looking directly at her, but I can see her from my peripheral vision, and it's taking everything in me to not turn entirely around to watch her. The way she moves on stage should be illegal, but at the same time, I can't deny that she is incredible up there. I can tell by the way that she moves that she loves being on the stage, and she draws every eye in the room, much to my chagrin.

Grabbing a barstool, I place an order with Jake, the bartender, of my usual rum and coke, still not looking at the stage. Jake, however, has no such qualms and is intently gazing in Macy's direction with a longing look in his eyes. I have the itch to knock him out right then and there, but then I remember that he is simply an innocent bystander in the standoff between Macy and I tonight. It doesn't make it any easier to watch him eye-fuck her from across the room though.

He glances back at me, noticing that I am definitely not facing the stage, and nods in her direction before saying, "Yo, McAllister. You seen Macy White lately? I mean, she was always cute, but fuck me. I'd like to get to know that one a little bit better, if you catch my drift."

I struggle to hide my reaction, but luckily he's not looking at me and is still staring toward the stage where the woman in question has finished her song and is laughing with Stella. I glance in her direction, noting just how right Jake is. She really does look like a goddamn goddess tonight. Her dark hair is in some sort of a half updo, with a gold clip holding the upper half on the crown of her head. The remaining hair cascades down her back in thick curls where it hits bare skin due to the sparkly backless number she is wearing. Her leather pants hug her ass in a way that reminds me of just how lush it felt in my hands the other day. I can't wait to rip them off of her later.

Just as I am about to look away, she meets my gaze, her own eyes darkening as she takes me in, her pupils so dilated I can barely see any of her emerald irises. Fuck, she is stunning. I don't know that there will ever come a day when my heart doesn't start racing at the sight of her. I already know that I've given up our game before it's even started. I can't even pretend to play indifferent with her, especially if my already hardening cock is any indication.

Her lips widen in a devastatingly beautiful smile, and she winks at me before snatching Stella's hand and jumping off of the stage to head in my direction. Every gaze in the room watches her, but she only has eyes for me.

Unfortunately for Jake, he seemed to think that the wink she sent my way was actually for him, and he says, "Holy shit, did you see that? She's totally flirting with me! I'm so getting laid tonight!" He goes to give me a high five, but I just glare at him, and he slowly lowers his hand. "What?"

"Hey, dipshit. Shut the fuck up before I break your fucking hand," I snap at him, unable to hold in my irritation, and slam the rest of my drink back angrily just as Macy sits down next to me. She takes note of my pissed off demeanor, and her brow creases.

"What's going on? Did Jake here make you question your masculinity by giving you diet Coke with your rum instead of the regular stuff?" She nudges me cheekily while tossing a conspiratorial smile at Jake. All it manages to do is remind me that he was planning on making a move on what's mine, and it pisses me off more. She shouldn't be having inside jokes with this fuckwit.

I clench my jaw and return my gaze back to Jake to say, "Hey, Jake. Get the fuck out of here."

He just shakes his head and huffs away muttering something about needing to restock the bar anyway. I turn my gaze back to Macy, decidedly less pissed off seeing her beautiful face looking back at me.

She just looks at me incredulously and says, "Um... okay? What the fuck was that?"

"Nothing you need to concern yourself with, songbird." I lean forward, offering her a sexy grin, showing her that I am not as pissy as I was a moment ago when another man was attempting to steal her attention away from me. I lean forward and tuck a lock of her hair behind her ear, brush my fingertips along her cheek, and move forward to whisper in her ear. "I'm the only man here who you need to focus your attention on tonight. And I can't fucking wait to hear exactly how rapt you are when I peel these damn pants off of you later."

She inhales sharply, nearing whimpering, at my suggestive words, and I feel her pulse quicken beneath my hand. I pull back, pinning her gaze with mine, and smack a featherlight kiss on her perfect pouty mouth.

"Aww, you guys are seriously so cute! Ace, are you sure I can't listen in later? I promise not to say anything. You won't even know I'm there." Stella bops her way over to us, slinging her arm around her best friend's shoulders, and smiles at me. "Hey, Mr. Perfect Penis. Having a good night?"

I raise my eyebrows at her and snort a laugh. "Mr. Perfect Penis?"

"Yeah! At least that's what Macy here seems to think! Wouldn't stop chattering on and on about much she wants to su–"

"Okay, okay! Stella, can you not? Seriously, no more fucking tequila for you!" Macy exclaims, eyes wide and cheeks a bright shade of red, clearly embarrassed.

I lean in again, and say, "Wait a minute. Stella, finish that thought. What did Macy say she wanted to do with my perfect penis?" Macy's face is nearly the color of a tomato, but I just smirk at her, taking another sip of my drink, reveling in the fact that she gets so worked up around me.

"Well, I think her exact words were 'I could gag on his giant cock all day and thank him for it when we are done!' or something like that," she says while Macy gapes at her friend, clearly shocked that she revealed her words so easily. I think I'm really starting to like Stella.

"I'm going to murder you! Go dance or something," Macy says, and she pushes Stella toward the dance floor in hopes that her friend will leave us in peace. To her credit, Stella doesn't walk away so easily and pushes Macy right back.

"Fine, fine. But remember, if you guys sneak off to the bar closet for a quickie, make sure to come snag me!" She smacks Macy on the ass and then saunters off to the dance floor before Macy can retaliate. I laugh, capturing Macy's attention once again, but she's not as happy to see me as she was before.

"Keep laughing buddy. See where that gets you."

She jabs her finger into my chest aggressively, and I just grab onto her hand and pull her into my chest so we are mere inches apart. I bring my lips back down to hers, close enough to brush across them, but not enough to actually be considered a kiss.

"Hopefully with you choking on my perfect cock and thanking me for it later," I say against her mouth, causing her to whip her head back and smack me on the arm. I laugh, showing her I'm just kidding, which causes her to laugh right along with me. I'll be damned if butterflies don't start fluttering in my belly at the sound and sight of her amusement. If I thought her singing voice was beautiful, it has nothing on the melody of her laughter. I pull her back toward me and wrap my arms around her waist. She threads her arms up and around my neck, bringing our faces close again.

"Well, I guess we'll just have to see where the night takes us now, won't we, Mr. McAllister?" she teases, the sound of my name on her lips forcing another grin to my face. "For now, can we start over? I'd really rather forget the whole choking on your giant dick thing for a minute, or we won't even make it out of this bar before I tear your shirt right off of you."

"I don't think I could forget it, even if I wanted to, babe. And I really, *really*, don't want to forget it." I wink at her and revel in the fact that her pupils blow out again and her cheeks flush at my words. "But sure, as long as you know that's where the night will end, we can move on. For now. Want me to snag you a drink?" I ask, though she's already sporting what is quickly becoming my favorite scent in the world, lavender with a hint of tequila.

She shakes her head. "No, thanks. Chase had me on a strict one drink policy since we left the house, and I already hit that limit about an hour and a half ago when we first got here."

"You've been here that long? Damn, I guess I lost track of time at the office again. I didn't realize it had been that long since you texted me." I run my hands through my hair, frustrated I wasted that much time away from her.

"Brody, it's fine. You have a job to do, and a paper to save and all that. Besides, the anticipation of your arrival was a serious turn on for me." She reaches up to run her own hands through my wavy locks, scratching her nails ever so slightly on my scalp. I groan at the sensation, and she smiles again, reaching up on her tip toes to snare my lips with hers. The minute she presses her lips against mine, I'm lost in the taste of her. The hint of lime and margarita mix on her mouth is driving me insane, and I lick my way into her mouth so I can capture even more. I could spend the rest of my life memorizing the shape of her lips and the taste of her kiss and never get sick of the feeling.

After a minute, she pulls away, a little breathless, and says, "Come on, big guy. Let's go dance!" She pulls me off to the dance floor, and I am once again struck by the thought that I would follow her anywhere she leads me.

macy

WHO INVENTED CAR HORNS, ANYWAY?

I EXPECT to get some resistance from Brody when I start to pull him onto the dance floor, but to my surprise, he comes easily, trailing right behind me. After the set that Stella and I did on karaoke, the guy put his machine away and switched the music over to whatever DJ was coming in for the night. Surprisingly, this bar gets pretty busy on the weekends, most of which I attribute to the various party buses that make stops here when they make the rounds in Southeast Minnesota. Whatever. It suits my taste just fine, though I wouldn't have thought Brody would be into the type of dancing that bachelorette and 30th birthday partiers are used to. Boy, was I wrong.

As soon as we hit the floor, he pulls me flush against him, pressing a quick yet deep kiss to my mouth that makes me hot and bothered all over again, and then whips me around to press his front to my back. His hands fall to my waist, grabbing possessively and forcing me to sway along to his rhythm. With my ass pressed firmly against him, I feel the not so subtle ridge of his length pressing against me.

Fuck. If it weren't for these leather pants, I imagine my

arousal would be causing all kinds of slippery friction along my thighs. Thank God for small mercies, I guess. Though, I'd be lying if I said wet leather wasn't at least a little bit uncomfortable and making me chafe.

As we rock our hips together and grind to the music, I reach one of my hands up behind his neck to anchor myself even closer to him, while one of his hands sneaks up and lightly, but firmly, grips the base of my throat. His other hand presses firmly into my stomach, bringing us as flush as we can be without him actually being inside me. I am seriously so turned on right now, it's insane.

We get lost to the music for a while, him pressing himself into me, and me torturing him with every sway of my hips. Or am I just torturing myself? It's really anybody's guess, because this seriously feels like my own personal form of torment. When the next song plays through, I turn my head, seeking his soft lips with my own, kissing him with every ounce of my being.

Our tongues clash as we are jostled around by the ever increasing number of bodies in this tiny bar. Who knew it could even fit this many people? Forgetting the crowd for a minute, I simply let myself taste Brody. His damn mouth still holds hints of the rum and Coke that he was drinking earlier, and I swear it might be my new favorite taste. I could kiss him forever and never get tired of the feel of his mouth and the slide of his tongue against mine.

Before either of us can go fully breathless, he pulls away, spinning me forward once again to keep us rocking along to the music. He leans his head down next to my ear, and whispers, "Keep kissing me like that, babe, and Stella won't be the only one getting a show in this bar."

I laugh at his subtle jab at Stella's jokes from earlier – at least I *think* she was joking, though with Stella you can never be fully certain – and press myself further back into his dick, causing him to groan. I throw my head back onto his shoulder and say, "I would think you'd know by now, big man, but I'm definitely not shy." I give him a wink, teasing him. His eyes darken as his pupils dilate even further than I thought possible. His hand, once again, finds its way up to my throat, but this time, he grips it even more firmly and uses his fingers to force my head his direction to gaze directly into my eyes.

"Careful, songbird. You may not be shy, but I won't share you with anyone. Not even a single glance at your perfect body is acceptable for any of these assholes," he practically growls in my ear. I should be annoyed at his possessiveness, but I'd be lying if I said it wasn't hot as fuck. His need to claim me just for himself makes my heart leap and my breathing stutter even further.

Before I can make a comment, he releases me from his hold, only to grab my hand and lead me back off of the dance floor. For a moment, I am sure he's leading us to the back room to make good on what is obviously going to be a spicy end to our evening, but then he turns to the left and heads for the door.

"Um... where are we going?" I ask, unsure why he's leading me outside. He doesn't say anything and just continues leading me toward his car. He still doesn't say anything as he opens the door and gestures for me to get in. I raise my brow at him but don't say anything, just following his lead.

I wait for him to get into the driver's seat, and then ask again, "Brody, where are we going? Planning on adding kidnapping to your roster tonight or what?" I smile to let him know that I don't actually think he's up to anything nefarious.

He glances over at me with a smirk and says, "I already told you. I won't share you with anyone, and that includes sharing your screams when I make you come five different ways before I even let you touch my dick."

"Goddamn," I breathe out, causing his smirk to widen before he turns his direction to the road. I swear the temperature in this fucking car just notched up at least ten degrees, and I am already sweating just thinking about it. This is shaping up to be an even better night than I could have imagined.

"Besides, I think it's about time I fill you up with my cock while in an actual bed. Much softer on the knees," he says with a slight laugh to his tone.

"The knees? What do you mean?" I ask, though I'm pretty sure I could figure out what exactly he means by that.

"You know. For when you're on them while choking on my dick, remember?" he says, not glancing my way, but letting a grin crack his face. Clearly, he finds Stella's confession of my deep, dark secret more amusing than I do.

I swat at his arm with a giggle and say, "Oh my God! You're never going to let that go, are you?"

"Not a chance in hell, love. At least not until we have that little fantasy of yours fulfilled. Wouldn't want you to be unsatisfied, now would we?" He winks at me and glances back out of the front of his car, navigating us to his place.

I huff a half-assed irritated sound but chuckle slightly and roll my eyes. He's not wrong; I do want to have his dick in my mouth again, so I can only be so mad that he keeps suggesting it. Forcing my thoughts away from that for the moment, I take a second to shoot Stella a text to let her know where I am. I'm sure she'd have the cavalry out searching for me if I didn't say anything to her. After I hit send, I watch out the window as we make our way through the streets back to his place, absent-mindedly humming along to the music on the radio.

"You can sing louder if you want to," Brody's voice cuts

through my blank thoughts, and I turn my head back to look at him. His gaze is still set ahead, so I get the incredible view of his perfectly chiseled jawline and flawless waves is his chestnut hair. In the moonlight, the profile he sets is enough to knock the breath out of my lungs. He quickly shoots me a look, his shockingly blue eyes meeting mine for just a moment before he turns. "I don't mind if you do. You have a beautiful voice, Macy."

I shake my head quickly, registering his compliment. "You – you think I have a beautiful voice?" I mean, I am a professional singer, so *I* know I have a wonderful singing voice, but he's never told me what he thinks of my voice before. Of all the things that he's said to me, this is the one that shocks me the most. I can feel butterflies fluttering all around in my stomach with the simple praise.

"Is that surprising to you? Fuck, babe. I've never heard anything like it. When you sing, it's not just your voice – although that is stunning on its own. It's the way that your tongue caresses the words that you're singing. It's the movement of your body as you lose yourself to the melody you're creating. It's the passion with which you belt each and every note. Every single fucking thing about you draws me in, Macy. I can't look away from you, not even for a second, for I worry that I will miss the subtle way you bunch your nose when you reach for the high notes or the shine to your eyes when you sing a particularly exciting bridge. You're incredible, songbird, and I could watch you for the rest of my life and discover something new each time I do."

I stare at him, not saying anything. I couldn't even if I tried right now, because holy fuck. My throat is tight with unshed tears at his words. I've always been complimented on my voice, but this is more than that. His words mean more to me than I could even put into words at this moment.

Thank God I'm saved from having to say anything as we pull into his driveway. He puts the car in park, and before he is able to get out, I unbuckle swiftly and practically throw myself across the center console onto his lap. To his credit, he simply catches me by the hips and pulls me in close to him.

I grip his face in both of my palms and whisper a quiet "thank you" before pressing my lips to his in what I had hoped would be a tender kiss but quickly evolves into one laced with wanton hunger.

His tongue dances across the seam of my lips, and I open them to allow him access to my mouth. He reaches up and grabs my hair, not enough to hurt but enough to hold me in place while he absolutely devours me. I feel a growl in the back of his throat that matches the moan I let out at his intrusion. With the little space I have between him and the steering wheel, I rock myself along his hard cock while his tongue continues vying for dominance against my own. Our breathing grows heavy and ragged, and I move my hips faster seeking friction, despite having two sets of pants between his cock and where I am craving it most.

Just as I hit his ridge in just the right spot and pull away from his mouth with a deep moan, my ass jerks back and hits the car horn, letting out a sharp peel into the otherwise quiet night, scaring the fuck out of me. I jump so fucking high, I rail my head against the top of the car sharply and let out a cry of pain.

"Ow, fuck! Why am I always hitting my fucking head on things?" I scream in frustration, recalling the amount of times I hit my head on the stage elevator during my performances. Am I really that clumsy? Seems unlikely.

I bring my hand up to press against the top of my head and glance back down at Brody who is full on laughing at my pain.

I swat him in the chest and say, "It's not funny, asshole! If I have a concussion, you're definitely not getting any tonight!"

That only makes him laugh harder, and I scowl at him in a failed attempt to be serious. After a minute, I find myself laughing right along with him. Despite his usual grouchy demeanor, he has a seriously infectious laugh. Maybe it's because he doesn't do it often, which only makes it that much more mesmerizing when he does. It's a sound I want to listen to the rest of my life.

Another minute goes by, and our laughter dies down. He reaches up to cup my cheeks in his hands and gives me a look that makes a certain four letter word flash through my mind before pressing a quick peck to my lips.

"Come on, songbird. Let's get inside and make sure you're not concussed."

With that, he opens the door and helps both of us out of the car. I expect him to set me on my feet, but he adjusts me so I am held bridal style as he makes his way into the house. I want to protest, but he cuts me off with a kiss and a muttered "don't" and continues walking toward the front door. Thank God he is holding me because if he wasn't, I would have totally swooned.

If I'm not careful, I'm going to fall in love with this man, and right now, I honestly can't think of a good reason why I shouldn't.

macy

I COULD DO THIS FOREVER

ONCE AGAIN PROVING to be far more romantic than I would have thought, Brody keeps holding me even after we enter the house. I thought that maybe the heated moment between us would be done and over with after my ass decided to wake the entire neighborhood with the car horn, but I was definitely wrong. As soon as we crossed the threshold into his house, his mouth was on mine once again, reigniting the heat that I'm almost positive is only ever at a simmer when this man is around.

Keeping contact with my mouth, he walks us further into the house, making his way toward the back to what I assume is his bedroom. The last time I was here, I didn't really get the chance to look around much, so it's like stepping into unfamiliar territory all over again. The thrill of him sharing his space with me again zips through me. I can't believe how much of himself he has given to me lately, especially since it's really only been a couple of weeks that we have gotten close, and he's been dealing with so much between the stress of the paper and losing his parents. It feels like we should still be practically strangers, but I feel the exact opposite when I am around him. It makes my heart squeeze to think about how I can't imagine what my days back home in Malibu would be like without him in my life.

Kicking his bedroom door open, he pulls his mouth away from mine, setting my feet on the floor with my back against the wall.

He looks down and gives me a quizzical, if not slightly dazed, look and asks, "What are you thinking about? I can practically hear your brain whizzing, and I'd like to keep you focused on me for just a bit longer, love."

He nips playfully at my lips, causing me to giggle.

"I was thinking about you," I say, pressing a quick kiss to his lips. "I was thinking about how it feels like we have known each other forever, even though it's only been a couple of weeks. It's weird, right? "

He rolls his eyes and says, "We *have* known each other forever. I used to be best friends with Chase, remember? You practically followed us everywhere."

"Yeah, I know, but we never really knew each other then. We were always just around each other. Now... now it feels like, I don't know. Like we should have been spending more time together then, like we are now. I can't imagine what my time here would be like without you, Brody, and I'm starting to get scared to leave you behind when I have to get back to my other life."

It's more on the money than he realizes, since I probably won't be able to reach out much when I step back into my role as Harper. I thought getting back to my life was what I wanted, but the more time I spend with Brody, I can't help but mourn my ordinary life, if he would be in it.

He doesn't say anything and just gazes down at me with stormy eyes. I almost worry that I said something wrong as he continues to stare, but then he reaches a hand up to lightly brush some of my hair behind my ear, allowing his fingers to linger along my cheekbone while his other hand rubs circles against my hip.

A small smile tugs at the corner of his lips, and he breathes out quietly, "You could never leave me behind, songbird. Don't you understand by now? You're *mine.* You were mine from the moment you set foot in this town. You were mine when you fell from that bar straight into my arms. You were mine the second your perfect pouty lips touched mine, and you've been mine every moment every moment that has happened since. Every second of every day. You. Are. Mine. So don't for one second start worrying about where this ends. Because I'll tell you right now. It doesn't. Got it?"

I don't know if he's actually looking for a response, but if he is, he won't be getting one from me anytime soon. His words hit me intensely and leave me so speechless that all I can do is stare at him and hope that the tears that are threatening to spill from my eyes don't fall down my cheeks. He keeps looking at me, with nothing but adoration shining in his eyes as he searches my own, waiting for me to give him some sort of acknowledgement. I notice a small spark of vulnerability in his azure eyes, telling me that he isn't quite sure how I will respond to his words.

I swallow thickly, and nod briefly, before breathing out a quiet, "Yes." He smiles fully now, leaving me even more breathless than before, and leans down, brushing his lips against mine.

"Good girl," he says, and his lips crash down fully on mine, causing me to moan at his praise and the feel of his lips. He still has that subtle rum taste that I love, but I need more of it, and I need it now. I open my lips to allow him into my mouth, and he takes full advantage, licking his way in with desperate strokes of his tongue.

He removes his hand from my cheek and moves both of them down to my ass, lifting me off of the ground once more while pressing me into the wall, and holds me in place with his body as I wrap my legs around his waist like a vice. I can feel just how hard he is as he slowly starts grinding against my center, making me realize just how wet I already am for him. His confession, combined with the way he is touching me, is driving me to the brink of insanity, and I start tearing frantically at his clothes.

Before I realize what is happening, my back hits the silky texture of his comforter, and he stretches his body along the length of my own. How he managed to move us so quickly without breaking our kiss is a marvel, but you won't catch me complaining. At least with our new position, I have a much easier time tearing his shirt from his perfectly sculpted chest. As I do, he tugs on my top, not remembering that it's a bodysuit.

"Not to ruin the moment, but you're going to have to take my pants off first. The bodysuit clasps at the bottom," I say, breaking off our kiss and attempting to shimmy out of my pants while underneath his massive frame.

"I think I can manage that," he growls, standing quickly and pulling my pants off in one swift motion. He runs the rough calluses of his hands up my bare legs, his nose gently grazing a path right behind them until he reaches the clasps that hold my bodysuit together. Before he undoes them, he breathes in slowly, kissing a path along the edges of the garment and driving me crazy.

"Oh, stop teasing me," I whimper, grabbing onto his hair in an attempt to get him to hurry along the process. He chuckles at my whining, not allowing me to guide his movements the way I am dying to.

"I could listen to you beg me all day," he says roughly, but he undoes the clasps anyway, taking a deep breath through his nose as I am exposed directly to him. I feel a chill in my most sensitive area, and it makes me shiver with anticipation.

I open my mouth to answer, but before I can make any sounds, he drags a leisurely stroke of his tongue through my core, making my body bow off of the bed and causing a loud moan escape from my lips. I use my grip on his hair to pull him impossibly closer, but his pace remains unhurried, as if he is trying to do anything in his power to savor the taste of me.

After another minute of my writhing and seeking of more friction, he adds one finger and curls in it, hitting my G-spot perfectly and causing my entire body to spasm. I scream out loudly as he does this a few more times. Just when I think he's going to add another finger, he removes the one from inside me and presses it into his mouth, his eyes on mine the entire time. I nearly combust from the sight of it, and I let out another whimper watching him intently. Before I can stop myself, I sit all the way up and drag my tongue through the grooves of his muscles, tasting his warm skin on my tongue.

"Fuck, songbird. You're stunning," he says, roughly grabbing my hair and leaning down to kiss me deeply again.

Before I can get lost in his mouth again, I pull away just enough so that we are still centimeters apart and say, "Less talking, more stripping. I think it's about time I make good on some promises from earlier."

"Fuck," he breathes out and unbuttons his jeans, stepping out of them and freeing his enormous cock. Of course he isn't wearing any boxers, and his shiny piercing gleams right in front of my face, making my mouth water with anticipation.

I lean forward, grabbing hold at the base of his shaft, and lick my way up the underside of him, swirling my tongue along the head before gently sucking it into my mouth and hollowing out my cheeks.

"Jesus, Macy, you and your fucking mouth," he growls out, watching me with hooded eyes.

I moan around him and take him even further into the back of my throat. His piercing runs along my tongue in the most delicious way, and I grab his ass to pull him as far as I can, following through on my earlier fantasies of choking on the size of him. I can hardly breathe, and I am loving every second of it.

"Goddamn, your mouth is like heaven. Can I please fuck it?" he asks nicely, despite the fact that I know he's moments away from doing just that without my explicit permission. His hard length is still in my mouth, so I can't exactly answer him, and instead I moan around him again while taking him as deep as I possibly can. That is all the permission he needs, and he starts fucking my mouth in earnest, making my pussy wetter with every thrust he gives.

Thank God I don't have much of a gag reflex, or his monster dick would be hitting it brutally as he fucks all the way to the back of my throat. I have to take huge deep breaths through my nose so I don't suffocate around his size, and tears leak from my eyes as he sets his pace. He looks down on me with such adoration that I almost come from the sight alone.

I reach down with my fingers to start rubbing my clit, but he grabs my hand before I can make contact.

"Ah, ah, ah. When I told you you were mine, Macy, I meant all of you. That means right now, I get to be the only one to touch your perfect pussy."

I try to whimper in protest, but he just pulls gruffly out of my mouth and flips me around to my stomach, shoving his cock directly into my cunt from behind and making me scream. I was already soaked from his earlier words and his dick in my mouth, so he glides in effortlessly, though his girth is large enough that it's still a tight fit.

"Shit, Brody! Oh my God, fuck me. Fuck me, hard NOW!" I nearly weep with the need for him to move inside of me. So far all he has done is that initial thrust, allowing me to adjust to his size, and I am absolutely not above begging for what I need from him right now.

"Careful what you wish for, love," he growls directly into my ear before he reaches down with his left hand to grab ahold of my throat. He threads his other hand underneath me to give some attention to my throbbing clit, and he thrusts deep and hard. I am so turned on, it takes almost nothing before I start to feel that familiar build.

With the angle that we are at, the head of his cock where his piercing sits hits me perfectly in my G-spot, driving me wild, while his ministrations on my clit continue their vicious pace. Out of nowhere, I hit the point of no return and shatter around him, screaming his name at the top of my lungs. My pussy clamps down on his cock, and he inhales sharply from the feel of me fluttering around him.

He doesn't for one second falter in his punishing thrusts inside of me, forcing my orgasm to go much longer than I have ever experienced before. I am near sobbing by the time I come down from my high, stars twinkling behind my eyelids.

"God, the sound of your voice when you come is my new favorite song," he says, and pulls out of me quickly, making me miss the feel of him inside of me. Before I can protest, he flips me around, leaning backwards on his knees, repositioning me across his lap, thrusting back inside of me. I cry out again and moan loudly as he bounces me up and down along his shaft. I am still a boneless heap, thanks to him, so he is fully in control of the pace of me riding his cock.

"Fuck, your pussy, Macy. I have never felt such peace as when you are wrapped around me fully and at my mercy. I wish I could spend the rest of the night inside of you, but I am getting close. Think you can come one more time for me before I do?" he asks, his brow pinching with the effort of holding back his own climax.

Beyond words at this point, I just nod along and moan. I have regained some of my muscle function again, so I put one hand on his shoulder and grab hold of his hair to take control as I start riding his dick with fervor. My added enthusiasm places my breasts right in front of his mouth, and he sucks in one of my nipples, teasing along with his teeth and biting it softly. He's watching me the entire time, and I feel another climax building at the sight and feel of him hitting me deeper than he was before.

The combination of my thrusts and how close we are brings my clit into contact with his pelvis in just the right way, and I feel myself close to shattering all over again. Just as I start to reach the top of my peak, he reaches between us and pinches my clit in the exact spot that pulls me over the edge with another sharp cry. He pulls me in for another kiss and swallows my moans of pleasure before thrusting hard up into me a few more times and joining me with his own climax.

With how big he is, his cum has very little space to go, and I can feel both of our orgasms running down my thighs and coating his stomach in the process. Fuck, it's just about the hottest thing I've ever seen.

I drop my head down to his shoulder, completely spent, and he strokes my hair so lovingly, I can feel myself getting choked up all over again. God, I adore this man. He pulls out of me, and I think he's about to get out of the bed to clean up, but he just tucks me into his side and lays both of us down to cuddle, kissing me on the head. I could spend forever just lying here with him like this, basking in the afterglow and reveling in the rise and fall of our chests together. Neither one of us says anything, but I feel Brody's lips brush along my hairline, causing goosebumps to erupt all over my skin in pleasure.

After another moment, I kiss his chest and look up at him to say, "You know, for someone who's so possessive of me, you still have yet to take me on a proper date. I'm starting to think maybe you just want me for sex." I wink at him to let him know I'm not serious, and he lifts his eyebrows in amusement.

"A date, huh? Hmm..." he ponders for a minute, and then he pulls me back down to his chest. "I think I can manage that." He kisses my forehead and drops his head back down to the pillow while closing his eyes.

"But just so we are clear, I do want you for sex," he says, smirking, and I bark out a laugh, nipping at his chest with my teeth.

"Take me on a date, and you might just get lucky," I say, peering up at him. He has a smile on his face, and I'll be damned if my heart doesn't do that squeezy thing again.

"Who says I didn't already? Give me a minute, and I can prove to you again just how lucky I am."

I want to protest, but what can I say? I love the sound of what he's offering.

brody

UNEXPECTED VISITS FROM DESIGNER ASSHOLES

SITTING in my office editing another puff piece about something nobody gives a fuck about is quite possibly the last place I want to be right now. After dropping Macy off at her Nana's house the day after karaoke night, I promised her I'd take her on an official date, as her official boyfriend. We haven't exactly put a label on our relationship just yet, but I figure that our conversation about her being mine more than makes up for the lack of discussion. She didn't seem to have any objections the other night either.

Instead of following through on that promise though, I have had to spend every fucking night this week chained to my desk trying to fill the gap between now and when we officially make the announcement about Harper Bloom's appearance in Oaken. It's been a bit of a struggle to find anything captivating enough, hence the long nights stuck in the office.

Thankfully, Macy has been content to hang out in my office, letting me eat her out on the sofa or fucking her in the copy room after everyone else has gone home. I am beyond insatiable for this woman, which is another reason why I have had to spend so much time working late hours. I tend to get a little distracted when she's around – not that I will ever complain about it.

Tonight, though, I asked her not to come by until I was almost finished working so I could just bang this piece out for tomorrow's paper. When it's finished, I promised her I would finally take her out on our date. I have something planned that I think she'll really enjoy, so I am doing my best to get these final edits done so I can get out of here.

After another hour, I am putting on the finishing touches when Macy waltzes through the door of my office, rocking a black dress that has a deep V down the front, showing off her ample cleavage, and a ruffled hem that hits just below her ass, drawing my gaze right to it. Her hair is pulled up in a curly pony on the crown of her head with small pieces hanging down in the front. She's wearing a shock of red lipstick that I can't help but imagine wrapped around my cock. Her beauty is just one of the many reasons I am irrevocably attracted to her, and I feel a sense of pride rush through my system at the real-ization that I get to call this woman mine.

"Keep staring at me like that, Brody, and we will have a repeat of Tuesday night," she says with a wink, reminding me how I fucked her on the floor of my office instead of taking her out for dinner like I had originally planned. To be honest, I think ordering take out Chinese food after making her come for me three times was a better way to spend our time anyway.

"Brody! Stop thinking what you're thinking, right now," she exclaims, snapping me out of my reverie, literally snapping her fingers in my direction. I clear my throat and adjust myself in my pants. Like I said, she makes me insatiable.

"Don't pretend like your mind isn't right there with me, love. I can read you like a book, and you're just as ready for a repeat performance as I am."

She rolls her eyes, and says, "Yes, well. You have to wine

and dine me first, Mr. McAllister. Otherwise, I'm going to start feeling like your dirty little secret, and Lord knows I have enough of those to last me a lifetime."

I huff out a laugh knowing that she's right. I can't imagine having to keep an entire secret identity, let alone one that would land me straight on the front page news if it ever got out.

Turning back to my laptop one last time, I press send and shoot the final edits over to our printer before closing it up for the rest of the night. I am beyond ready to spend some time with my girl and to give her a date that will knock her thigh high boots off of her perfect legs.

I am just grabbing my jacket when a sudden knock at my office door catches my attention. I hadn't realized that anybody was still here, but I should have known Josie would be burning the midnight oil right alongside me.

"Uh, hey. Sorry to bother you guys. Hey, Macy," Josie says, giving her a smile. I keep forgetting that these two have sparked a friendship since Macy has been spending so much time in the office, and I try to keep my ridiculous jealousy in check. Macy's allowed to have friends, and I should feel grateful that she found such a wonderful one in Josie. If only they didn't have those damn inside jokes together about me...

Macy just smiles a broad grin at Josie and waves enthusiastically at her.

"Brody, there's a guy here to see you. Said he wants to talk about Harper Bloom?" Josie says, with a question in her tone. Clearly, whoever it is isn't someone I had on my calendar, which makes me instantly wary, especially considering Macy is standing right here with me.

I scowl at her, confused. We haven't announced anything about Harper coming to town yet. Why would some random guy want to talk to me about her of all people, completely out of the blue?

Just as I am about to ask Josie about it, a man I assume is the guy she was just referring to waltzes through my office door and plops himself down on my sofa like it's his office instead of mine. He practically bowls Macy over on his way to sit down, which instantly pisses me off. Who the fuck is this guy?

"Who the fuck are you?" I ask, not bothering to be polite. He doesn't get to just stroll in here like he owns the place and disrespect my girl by striding right past her and acting like she's less than the carpet beneath his ugly ass shoes. If he only knew who he just treated like that, he'd probably shit a brick.

He leans forward, extending his hand to shake mine, not even bothering to stand up. Arrogant fuck. I just glare at his hand until he lowers it, not seeming fazed in the slightest by my reluctance to shake his hand.

"Leopold Regis, at your service," he says, confident that I should know his name. It's vaguely familiar, but I can't quite place it. I just continue glaring at him until he continues. "Editor of *The Regis Report.*"

Ah, so that's where I recognize him from. That goddamn gossip site that makes all of America's Sweethearts look like scum of the earth with his career ending clickbait articles. He's the one that wrote the article and leaked the audio of Macy's sex tape a few weeks ago. That alone should be enough for me to drag him out of my office by the neck. For appearance sake, I don't take this course of action, though I am highly tempted.

"Alright, Regis. What are you doing *here?*" I ask, in my most dangerous tone of voice, making it clear that I am less than interested in exchanging niceties with him. To his credit, he doesn't seem fazed by my demeanor. Either he's incredibly brave or shockingly stupid.

"Well, word on the gossip blogs is that Harper Bloom is planning to make her grand comeback in this rinky-dink, teensy patch of nowhere. What I want to know is *why?* and how your little nothing of a paper managed to snag an exclusive on the details," he says with a matter of fact tone like everything he said is a fact and not one of the rudest things he could have led with. He's confirming all of my prior suspicions that he's a total dick, and I am no longer interested in entertaining this conversation.

"First of all, don't fucking talk down to me like I'm the gum beneath your designer shoe. Second of all, how did you even find that out? We haven't printed a single thing yet about Harper Bloom," I snap at him. I am equally as pissed that he's here talking to me like I am barely worthy of his time as I am that somehow the story has leaked before I got the chance to print a single thing about it. How could that have happened?

"Oh please. Like a single thing that happens in the lives of celebrities goes unnoticed on my radar. I have people and connections in all corners of the world. You really thought a story this juicy wouldn't cross my path? You really are out of your league," he scoffs, dismissing me and my work even further in his mind. I will have to ponder over how exactly he managed to find out about Harper's performance in town later. Right now, my primary concern is getting him the fuck out of my space and away from the one person who he shouldn't be crossing paths with at all.

"Well, excuse me if I don't give a fuck about sharing any details with you. I guess you'll just have to use your fancy connections to figure out your own story about Harper. You know...*after* I get the exclusive directly from her and her team," I grit out. "In the meantime, you'll have to excuse me. I have a date planned with my girl, and you're getting in my damn way."

Regis seems to finally register that Macy is still in the room with us and glances in her direction. He gives her a once over, making me grind my teeth even further as he takes her in like a specimen under a microscope. Fucking prick. As he continues scrutinizing her, his brows pull together, and he taps his pointer finger against his chin like a cartoon supervillain.

"You seem really familiar to me. Have we met before?" he questions her.

I look at her, and she is pale as a ghost, her mouth flapping open and shut like a fish. It might be the most surprised I've ever seen her, and it's making me anxious to see her so distraught. I can only imagine what scenarios are running through her head at this moment, and I can't wait to get her out of here so she can breathe again.

"Um... I don't think so," she breathes out, almost imperceptibly. She slightly looks like she's shaking, and it makes me see red that this prick is the reason she might be upset. I reach out and wrap my arm around her waist and make my way toward the door hoping Regis senses the dismissal.

"Macy is none of your fucking concern. I think it's time for you to leave," I say to Regis, hoping to discourage him from asking her more questions. I'm not exactly worried that he's going to do anything to hurt her. I just don't fucking like him, and he doesn't deserve to look at my beautiful songbird.

He scratches his chin again and eyes her up and down once more before turning back to me. "Well, if you change your mind and want to work together, here's my card. I will be sticking around a while to see if I can catch Ms. Bloom with her pants around her ankles. Again."

He gives me a conspiratorial wink, like we are in on a joke together, and hands me his business card. He leaves without another word, making me curl my lip in disgust. I briefly consider tossing his card in the trash, where it belongs, but throw it on my desk instead.

I turn back to Macy, finding her still stuck in her own head. "Hey, sorry about that. Ready to go?"

She doesn't answer and just stares where Regis exited, looking entirely disheveled. I reach my hand out and put it against her cheek, gently turning her head so her eyes meet mine. I register the panic in them, making me even more concerned.

"Are you okay?"

She blinks a few times and then nods her head. "Y-yes. Sorry. I just wasn't expecting to see him here, that's all. He's the last person I want to be sniffing around here."

"Don't worry, songbird. We'll stay away from that fucking asshole. Trust me."

"Are you ready to go? I'd like to forget about him, if we can," she says, though I can still hear the slight anxiety in her tone.

I grab her hand and pull her close to me so that I can bring my mouth close to her ear and whisper, "Yeah, babe. I hope you're ready, because I'm about to date the fuck out of you."

She follows me easily out of the room and gives me a genuine laugh. Exactly what I need to hear to boost my confidence going into the evening with my favorite songbird right alongside me.

macy

WILL THIS MAN EVER STOP SURPRISING ME?

FUCK, *fuckity, fucking, fuck.* What in the actual fuck is Leopold Regis doing here? I have been in full blown panic mode since that sleazy piece of shit blew into Brody's office like he owned the place. He's here to dig up dirt on Harper and stir the fucking pot, and I am freaking the hell out! How did he even find out about her coming to town? Aside from my inner circle, I haven't told a single soul about the impromptu benefit concert.

Despite telling Brody that I wanted to forget about it, I can't help but ruminate over the fact that he's here, and we have to figure out a way to avoid him at all costs if we want to keep the exclusive with the paper. As we roll toward wherever Brody is taking me on our date, I ponder who could have possibly let this slip and come up with a total blank. I will just have to talk to Chase about it when we get back to Nana's.

Brody glances over at me from the driver's seat of his car, a look of concern creasing his eyebrows at my state of distress.

"What's rattling around in that head of yours, Macy?" he asks, reaching over to give my hand a quick reassuring squeeze.

"I was just trying to figure out how fucking Regis found out about Harper coming here, and I'm totally drawing a blank. The only people who know about it are the two of us, Chase, and Stella, and none of us would tell a single soul. I just don't get how he figured it out," I say, chewing on my lower lip in frustration.

His eyes soften, and he reaches his hand up to drag my lip out from beneath my teeth with his thumb. He grabs my hand and brings it to his lips, kissing the back of it in a gesture that sends the butterflies in my belly into a frenzy.

"I'm so sorry, Brody. I will talk to Chase and be 100% sure that you get the exclusive on all things Harper. I promise," I say, pleading with him not to be too angry.

"I'm not worried about it, love. That fuckwit can go sniffing around here all he wants. I know you and your brother. Not only that, but you trusted me completely with your secret and that means I know I can trust you to share everything with me. We'll figure it out, okay?"

I nod, though I'm not quite sure I can let go of my anxiety just yet. Brody says he's cool with all of this, but what if he's not? What if he ends up thinking this is all just a little too much? What if he doesn't want me when this is all ov–

"Hey," Brody says, stopping my frantic thoughts and forcing me to focus on him once again. He offers me a small smile and continues. "Stop thinking whatever it is that you're thinking. I'm not upset. Well not about the story anyway. I could do without that prick running around in my town, but for now, I want you to forget about him and all of that stress that's marring your beautiful face and focus on our date night. I, for one, can't wait to show off my stunning girlfriend."

"Girlfriend? We are at that stage now, are we?" I make a lovestruck face at him, smiling at his official claim of me as his.

"Babe, we've already discussed this. You're mine. End of

discussion. Now, turn off your damn brain for the next few hours, and let me prove to you just how thrilled I am to call you mine," he says, placing another kiss to the back of my hand and looking out of the windshield to focus on driving once more.

I sigh, but shake off the lingering anxiety I am feeling. "Okay. So, what style of doting do you have planned for me tonight, *boyfriend?*"

He just smiles that devastatingly handsome grin I love so much at my use of the label, but he doesn't give me an answer. He just shakes his head and presses a finger to his lips in a gesture meant to convey that it's a secret. I guess I will have to wait to find out.

* * *

"You know, if I had known this is where you were going to bring me, I would have worn some pants or something. I am totally going to fall on my ass and flash the DJ the goods!" I exclaim in Brody's direction, trying, and failing, to keep up with him on these damn roller skates.

Ever the confusing man, he brought me to a roller rink for our date. Super cute and everything, but it turns out that I am crazy unsteady on skates. You'd think I'd be better on them given all of the crazy stunts I've had to do for my concerts and music videos, but I am a disaster on these things. Guess I won't be adding a rollerskating act to my stage set anytime soon.

"No need to worry, love. I connected my bluetooth to the surround sound for my perfectly curated playlist, and he's leaving. It'll be just the two of us here tonight, so the only person you'll be flashing the goods to is me," he says, chuckling at me from across the rink. Somehow, he's managing to skate circles around me. How is he so fucking good at this?

I try to skate toward him again, but the skates roll out from underneath me, and the world starts to tip as I fall. I practically see my life flash before my eyes, and thank the universe for all of the wonderful things I got to do in my life as I freefall toward the floor. But before I make contact, a pair of strong, muscly arms wrap around me, holding me steady.

"You know, I have to admit I thought you'd be better at this. How is it possible that the great Harper Bloom is able to do aerial gymnastics while belting high notes, but she can't rollerskate more than 6 inches without falling on her perfect ass?" he teases me, but he holds on, gliding both of us along the rink.

"Not all of us moonlight as John Travolta in *Saturday Night Fever*! How did you manage to learn how to skate so well, anyway?" I huff at him, irritated. I would have thought I'd be better at this, too, and it's making me cranky that I can't get the hang of it.

"My parents used to bring me here a lot as a kid. It was one of their favorite places. Some of my best memories are from when we would take family outings to the rink," he says, getting lost in the recollection for a minute. He shakes his head, laughing, and continues. "I swear my tailbone is misshapen from all of the times that I fell on my ass learning how to skate. Mom would always rush right over, but dad would stop her, saying I needed to keep practicing or I wasn't ever going to figure out how to stay on my feet. At the time, it made me so mad, but, of course, he was right. I figured it out, and I started skating circles around them not long after the first time they brought me." He falls quiet, just pulling me along with him and gazing down at me.

"You must really miss them," I say, squeezing his hand and looking up at him. I can see the brief flashes of grief in his eyes, and it makes me hurt for him. He keeps so much of his past bottled up, and I know it causes him more pain than he realizes to not talk about them.

For a moment, I worry that he's not going to say anything, but then he gives me a sad smile and says, "Yeah. They were amazing, and I can't help but feel like I will never be able to live up to their legacy. Being here makes me feel close to them again, and being here with you reminds me of why this was always one of my favorite places."

I pull on his hand, forcing him to stop moving, and bring him chest to chest with me. I hold both of his hands in mine and gaze into his eyes so that he knows just how serious I am about what I am about to say.

"They would be so proud of you, Brody. Don't for one second let yourself believe that you are failing them. You are keeping their memory alive through your work and the time that you spend doing their favorite things," I say with sincerity, keeping my eyes directly on his. He closes them and breathes out a sigh. For a moment, I think I've upset him, but then his eyes flash open, and he leans down pressing a tender kiss to my lips. It's not the same as the heated kisses we usually exchange, but it feels even more intense with all of the lingering emotions surrounding us.

After too brief a moment, he pulls away and leans his forehead against mine to look into my eyes again, breathing out, "Thank you."

"You're welcome. Now, come on and show me some moves! I know you're holding back to make me feel better. I wanna see what you can do on these rolling death traps, babe," I say, smiling at him playfully and pushing him away from me. I nearly lose my balance at the sudden movement but manage to catch myself before I tumble to the floor.

"Oh, love, you have no idea the moves I have planned for you," he says, and I shiver, remembering a few of the moves that we have already practiced earlier this week. He gives me a knowing smirk and keeps skating backwards like a pro.

"Now, sit your ass in that chair and prepare yourself for the show of a lifetime," he shouts out and skates away from me at top speed.

I notice, for the first time, the chair that's not too far off to the side of the rink and make my way to it, precariously. He fiddles with his phone, choosing a song, and turns back to me with a devilish look on his face.

As the music starts playing through the speakers, I start laughing. The whispered voice of Marvin Gaye croons through the surround sound, imploring me to "get up, get up, get up, get up." Just as the opening verse of "Sexual Healing" starts, Brody begins his routine, making his way around the rink.

Despite his incredibly intricate moves, his eyes never leave mine, heating me from the inside out. His choice of song may be somewhat hilarious, but it's doing a pretty good job of getting me all hot and bothered as he makes his way toward me, gyrating his hips along with the lyrics. I continue laughing as he lip syncs along with the music, crooning at me while also skating like a pro-rollerskating dancer or whatever they call themselves. He keeps going through the entirety of the song while I hoop and holler at him in encouragement.

Just as the song begins to fade out, Brody skates right up to me and drops to his knees in front of me in the chair. I offer him a round of applause and beam at him.

"That was incredible! You are full of many secret talents, Brody McAllister," I say, leaning down and wrapping my arms around his neck while he grins up at me. I feel a thrill of excitement heat my blood at the uncontained joy on his face.

"You're the only one that will ever see them, songbird," he says, smacking a quick kiss on my lips. This man is full of surprises, and I can't wait to uncover every single one of them.

He abruptly stands, pulling me up to standing with him. "Now, come on. I have one more surprise for you."

"I don't think anything could top what I just saw. That was indescribable," I say as he drags me toward the center of the rink once again. This time, I manage to make it there somewhat gracefully, though I imagine that has more to do with his hands guiding me than my own talent on the skates.

"I'm going to take that as a compliment. Now sit," he commands, helping me to sit down right in the middle of the room and following me down. "Lie back, love."

I do as he asks, and he reaches back into his pocket to pull his phone out again and taps on it a few times. The lights in the rink go out, bathing us in total darkness. I am about to ask what the hell is going on, but then the LED lights that normally cast a disco atmosphere around the room turn to face the ceiling and cast a galaxy across the broad white ceiling, bathing us in artificial starlight. I gasp at the sight while Taylor Swift's "Lover" plays through the speakers as we lie there staring at the constellations above us.

I turn my head to look at Brody, finding him already gazing at me with a look of yearning painting his perfect features. I reach my hand out and run my palm along his face, brushing my fingertips along his lips, scooting my body closer to his until he reaches out to pull me toward him. His eyes never leave mine, and we are just watching each other, breathing in the scent of the other.

My eyes flick down to his lips, and I whisper, "Brody..."

"I want you to know, songbird, that I plan for every one of my future favorite memories to be centered around you. After my parents died, I became a ghost. Just going through the motions, never allowing myself to feel anything besides anger and self-loathing, until you breezed your way into my miserable world. You are bringing me back to life, Macy, and I never want to let you go," he says, his eyes glittering with emotion as he looks at me. His words are sincere, but for some reason I feel a rush of insecurity roll through my body.

"Are you sure I'm the one that you want? It's only been a few weeks. You might change your mind," I say, not sure why I'm trying to convince him to be skeptical. "We're still getting to know each other as adults. What if you don't like what you get later?"

He looks at me incredulously, as if I just said the craziest thing in the entire world.

"Songbird, I have spent the last two months memorizing every single thing about you. I've memorized the sound of your laughter when you genuinely find something funny. I've memorized the exact moment when you've had just the right amount of tequila to start dancing on tables, regardless of who's watching. I've memorized the sensation of you walking into the room like I've wandered too close to the sun, and my eyes immediately find you like you're a beacon that was created just for me," he says, leaving me completely stunned. "There is nothing about you that I could ever dislike."

His words strike me like a physical blow, and it feels like my heart swells impossibly large in my chest. In lieu of responding, I close the distance between us, and lose myself in him, as he rolls himself over me to deepen our kiss. My body is flush with emotion, and it hits me like a freight train.

In just a few short weeks, I've managed to fall in love with this man. And in just a few weeks, I will have to leave him behind to become Harper Bloom all over again.

brody

MESSING AROUND AT THE OFFICE IS A RECIPE FOR GETTING CAUGHT

FOR THE NEXT couple of weeks, I spend nearly every night taking Macy all around Oaken and reminding her of the places from our past. Sometimes I forget that she's not used to the small town lifestyle anymore, and watching her re-experience life on the slower side of things is nothing short of mesmerizing.

She's mentioned a few times what her life is like as Harper, and it sounds like she barely has had a chance to breathe since she and Chase jetted off for the glitz and glamor of rubbing elbows with the stars all those years ago. Not only that, but managing to keep a low profile when she chooses to go out into the world as Macy couldn't have been a walk in the park either.

Despite my earlier confidence about her being mine, and mine alone, I do worry that once the town festival is over, she will jet out of here back to life in the fast lane and forget all about me. I just have to do a really good job of convincing her that I can handle both worlds, even if that means that I have to get comfortable being in the spotlight myself.

"Penny for your thoughts?" Macy mumbles from the corner

of my office. She's been here helping me prepare for the festival, setting all of the plans in motion so it goes as smoothly as possible when "Harper" is set to arrive in town.

I glance up at her, briefly taking her in, as she lounges upside-down on my office couch with her feet on the back of the sofa and her head hanging off of the seat, her long hair resting on the floor. I chuckle at her, shaking my head.

"You know, you're going to get a headache if you keep sitting like that, forcing all of the blood to rush into your head," I tease her. "They design couches for your ass to sit on the seat for a reason, Macy."

"Well, those reasons are stupid, and they definitely don't take into account the fact that the best thinking is done when you literally turn your world upside-down," she says, flicking through her phone above her head. "Besides, it's comfy to lay— OUCH, fuck!"

She exclaims loudly as her phone slips out of her grip and lands directly on her face with a loud smack. In her pain, she slips even further down the sofa, causing her head to bang on the floor and her legs to go flying, splaying her out in a position she will be hard-pressed to get herself out of alone. I laugh loudly at the image she is presenting right now.

"Stop laughing, asshole, and help me!" she snaps, wiggling around on the floor to try and get herself into a more comfortable position on her own. All she succeeds in doing is getting herself in an even worse position than before. I stand up from my desk, shake my head, and move over to help her.

"You know, for someone who is said to be one of the best performers in the world, you really are one of the clumsiest people I've ever met," I tease her. I swear, I've seen her run into something or drop things on her face more times in the last few weeks than I have seen anyone do in a lifetime.

She manages to get her legs stretched out, so she's just

laying there waiting for me to give her a hand to stand up from the floor. I reach down and grasp her tiny hands in mine, but as soon as they touch, she uses her position and all of her strength to pull me off of my feet to join her on the floor.

I land on her, hard, with a muffled "oof," but she just laughs as I do, gazing up at me. I am lying sprawled out completely on top of her, but she doesn't seem to mind.

"Ha! Now who's the clumsy one?" she jabs, clearly pleased that she was able to get the best of me. I grab both of her hands again, bringing her arms above her head, so I can pin her into the floor even further with my body.

I lower my mouth close to her face, and say, "Good effort, songbird, but now you're at my mercy."

Her laughter dies off and her eyes go hooded at my suggestive tone, flicking down to my lips as I move closer to her. Just as our lips are about to touch, I let her hands go and start tickling her mercilessly, eliciting more of that tinkling laughter from her flawless lips.

"S-stop! Brody! I can't take it! Please!" She manages to huff out in between laughs and deep breaths.

"Woah, okay, I will just come back later then, I guess," Josie says, and I lift my head up to see her standing in the doorway holding papers over her eyes to shield her from our shenanigans on the floor. I push myself up off of Macy, grabbing her hands to drag her up with me.

"No, that's not necessary. What's up, Jos?" I say gruffly, attempting to hold back my irritation at being interrupted, even if Josie was just doing her job. I head back to take a seat at my desk while Macy takes her same position back on the sofa. Stubborn girl clearly didn't learn her lesson the first time.

Josie's still holding her stack of papers to avoid looking at us, worried about what she might see.

"Are you guys... decent? I'd really rather not see a dick this early in the day, thank you very much," she says, and she visibly shudders as if the sight of my dick is physically appalling to her.

"Jesus, Josie. The entire office is here, and my door is open. Do you have such a low opinion of me?" I ask her, my tone suggesting I am actually offended by her assumption that I can't keep it professional while at work.

"Oh, fuck off, Brody. Don't act like you haven't messed around with all of us here before," she snaps at me, but lowers her papers so she can look me in the eyes. Admittedly, she's not wrong, so I just huff at her words and roll my eyes. She looks over to Macy, who's back to scrolling on her phone, probably busy making all of the arrangements for next week. "Hey, Macy. Are we still on for drinks later?"

"Hell yeah, girl! I am in serious need of some girl time, and I know Stella has been itching for another night on the town. Plus, I could use a break from Mr. Scowly Face over there," Macy says, smiling up at Josie, and casting me a teasing look.

"I don't scowl," I mumble under my breath, definitely scowling. "What did you need, Josie? We are busy here." I am being a touch gruff, but Josie should be used to that by now. Macy might bring out the very best in me, but I am definitely still a grouch when I am at work.

"I just came to check in and see how the plans for Harper Bloom's arrival are coming along? I know we made the announcement earlier in the week about her coming to town for the festival, which gave us an incredible boost in sales, but now people want to know exactly what events she will be participating in and when they get to see her. I assume we have a plan of action? I'd like to get that printed in Thursday's paper."

"I can help with that," Macy chirps, sitting upright on the sofa for the first time since she arrived an hour ago. "So,

Chase and I have planned for her to arrive in town on Monday morning, and she will spend the day with us, just going over everything – security, logistics, and all of the other boring stuff. She's taking a red-eye, so we figure she's probably going to be pretty jetlagged and won't want anyone else around. Then, Tuesday, she will make an appearance at the grape-treading event the winery is doing, mash some grapes, and do some photo ops. Wednesday, we have her slotted to read to the kids at the local library. Thursday, dinner with the Mayor, and then Friday is the concert. How does that all sound?"

Josie is writing away on her notebook, mouthing along as she does, taking in everything Macy just listed off. It's a pretty jam packed schedule, but we wanted to capitalize on how much time she's spending here, and Chase agreed that all of it sounds like the perfect, wholesome agenda that will boost Harper's image and make people forget about the whole sex tape thing.

"That sounds great! And Macy, you'll be there to help facilitate everything, right?" Josie asks, looking up from her notebook to glance at Macy. We still haven't told Josie the big secret, so we had to come up with an excuse as to why she won't be around when Harper is here.

"Um... actually I think Chase was planning on handling all of that. I have some appointments next week that I have to go to, so I won't be around much."

Josie's eyebrows crease in confusion. "What? You're not going to be around for all of this? You're the one that made it all happen in the first place. Won't Chase want you around to help facilitate?"

"Nah, he'll understand. I've got some other things I need to take care of, but I will be around after the concert." She looks away, quickly, I assume in hopes that Josie won't question her further on the issue. Any other day, she'd be shit out of luck, but Josie surprises me by letting it drop.

"Okay, cool. So we will run everything through Chase." I swear I see her cheeks heat as she mentions his name, but I wonder if it's just a trick of the light or something. "In the meantime, how are we handling the Leopold Regis situation?"

I growl at the mention of that asshole's name. I had forgotten about him in the days following his visit to my office. Now with Harper's arrival getting closer, he's probably going to be sniffing around even more. Macy answers before I get the chance to say something nasty about him.

"I think Chase is working on damage control with him, so you guys don't need to worry about it at all. He's dealt with Regis for years and knows how to throw him off a trail, so no need to stress."

"Sweet! So that's all covered. I will get working on the article tomorrow that will lay out the agenda for Harper, and we will be ready to roll through everything next week. I'm going to go wrap that up, and then Macy, wanna head out with me?" Josie asks, snapping her notebook closed.

"Actually, I'm going to get going here pretty soon. I told Stella I would meet up with her to grab something from the coffee shop before we all meet up at the bar. I will meet you there, if that's alright?"

"Yeah, that's totally fine! It shouldn't be more than a couple of hours, so meet at Main Street at like... 6?" Josie asks, looking up at the clock to gauge the time. I hadn't realized that it was already so late in the afternoon.

"Perfect! See you then!" Macy chirps, and Josie nods, leaving my office.

I stand up from my desk, and make my way over to Macy still sitting on the sofa. I lean down, placing my hands on either side of her legs, while she threads her hands up and around my neck. "Girl's night, huh? What am I supposed to do tonight then?"

"That sounds a lot like a *you* problem, buddy. But I could maybe be convinced to come over to your place after I leave the bar," she teases, her emerald eyes twinkling at me and a smile lighting up her face.

"Oh yeah? Tell me what I have to do to convince you, songbird," I rumble, smirking at her and letting my eyes flick down to her lips. It has the intended effect, and her eyes go molten with desire. She pulls me closer to her and mumbles against my mouth.

"Close the fucking door, and get on your knees," she says, instantly making my dick rock hard. "You have five minutes before I have to meet Stella. Better make them count." She winks at me, and I feel the blood in my veins zip with excitement. Macy is my favorite flavor, and I can't wait to get a taste.

I smack a kiss to her lips. "Yes, ma'am."

I follow through on her request to close the door, locking it behind me, and turn back to her. "But just so we are clear, I only need three to make you scream my name."

She laughs, and I follow through on my promise, slapping my hand over her mouth to muffle her cries as she comes on my tongue in less than two minutes.

macy

LEOPOLD FUCKING REGIS AGAIN?

"SO, have you figured out how you're going to deal with the whole Leopold Dipshit situation yet?" Stella asks, sipping on her bright green matcha latte. I chew on a chocolate chip scone to avoid answering her question. She just raises her eyebrows at me, knowing I'm deliberately trying not to answer the question because I still have no fucking clue what we are going to do about him snooping around town.

"Macy!" she yells out, slapping me on the shoulder. "I know that you told Brody everything and all that, but aren't you at least a little bit concerned that more people are going to figure it out with that asshole skulking around town trying to dig up dirt?"

I drop my head into my hands, allowing a loud groan to slip through my lips. "Ugh, I know! I just haven't had a ton of time to think of a plan. Between prepping for Harper's arrival and spending all of my time with Brody, it's just kind of been on the back burner."

"Well, I guess I can't fault you for that. If I were getting dicked down every which way to Sunday, I'd probably put

Regis out of my mind, too," she says, winking at me and taking a sip of her latte. I scowl and swat at her from across the table.

"Not helpful, Stel," I grumble, sipping my drink through my straw. "What do *you* think I should do? You've had nothing but down time since you've been here. Come up with any ideas while you were on your deep dive into trashy Netflix reality TV shows?"

"Not in the slightest," she says, sighing like the weight of the world is on her shoulders and not mine. "Those people can barely make a relationship last for more than 10 days, let alone come up with a scheme to take somebody down. But if I were you, I'd hunker down with my muscle man, have him tie me to a bed, and let him have his way with me all hours of the day until it's time to don the disguise."

"Stella..." I groan, glancing around the room to make sure that nobody overheard her rated R suggestion for dealing with the situation.

Thankfully, there's only, like, three people in this coffee shop, and they are one of those places that blasts the music so loudly you can barely hold a conversation with the person directly across from you, let alone overhear someone else's from across the room.

"What? Nobody can hear us all the way over here, and I think my idea is foolproof. Regis can't dig up any dirt on you if you're not around to dig on," she says, her tone saying that she believes her plan is rock solid. My eyebrows bunch together, and I give her a look that I hope conveys just how ridiculous her previous statement was.

"Okay, fine. If hunkering down isn't an option, then what you need to do is take the fight to him. Deal with the situation head on, and get rid of him for good," Stella adds, shrugging her shoulders.

"You're right, but how do we do that? It's not like I have a ton of blackmail to use on him or anything like that," I say, exasperated with how I feel like I'm constantly going in circles over this situation. It shouldn't be this hard to get one guy to leave you alone, right? Even if you're an international pop star with a secret identity.

"That's it! You have to find some blackmail on this fucker. Figure out a way to use it against him so that he leaves Harper alone for good," Stella says, smacking her hands on the table excitedly. Not only does she love her reality shows, she's always up for a little revenge drama, so I am unsurprised by her suggestion.

"You make it sound so easy, Stella. It's not like Regis just leaves his personal diary lying around for anyone to grab and read. How would we even do that?"

"I don't know, but I think that's the way to go. Give him a taste of his own medicine. The prick," she scoffs, grinding her teeth in irritation. Harper may have gotten most of his ire over the years, but Stella, being her close friend, picked up some of the heat as well. She might even hate him more than I do, and that's saying something.

"I'll figure out a way to deal with Regis soon enough," I say, finishing off the last of my iced coffee. "For now, let's set that drama off to the side and make our way over to the bar. Josie should be getting there any minute, and I am beyond ready for some girl time. Plus, I think they have karaoke again tonight! You ready?"

"Yeah, yeah, yeah, let's go," she agrees, slurping the rest of her matcha latte with a loud sound. She garners a few looks from the few people around the shop, but true to form, she doesn't seem to care. I love Stella for her ability to be unapologetically herself.

Thankfully the coffee shop isn't too far from the bar, so we are able to walk there. The entire time, I ruminate over how exactly I'm going to deal with the Regis situation, and what information I could even drag out of him to get him off of my back once and for all.

Before I can spend too much time making myself even more depressed thinking about it, we arrive at Main Street Tavern. As expected, Josie is already here. We are a few minutes late, so she's sitting at the bar chatting with Jake, the bartender.

When she sees us come through the door, she gives a huge smile and waves us over. We make our way to her, bypassing several gawking dude-bros who are playing pool in the corner. Nothing like a few new faces in a small town bar to stir up interest, especially amongst the male population.

Sidling up to the bar, I squeeze myself onto the stool next to Josie, and Stella does the same on my other side.

"Hey! Everything ready to go for the paper tomorrow?" I ask Josie.

"Yep! All set. But I don't want to talk about that damn paper anymore. I am ready to leave it behind for the night. It's been too damn long since I've had a girls' night, and I am ready to party!" she says loudly, quoting *Bridesmaids*. It's a side of Josie I haven't seen, and I laugh along with her.

"Yes, girl! I am so ready!" I say, waving Jake back over, so I can order a drink. Tequila preferred, of course. Stella does the same on my other side, ordering a strawberry margarita to match mine.

"I think we should cheers! To the tequila gods for creating the most delicious drink on planet Earth, and to girls' nights with new friends!" I shout out loudly, and both Stella and Josie clink glasses with me, whooping along. We each take a huge sip from our drinks, and then set them back down, tapping my hands on the bar. "Okay! So karaoke, then? I'm officially making it our girls' night tradition."

Stella snaps her fingers and lets out a loud "yes!" while Josie claps and nods her head vigorously. I admit that I wouldn't have pegged her as a karaoke girl, but I am stoked that she's going along with it. I remember that in high school choir she had a pretty good singing voice, and I'm excited to be singing with her again. It feels like I've found another soul sister right here in my hometown, and I am loving every second of it.

"I think in honor of the pop princess herself coming to town, we should do a Harper Bloom song!" Josie exclaims loudly and hops off of her bar stool to head over to give the DJ her song choice. A shot of panic runs through me at the idea of singing one of my own songs, and I reach out to grab her arm, stopping her progression.

"Wait, Josie! Don't you think people will hear enough of her music at the concert next week?" I implore her, trying to get her to choose a different artist. I've strategically avoided singing any of my own songs for fear that someone would be able to put two and two together. My history with secretly recorded sound bites hasn't served me well in the past.

"Oh, come on, Macy. The people in this town will likely be playing her album on repeat from now until she sets foot on that stage. Besides, this is the perfect way to get people hyped!" She shakes me off and heads to the DJ.

Stella grabs my arm, drawing my attention back to her. "Chill out, Ace. Nobody's going to be able to tell that it's you. Even if they have suspicions, they'll just chalk it up to you sounding shockingly similar to Harper. But if you're that spooked, just take a shot of tequila with me to loosen up. You can sing one of your songs without the entire world figuring out your secret, I promise."

I shake my head to dispel the anxiety. Maybe she's right. It's probably not as a big of a deal as I am making it out to be. I can't imagine most people are on the lookout for secret pop stars doing karaoke in the middle of Oaken, Minnesota.

"Fine, you're right. But I still want the shot, please and thank you. Jake! Two tequila shots, please! Extra lime on the side!"

* * *

I belt out the lyrics to Harper's – *my* – latest hit, bopping along with Josie and Stella on the stage. I'd like to say that I toned it down in hopes nobody would recognize my voice, but what can I say? Once I get a microphone in my hand and hear the opening notes of a song that I wrote, I just can't hold back. I am definitely banking on the fact that I am virtually a nobody in this town, and everyone will just think "huh, she sounds a lot like Harper Bloom" in their heads before totally dismissing the idea. I mean, people can sound like other people. There are impersonators and everything, right?

I'm just in the throes of wrapping up the song, flinging Josie out in a spin move, when I notice someone sitting at the bar, assessing our trio with scrutinizing eyes. Leopold Fucking Regis is here, and my note falters for a second as I make eye contact with him. I skip my gaze away quickly, and shimmy with Stella, finishing up the song to a loud applause from the crowd of people that have gathered in the bar since we got here. We laugh and grasp our hands together, taking a slightly drunken bow.

We razz each other, hugging and laughing as we head back up to take our seats at the bar once more. We order another round of drinks, high on the feeling of girls' night and dancing around like crazy people on the stage.

Out of the corner of my eye, I see someone pull up right next to me, facing me head on, while I do my best to focus on

Jake making our drinks. When it's clear that I'm not going to look in his direction, he speaks up, catching my attention.

"You're Brody McAllister's girl, right? Macy, was it?" he asks, intentionally giving the wrong name to ruffle my feathers like the insufferable ass that he is. Unfortunately, it works.

I glare at him, clicking my tongue against my teeth in irritation. This asshole doesn't deserve an ounce of my respect, especially after calling me the wrong name. "Macy."

"Ah, Macy. Right. You've got quite the set of pipes on you, Macy. Singing that song, I almost thought I was listening to the infamous Harper herself. Alas, it was just you," he says that last bit with disdain as if he couldn't even begin to imagine that someone like me would be good enough for the stage. If only the asshole knew.

Regardless of his clearly low opinion of me, I plaster a saccharine smile on my face and say, "Yep! Just little old me. Now, if you'll excuse me, your presence is putting a major damper on my otherwise incredible night so..." I go to turn away from him, but he grabs hold of my elbow, and I zero in on the contact of his hand on me.

"Your boyfriend didn't seem all that excited to share information with me, but I wonder if you might be more open with me. You're Chase White's sister, so you must know Harper, too, right? Care to share some of her secrets with the world?" he asks with a smarmy tone to his voice. Clearly he thinks I am one of Harper Bloom's groupies looking to make a quick buck out of airing her dirty laundry. I pull my elbow out of his grip and level him with another glare.

"Look, buddy. You're barking up the wrong tree if you think that I'm going to air out any skeletons in Harper's closet," I snap at him, but he just smiles back at me with amusement, unbothered by my reaction. "I don't like you. I've never liked you, and you should be ashamed of yourself for making a living out of ruining other people's lives."

His eyebrows lift in a condescending gesture, and he throws back the rest of whatever drink he was sipping on, before his gaze returns to mine. "You don't have to like me, sweetheart. But I can tell you're hiding something, and you can put money on it that I'm going to figure out what it is. I can't wait for Harper to get into town, and I can finally figure out exactly what she's been up to for the last several weeks. I'm sure whatever it is will make me another cool few millions when the scandal breaks."

With that, he gives me a huge grin, grabs his jacket, and leaves the bar, not even giving me the chance to reply to his jabs.

I release a breath, watching him go with anger coursing through my veins, making me shaky. Fucker.

"Oh my God! Was that Leopold Regis?" Stella hisses in my ear. "What did he say to you? I was hoping he had left town for a little bit and would be back for the festivities."

I scoff, "You really thought that slimy fuck was going to go back to Malibu instead of sticking around to do his best to dig up more dirt on Harper? Which is exactly what he was just doing, by the way. Trying to get me to spill secrets on her. God, I fucking hate that guy!"

"Which guy?" Josie asks, returning from what I assume was the bathroom.

"Leopold Regis," Stella says. "We have had many a run-in with that asshole over the years, and he never gets any better. He really hit a new low airing out Harper's private sexcapades all over the internet, though."

"Yeah, he seemed like a total prick when he came by the paper last week. Fucking gossip sites," Josie grumbles. "They make the rest of the news look bad with their clickbait *gotcha!* tactics."

"Whatever, fuck that guy. I think I have a few more songs in me tonight. Ready for our encore ladies?" I say, raising my glass to clink with them again. They cheers with me, and we make our way back up to the DJ to input another few songs to sing.

Despite the fact that I want to just shake off my interaction with Regis, though, I can't help but worry that he's going to put enough effort into uncovering something that he may just stumble upon the truth. And I simply cannot let that happen.

macy

DID I REALLY JUST SAY THAT?

I WAKE up to the smell of coffee and the sounds of someone shuffling around my room. I let out a heavy groan, squeezing my eyes shut, and realize just how much my head is pounding. The stale taste of lime in my mouth lets me know that I got too drunk last night to give a fuck about brushing my teeth. Huge mistake.

"Now, this seems a little bit familiar," the presence in the room says, and I realize Brody is the person I hear moving around. I groan again, lifting the covers up over my head to block out the light, and I feel the bed dip as he sits down next to me.

"Oh my God, I think I'm dead. Am I dead? I must be, right? Dead. Dead. Dead," I complain, my voice muffled by the blanket, and I hear him laugh at my antics. Sure, he can laugh. He's not the one whose brain is currently trying to escape through the top of their skull.

I flip the covers down abruptly and look up at him leaning over me with a huge smile on his face. "Don't laugh! Who's going to give you amazing head if I'm gone? You know you're never going to find someone as willing to suck your cock as I am. Better start counting your blessings now that you got it while you could. You know, before I die."

He just smiles wider at me and reaches down to brush some of my errant hair out of my face. I can only imagine what it looks like right now, but he doesn't seem to mind. He leans down and kisses my forehead. Thank God the blanket is still covering my mouth, or he'd probably pass out from the smell of my tequila infused morning breath.

"You're cute when you're hungover, love. And you're not dead, though you did drink Jake out of every bit of tequila he possessed last night. An impressive feat. for sure." He leans over and grabs the coffee off of the bedside table, handing it to me. "Here, drink some of this, I promise you'll feel better. And take these."

He passes me some ibuprofen, and I swear I would marry him right on the spot for that small gesture alone.

"Oh my God, I love you," I say, popping the pills into my mouth, and take a huge gulp of the steaming cup of coffee. I moan around the taste of it and feel marginally better as the hot liquid rushes down my throat and heats me from the inside out. After another sip, I look over to him and notice that he is staring at me with a look of shock on his face.

My brows crease at that look. "What? Do I have something on my face?" I swipe furiously at my cheeks, hoping to dispel whatever it is that's making him look at me like that.

"What did you just say?" he asks me, his eyes shifting rapidly between mine, and his chest rising and falling quickly with his short intakes of breath.

I look away, replaying the last few minutes of our conversation in my mind, wondering what I could have said to make him look at me like that. All at once, it hits me, and I snap my gaze back to him where his eyes haven't left mine. I take a huge intake of breath, a feeling of panic zipping through me.

Oh my God. Oh. My. Fucking. God. Did I really just let that slip out of my mouth like that? I am a goddamn Grammy winning artist and songwriter, and I just let those three words fall out of my mouth like they were nothing? What the fuck is wrong with me?

"Oh, um... what? Nothing. I didn't say anything at all. Probably the weather, yeah something about the weather. 100% that's what I said," I stammer out trying to distract him away from what I actually said with nonsense. He grabs my chin in his hand, his thumb reaching up to pull on my lower lip. He swallows deeply, allowing his eyes to flick down to my lips for a moment, before looking me in the eyes again.

"That's not what I heard, songbird," he says, gravel in his tone. "What I heard you say are the words that have been imprinted on my mind for weeks just waiting for the right time to confess them to you. What I heard is that you finally realize that you're the only person in the world that makes me feel like the sun never sets when you're around. What I heard you say, songbird, is that you love me. Did I hear you wrong?" His gaze searches mine, giving me the space to take the words back if I so choose to, but with a vulnerability that belies just how scared he is that I will. He thinks he's an emotionally closed off person, but in just a few weeks, he's shown me a different side to him that I can't help but want to dive right into.

Noting his gaze is still hanging on mine in anticipation, I don't give him any more room to worry and whisper a quick, "Yes. Of course I do, Brody. I love you."

The smile that breaks across his face wipes away the last of my hangover and causes heat to zip through every fiber of my being. He's so devastatingly handsome when he looks at me like that, and I feel my knees get weak, even lying down in the bed. If I were standing, I swear I would melt into a puddle on the floor.

He grabs hold of my face with both of his enormous hands, and kisses me like I am the air he breathes. I sigh into him, whimpering at the back of my throat at the feel of his silky lips moving across mine. The kiss only lasts a few short seconds, and then he pulls back to gaze at me again.

"I have never and will never love anyone the way that I love you, Macy. I crave you every second of every day, and I know that my life will never be complete if you're not in the center of it," his voice breaks slightly at the end of his words, like he is on the edge of shattering just thinking about that possibility. It gives me hope that when the concert is over and it's time for me to get back to my life, he will want to still be a part of it even if I'm not in Oaken anymore.

"I love you," I say again, stronger so he knows that I am one hundred percent sincere, and pull him back down for a kiss. I intend for it to be a sweet moment for our post-declaration, but it very quickly turns heated.

With a groan, he presses the length of his body against mine and licks his way into my mouth with his tongue. I allow my legs to spread to accommodate him, wrapping them around his back, so I can feel all of him against me.

A whimper escapes from the back of my throat as he grinds his hips against my center, allowing his dick to hit my clit in just the right way, despite the fact that my panties and his sweatpants are currently putting up a barrier to our touch.

His hands run up my sides, dragging the t-shirt he must have dressed me in last night up along with them until he pulls it completely off of me, exposing my naked chest to him. With my arms above my head, he grabs my wrists and pins them to the bed, lacing his fingers with mine as his hips continue to grind into me.

He breaks the kiss, forcing a sound of protest from my lips that quickly turns into a moan as he pulls one of my nipples into his mouth and gently runs it through his teeth. He does the same to the other side, and I inhale a sharp breath at the sting of pain it gives as he nips slightly too hard.

"Brody," I breathe out, unsure of what I want to say but knowing that he is at the center of all of my thoughts right now.

He doesn't answer me, just groans and releases my hands so he can press kisses down my body. He starts at my breasts and slowly kisses along my ribs and down my stomach.

"I love you. I love you. I love you," he whispers out after each kiss along my skin, and I feel each declaration from the top of my head to my toes, filling me up until I swear I will burst from happiness at his words.

Just as he reaches the top of my panties, he glances up, locking eyes with me where I gaze down at him. I feel a zip of anticipation run through me as our eyes connect, and he sucks in a sharp breath before sliding his hands up my legs to grab the fabric and bring it down, baring me to him fully.

"God, songbird," He says quietly, his eyes locked on the apex of my legs in reverence. "Perfect." With that, he drags his tongue up the center of me, tasting the arousal he was just admiring ever so gently, and I roll my head back with a moan.

"I could spend the rest of my life surviving on nothing but the taste of you," he says, a possessive growl in his tone as he does.

"Brody. Please," I plead, begging him to relieve the ache. If he makes me wait another second, I swear I may die of antic-ipation.

"I love it when you beg," he says, triumphantly, with a knowing smirk. Then, he lowers his mouth again and goes to work on my throbbing clit.

"Oh, fuck," I nearly scream out as he licks and sucks me with more enthusiasm than before.

The way his tongue is swirling along my clit is nearly enough to undo me, but before I can get too close, he pulls away and runs his fingers through my slick cunt, wetting them as he goes. His fingers briefly dance along my clit, before he brings them back down and curls one of them directly inside of my pussy, forcing another loud moan from me.

"That's it, songbird. Sing for me," Brody says, adding another finger and curling it in just the right spot to cause another sharp zip of arousal to flood to my core. I imagine his hand is nearly dripping at this point, but I am beyond caring. He brings his mouth back to my clit, attacking with fervor once again, never pausing on the move of his fingers inside me.

It takes all of two seconds of this before I detonate, screaming loudly as I come, clenching down on him as my back bows off of the bed. He keeps his mouth on me, drawing out my orgasm as long as he possibly can.

"Holy fuck," I say, my eyes still seeing stars from the intensity of my climax.

Brody crawls back up my body, and I feel the press of his cock along my freshly soaked core. I hadn't even realized he took his pants off, but I suppose that's not surprising considering I basically saw through time and space during my orgasm.

He runs the tip of his cock along the entrance of my pussy, his piercing hitting my clit, as he coats himself in my arousal. He does this a few times, kissing me deeply as he grinds into me, not yet filling me in the way that I wish he would.

I let out an impatient sound as he runs his cock along me again, and he draws back to look me in the eyes, a smirk dancing across his perfect lips.

"Say it again, songbird," he whispers out, lowering his face until his mouth is only centimeters from my own.

"I love you, Brody," I say looking him straight in the eyes, conveying every bit of that truth with them as he gazes down at me with his own adoration shining in his.

"I love you," he says before kissing me again deeply and sliding home in one strong thrust. We both let out moans as he does, feeling the fullness of him completely inside me.

I expect him to fuck me hard and gruff like he usually does, but he keeps his cock seated and gives shallow thrusts, kissing me through all of them. He slides in and out slowly, hitting me slightly deeper each time he moves, slowly building another climax within me as he does.

His lips never leave mine, but he pulls one of my legs up to wrap his arm underneath my knee so he can get even deeper, his other hand threading between us so he can play with my clit. It's not the rough and hard sex that I'm used to, but somehow this is even better as we both feel the emotions swirling between us. He speeds up slightly, hitting me deeply as he does, nipping along my neck as I moan out his name.

I can feel my orgasm building even further as he continues his thrusts inside of me while his other hand works my clit. I scratch my nails down his back and grab ahold of his ass, forcing him to go even harder in his thrusts.

With a few more, I am right there, and I feel the telltale tingles building in my lower belly.

"Brody," I whisper, my lips pressed to his neck. "I'm so close."

"Come for me, Macy," he says, thrusting even harder than before and I come again when his lips press against mine. My pussy squeezes around him, and I feel his pace start to falter as he comes right along with me. He groans out, slightly breathless, as he thrusts a few more times, filling me with his cum.

His head falls to the crook of my shoulder, and he bites me softly as he comes down from his orgasm, and I take deep breaths to come down from mine. After a minute of us just breathing, he lifts his head and gazes down at me with so much love painting his features, it's enough to steal the very little breath I have left.

He kisses me softly again and says, "I love you, Macy. Always."

He then rolls to the side, sliding out of me, and pulls me into his. We are both spent from the high of our emotions coupled with incredible sex, so it takes no time at all before I feel sleep tugging at me again. Just before I think both of us are going to fall back asleep, I feel him press another kiss to my hair and whisper something.

"Always, Macy. No matter what," Brody says, and I fall back to sleep with those words echoing through my mind.

macy

NANA KNOWS BEST

THE WEEKEND FLEW BY MUCH FASTER than I would have wanted. Brody and I spent the entirety of it basking in our love for one another, fucking like we would die without it, and just enjoying the calm before the storm of festival week. I watch him leave through the door to my Nana's house and only close the door as his car turns onto the highway, heading back into town. I close the door quickly and lean back with a sigh like I'm the heroine in a Hallmark movie or something equally as cheesy. That's how Brody makes me feel, and I am loving every second of it.

"Wow. You look positively lovestruck. I remember when I used to look like that," Nana says, as she walks through the hallway with a basket of laundry in her hands. She has a nostalgic smile on her face, as she no doubt recalls when Pop Pop was still here, and they got to bask in the glow of being totally infatuated with each other. The thought makes me happy for them, but heartbroken that their love story got cut short. I can only hope that mine and Brody's will last a lifetime.

I push myself up off of the door and make my way over to her, grabbing the basket from her hands and bringing it into the living room to help her fold. I sit on the sofa, and she joins me, running her hands along my shoulders offering me her affection.

"I love him, Nana. I love him so much, it's making it hard to breathe," I say, grabbing one of her shirts and folding it the way I know she likes. I never would have thought there was a right and wrong way to fold tee shirts, but in Nana's house, there definitely is.

"That's how it goes, darling. If it's a love that doesn't make you a little bit insane, then you're not doing it right."

I feel a shy smile tug at the corner of my lips at her words, and then I remember that we still have a lot to figure out on top of having to deal with Regis. We haven't yet had the conversation about what happens after I go back to my life, and I will admit that I'm anxious he won't want to stay with me. My smile drops into a frown, and I feel my eyebrows pull together at the turn my thoughts have taken.

"Uh, oh. That's not the face of someone who's basking in the glow of new love. What's wrong?" she questions me, snagging a pair of jeans from the basket and folding them.

I heave a sigh and angrily reach into the basket again, grabbing the first thing within reach. I sloppily fold the pair of pants, and she reaches over to steal them from me to refold, casting a scowl in my direction for the abuse of her clothing. Apparently I am too distracted by my frustration and not folding up to her standards.

"Now, now. Tell me what's got you into a tizzy, but for the love of God, don't take it out on my clothes!" she berates me with no real heat to her words. She smiles at me to make sure I know that she's kidding. At least, mostly kidding anyway.

I lean back on the sofa and allow my head to drop back until my gaze is focused on the ceiling.

"I love him, Nana. I love him so much, my heart squeezes a

little bit every time he walks into the room or I even think about him. And he knows my secret, but what if he doesn't want to stay together after I leave here? What if the idea of being with someone in the spotlight at least half of the time is too much for him? What if Regis writes something terrible about us, and he realizes that I'm not worth—"

"I'm gonna stop you right there, darlin'. I have never seen a man more in love with a woman than Brody McAllister is with you, and that includes your Pop Pop," Nana says, cutting off my panic spiral. "He's not going to give two hoots about some jackass who writes nothing but slop for a living. All he wants is to be with you. You're it for him, Macy, and he'll do whatever he can to keep you. Even I can see that."

I swing my head to look at her. "Yeah, but I'm leaving so soon, Nana. I have a tour to get back to and a life that I love waiting for me in California. I can't just expect him to come with me, can I?"

"I don't know, Macy. What I do know is you need to talk with him and let him make his own decision about his life. You can't go assuming that you know what he's thinking if you haven't asked him."

I groan again, knowing she's right. Brody hasn't given me any reason to doubt that he would stay by my side, so I don't need to be projecting my fears onto him. We do need to talk about what comes next soon, but first, we need to deal with Regis. I need to temporarily let go of my anxiety about my future with Brody and do my best to take it one problem at a time.

"How are you feeling about stepping back into the spotlight? I know you weren't very excited to be back in town," Nana asks, changing the subject slightly. I try to protest, but she cuts me off. "Now, don't give me that. You might love your old Nana, but you definitely had an attitude about being back here, and we all know it."

I give her a sheepish look, knowing she's not wrong. I wasn't exactly thrilled to be back here when I first arrived, and I must not have done that great of a job of hiding it. I mutter a sorry under my breath, and she continues speaking.

"You were practically jumping out of your skin to get out of here. Now, it seems like maybe you're not as jazzed to get out of here as you were then, am I right?"

I ponder her question for a minute before answering. It's true that I didn't want to be back here, especially not for as long as we have been, but am I still that unhappy? Immediately my mind shouts a resounding "no."

"You know, I think it's actually been a much nicer break than I was expecting. I love being Harper, and I would never give that up, but being back here, I am reminded that sometimes it's nice to be able to step out of the spotlight and just...be for a while. You know?"

"I can't say that I do, because I live like this all the time, but I think I get what you're saying. Plus, getting a little action from a certain tattooed muscle man doesn't hurt, right?" Nana teases me.

"Nana, oh my God!"

"Oh shush, I'm old, not blind. Nor am I deaf, and you two are definitely not shy about your shenanigans. No wonder you got yourself into that sticky situation before you came home. You really should be more aware of who's around you, darlin'. You might find yourself in the press a lot less," she says, laughing a little to ease the sting of her assessment.

My jaw drops as she not only manages to embarrass me with the knowledge that she has heard Brody and me messing around but also by berating me for being too wild around the paparazzi. Maybe I should be more careful.

I quickly dispel the thought, shaking my head at her. "Nah. That sounds crazy boring, Nana. Besides, what's the use of being an international pop star if I don't get to have any fun, huh?"

She huffs out a sigh that ends in a laugh, rolling her eyes at me. "You always were a wild child, that's for sure. Well, I suppose I can't stop you, especially when you have the world at your feet and endless money to get into shenanigans. Just promise me you'll manage to take an extra couple seconds to think the next time you want to do something crazy, alright? My old heart can only handle so much at this point in my life, and hearing your sex sounds isn't something I care to repeat anymore, thank you very much."

"Deal," I say with a laugh, standing from the couch to head upstairs and settle in for the night before shit hits the fan tomorrow.

"Macy," Nana says, stopping me in my tracks, and I turn to look at her with my eyebrows raised. "Talk to Brody about your fears for the future of your relationship. It will put you at ease going into this week, which I think you're going to need. Lord knows I'd be shitting a brick if I had to pretend to be someone else in front of all of my former friends and classmates."

I laugh at her phrasing and press a kiss to her forehead. "You're right, Nana. I'm going to go take a shower. I love you."

"I love you, too, darlin'. You'll figure it out, and I promise it will go much better than you think."

I sure fucking hope so, because I am halfway considering not going back to my life if it means I'll have to leave Brody behind.

macy

NOTE TO SELF: CRUSHING GRAPES IS NOT FOR THE CLUMSY

"OH MY GOD, I am so fucking excited!" Stella squeals in my ear, jumping up and down as we put the finishing touches on my look. My signature red wig is in place again, and I am glitzed out in all kinds of glitter and my signature full glam makeup. It's amazing what an expensive wig and heavy foundation and lashes will do for a girl, and I think I look pretty fucking amazing. Hopefully it's enough to make sure that nobody recognizes me as Macy. But just in case, I have an oversized pair of sunglasses ready to go. We definitely aren't taking any more chances than necessary.

"God, it feels like forever since we've gotten totally dolled up! You know, I have loved just hanging around your hometown with you, babe, but nothing beats the rush of being backstage with all of the Harper Bloom groupies," Stella continues on, touching up her lip gloss in the mirror while I fiddle with the sparkly mesh dress I have layered over a black bustier and high waisted black shorts.

It's a little over the top compared to the relatively simple outfits I have been wearing around town lately, but stepping back into my pop star life means I get to step back into all of my crazy outfits, too. I love every second of it. Besides, I figure the bigger the difference between myself as Macy and myself as Harper, the less of a chance that someone will recognize me. Which is definitely critical considering Regis is still snooping around town somewhere.

I still haven't totally figured out what we are going to do about that situation, but luckily, for the thing at the winery, I only have to worry about hiding from Josie. Brody texted and said that he is sending her to cover this today, and he's spending the day working on coming up with some ideas to get Regis out of town for good. Hopefully he comes up with something, because I'm beyond over stressing about that asshole ruining my life.

Pushing that thought from my mind, I do one last once over of my choice of outfit, and smile at myself in the mirror. From here on out, I am officially Harper Bloom once again, and I would be lying if I said it didn't feel damn good. I've missed this sparkly bitch, that's for sure.

"Ready to go?" I ask, eyeing Stella. She looks like a freaking goddess in her ensemble too, and I am momentarily jealous that she doesn't have to bother hiding who she is, since she never lied about being friends with Harper. She can just walk into the day knowing that every person she encounters throughout the day knows exactly who she is. Lucky bitch.

"Fuck yeah, girl! Let's go raise some hell in this town! Woo!" she shouts, jumping up and down in her excitement as we head out the door of my bedroom.

Chase is waiting for us at the bottom of the stairs with his hands on his hips like the giant stick in the mud that he is. Clearly, he caught Stella's exclamation because he's stepped right back into his role as the resident pooper of parties. I thought we had broken past some of that with all of the time away, but apparently, he's not letting go of his protectiveness so easily. We'll have to work on that.

"Let's get one thing straight, you two. There will be absolutely no raising hell. You are here for some good press, not to go right back to the partying that got us into this mess in the first place. Is that clear? We have to play this just right, or the secret you built your life around goes up in smoke, Ace. Are you ready for that?" he admonishes, narrowing his eyes on me. I know his warnings are just out of concern for me and my secret, but I don't need the added pressure right before I have to go pretend to be someone entirely different in front of people who have known my family for years.

I give a dramatic roll of my eyes before answering him, "Seriously, Chase, have you ever considered smoking weed? You could do with some chilling out."

His deadpan look tells me he isn't too thrilled about my advice, though I still think he would be wise to take it.

I throw my hands up and continue. "Okay, dad. We pinky swear we won't get into trouble. Satisfied?"

"Not even slightly, but we don't have time to argue right now. You're already late for this grape squishing thing, so we gotta keep it moving. I have hired a few bodyguards that will be with you for the rest of the week, and they're waiting in the Escalade outside, so I suggest you get moving," he says gruffly, back into his usual no nonsense persona. "Bye, Nana! Love you!" he yells, and then he ushers us out toward the giant black SUV surrounded by four giant dudes.

I had almost forgotten that I needed some security to come with me. I've gotten so used to going wherever I wanted when I wanted, and it's a shock needing to be surrounded by a bunch of random guys I don't really know. This part I didn't miss, but it's a necessary evil I suppose.

"Boys," I salute them as I get into the car. I swear I see one of them blush, but none of them say anything and just help the three of us into the back of the car. We head out, leaving Nana's house behind as we make our way to the winery.

The closer we get, the higher my anxiety spikes until I'm practically shaking like a leaf in a freaking hurricane. My knees are bouncing like crazy in the backseat, and I can feel the car rattling underneath the aggressive action.

"Ace," Chase says, snagging my attention. I note the look of concern in his eyes. "You seriously need to try and relax. You've done this a thousand times before. This is no different."

"The fuck it isn't, Chase! I know these people. Josie and I are friends now. It's not like when I get to throw on a wig in front of thousands of random strangers. The stakes are so much higher, and we both know it."

I wring my hands in front of me realizing just how fucking stupid this idea was. I mean, really. Did I seriously think people wouldn't recognize me? Especially someone who has spent nearly every day with me for the last several weeks? What was I thinking suggesting this as a solution?

"Girl, for real, you need to take a few deep breaths and calm down. Just let me do the talking. We can pretend that you're resting your vocal cords so you don't have to talk much, and if you keep your sunglasses on, she'll be none the wiser! It's foolproof," Stella chirps from my other side, squeezing my hands in reassurance and in an attempt to get me to calm the fuck down. Easy for her to say.

It most definitely is *not* foolproof, but I guess at this point, I don't have much of a choice. So, instead of continuing my freak out, I take five deep breaths just as we are pulling up to the winery. I see Josie bouncing on her feet, probably with excitement at meeting the party pop princess in the flesh. Little does she know.

The tough looking bros who are playing the role of my

body guards today open the door, helping myself and Stella out, but leave Chase to fend for himself. I'd be offended if I wasn't hyper aware of the size of the heels I'm currently wearing.

After exiting the car, Stella rushes over to Josie and wraps her up in a massive hug while I smooth out my outfit to ensure it doesn't have any wrinkles. Not that it really matters. I will be knee deep in grapes soon enough, so I shouldn't have bothered putting on nice shoes at all.

"Harper! Get your pretty ass over here!" Stella shouts over to where I am still standing near the car. I'd be lying if I said I wasn't procrastinating just a little bit. I steel myself quickly, stepping back into the confident queen Harper Bloom is known for, and head over to greet them.

"Oh my fucking God! This is actually insane! Harper Bloom. Here. Talking to Me. Holy Fuck," Josie says by way of greeting, and I can't say that I blame her. It is a little crazy to think about how just three months ago I was gearing up for the international leg of my tour, and now here I am in Oaken prepping to squish a bunch of grapes with my bare feet. It's amazing how much can change in such a short period of time.

I don't say anything, sticking with my plan to talk as little as possible over the next few days, but I flash her a megawatt smile and wave at her.

"Gah, I'm so sorry. I'm making a total fool of myself over here, gushing like a thirteen-year-old girl. I'm Josie," she continues, visibly shaking her head out to clear herself out of her fangirl moment. "My boss, Brody, will be the one covering the big events at the end of the week, but I will be here today and tomorrow doing these smaller ones. It's insane that I am meeting you in person. How was your flight? Are you settling in okay? I know this isn't exactly your normal scene."

I open my mouth to say something, but Stella cuts in

quickly before I'm able to say anything, "Everything has gone smoothly so far, Jos! Harp's been laying low lately, so you'd be surprised how used to this scene she is. You know... since needing to take a break post-sex tape."

I huff an annoyed sound and shake my head in irritation. Apparently, I will never be able to live down that fucking pseudo-sex tape nonsense. Leopold Fucking Regis and his stupid gossip site. I swear the man should be in jail.

"Anyway, I'm not sure if Macy mentioned anything to you, but Harper is actually on vocal rest until the concert, so she's going to be pretty tight lipped from now until then. We hope that's okay?"

Thank God for my best friend. I definitely didn't want to come off as a total diva in front of Josie, lest she writes a story about how I barely spoke the entire week. That definitely wouldn't give the desired press I am looking for with this giant scheme.

"Oh! Yeah, yes, of course, no biggie. Will your voice be good to go for the reading at the library tomorrow?" Josie asks.

Fuck. I forgot about the reading. It's not like I'm going to be able to stay completely silent while I'm reading books to a bunch of six year olds. I nod along anyway, giving her another encouraging smile and a thumbs up to indicate that I'll be good to go by then. We'll figure it out. I will just have to practice my vocal impressions tonight or something.

"She'll be great! So, anyway, should we get this road on the show or whatever? I'm ready to get my wine tasting on, that's for sure," Stella chirps, grabbing both of our hands and guiding us toward the giant barrels full of grapes. There's a woman waiting there to show us what to do, and I smile as we make our way over.

"Awesome, so how this is going to work, Harper, is you'll take off your shoes and sanitize your feet, then hop in and start squishing. You'll be racing against the owner, Darla." She indicates a woman off to the side who's filling a second barrel, and I wave at her. She smiles and nods but continues filling the barrel that she will be using.

There's a pretty significant crowd of people gathered as this race is basically the kickstart of festival week for most of the town, and with the added interest of one of the most famous women in the world being here, we've garnered a good amount of attention. My bodyguard team is keeping the crowd behind a line of barriers, but they're screaming at me trying to get my attention. I wave and blow kisses at all of them before turning my focus back to Darla and Josie, noticing both of the barrels are now nearly full.

"Alright, are you ready? I will be recording and covering the event, which will hopefully go up on the paper's website later this afternoon. Cool?"

I nod briskly and start pulling my shoes off, washing my feet and hopping into the barrel next to Darla, offering her an encouraging smile.

I breathe out a quiet "May the best squisher win," and she laughs at me a little bit.

Ready as I'll ever be, I take a deep breath and get comfortable on my feet inside the barrel. We both look out to the crowd as they count down a loud *3, 2, 1, go,* and I start squishing to the cacophony of the crowd's cheers.

As it turns out, I was one hundred percent *not* prepared for how difficult squishing grapes would be, nor how slippery the tiny fruits become when you squish out their insides. I got into the groove quickly, but after about 45 seconds of hardcore stomping, I started to feel the goop beneath my feet grow more and more slick. I made the mistake of glancing over at Darla to see how she was faring, and that's when things took a turn for the worse, literally.

As soon as I made eye contact with her, my left foot hit a particularly slippery patch in my barrel, and the world started to tilt on its axis. Before I could stop it, I fell backwards and out of the barrel, grapes flying everywhere and my sunglasses flying right off of my face. I let out a loud squeak as I fell, and the crowd let out a comical gasp as I did. I swear things moved in slow motion, but maybe that's just how it seemed to me.

Once on the ground, it took me a second and then I started laughing uncontrollably. How utterly ridiculous I must look right now, decked out in my designer gear, covered in grapes and on my ass in front of a massive crowd of people. Brody is right. I am definitely clumsy.

"Oh my God, Harper! Are you okay?" Josie comes rushing over, turning her camera off in the process and reaching out to help me stand up. I am still dissolved in a fit of laughter, so all I can do is nod vigorously, and take her outstretched hands and stand up.

After I am standing, she reaches down to grab something and reaches over to hand it to me. "Well, I admit, that wasn't exactly how I saw that going, but I hope you're okay if I still..." she trails off, giving me a confused look, her gaze running over all of my features.

"What? Do I have grapes on my face?" I say, swiping vigorously at my cheeks to dislodge the offending fruit. I don't feel anything, but I'm sure I didn't come out of this unscathed.

"I-Macy?" Josie asks, and my stomach lurches uncomfortably. I quickly snag the item out of her hands, now realizing they are my sunglasses that I completely forgot went flying in the process of falling on my ass. I push them back up on my face and look away from her as fast I can.

"Um... anyway, I should go get cleaned up," I rush out in a voice much higher than my normal speaking voice in an attempt to disguise myself once again. Josie gives me a once over and then shakes her head, dislodging what she thought she saw. At least, I hope she does.

"Right, yes, sorry. I hope it's okay for me to post the video still? I can cut out the last bit if you want me to," she says, and I nod, shooting her a thumbs up, and hurry back to the car with my security in tow. I wipe off as much of the grapes as I can and jump in, taking a huge deep breath and letting out a curse.

"Holy shit, Ace, that was fucking hilarious. I can't tell you how happy I am that Josie got that on camera! I will for SURE be bringing that up in my maid of honor speech at your inevitable wedding to Brody. Comedy gold, babe," Stella razzes me as she gets into the car. She glances over at me, taking note of my expression, her brows furrowing. "What? You look like you've seen a ghost."

"I-I think Josie may have recognized me," I stammer out in a shaky voice.

"What did you just say?" Chase says, getting into the front seat and whipping his head around to confirm what he just heard.

"I mean, I can't be sure. My sunglasses only fell off for like... a second, but she said my real name before I was able to put them back on. I think I managed to throw her off of the trail though."

I hoped, anyway.

Chase takes a deep breath, his jaw working furiously in contemplation. "Well, I hope so, but I guess there's nothing we can do about that now. Let's just get you home and cleaned up. Then we can focus on getting through the rest of this week without any more mishaps. Okay?"

The car starts moving, and I look out of the window at Josie again. She can't see me, but I can see her. She looks toward the car, her lips pursing in thought before she shakes her head, seeming to shake off the thought before heading back to talk to Darla. I can only hope that she is dismissing what she thinks she saw as a trick of the light.

brody

I'M GONNA GET THAT PRICK

AFTER GETTING CLEANED up at her Nana's place, Macy beelined it over to my place and immediately proceeded to freak out on my living room sofa about the mishap with Josie.

"Macy, I promise you it's going to be okay. You said she only saw your face for like a second, right?"

"Yes, but she literally said my name, Brody. What if she keeps digging? I feel like I should just avoid her as best as I can for the next week. You should just take over being the journalist for my next few events," she says, pouting her perfect lips at me in hopes that I will give in.

"Then she would definitely know something's up, love. Maybe it wouldn't be such a bad idea to just... tell her?" I say, thinking maybe it's time to get it out of the way. Josie is smart as a whip, so it's probably inevitable anyway.

"Yeah, okay," she says, heavy on the sarcasm. "Should I also rip my wig off on stage and write a love ballad to Leopold Regis, too?"

I lean over her from the back of the sofa and whisper in her ear, "Keep using that smart mouth of yours to sass me, and I'll have to fill it with something other than quick remarks."

She inhales sharply, and I can see her chest rising more rapidly than it was before. I love how turned on my girl gets when she is anticipating taking me. She turns her head to press her lips to mine, but before she is able to, I pull away from her, and she huffs in irritation at being denied.

"As far as the Josie thing goes, I say just play it cool and do your best to keep away from her if you can. It's not that big of a deal, I promise."

"Fine," she agrees, though I can tell she's still stressed about it. I make a mental note to provide some stress relief for her later.

"Speaking of Regis, I haven't seen him around town much in the last few days. He hasn't been bothering you much, has he? I have half a mind to rip his balls clean off his scrawny body if he crosses my path again," I say, knowing full damn well I should do worse than that to him. I hate that he's another stressor for Macy, and I want to be able to fix it.

"No, I haven't seen him, thank the almighty heavens. Seeing him in town has seriously triggered my feelings about how violated I felt when that tape was released," she shudders as she says this, and it pisses me off even more than before that he disrespected her in this way.

She continues before I can say anything. "I mean, I'm super sex positive and everything, and I'm not ashamed of my sex life in any way... especially now," she winks at me quickly before continuing, "but, I just feel so gross about the fact that he recorded me in such a vulnerable moment and then used it to further his own career. It's such a helpless feeling, thinking that he's always lurking around when I don't want him to be, you know?"

I don't know. I can't even begin to imagine what that feels

like, and my body flushes with rage that she is feeling this way because of that asshole. I vow to make him pay for everything he has ever done to hurt her, and I start making a mental list of ways we can get back at him and get him away from her for good.

"I can't tell you how much I want to tear him apart for everything he's done to you, songbird. I promise you, I will figure out a way to get him out of town and out of your life."

Her eyes soften as she looks at me, and I see so much love shimmering in her gaze that I feel my heart squeeze. I never thought I would be the type of person who felt like this about another person, but I love her so much I can't help but be obsessive about her all the way down to my bones.

"I love you, Brody," she says, giving me a look that is hopeful yet tentative. I know she's been dealing with him for years, so I don't blame her for being cautious. I want to give her more assurance that I will always take care of her, even if it gets me in trouble, but she cuts me off before I can say any more on the subject.

"Now, enough of the doom and gloom. I want to just relax, and I recall something about my mouth being filled with more than quick remarks?" she asks, her eyes starting to heat in a way I will never be able to resist.

I will never deny her a single damn thing that she wants, and I am more than okay with that.

brody

JESUS, JOSIE

THE NIGHT of the mayor's dinner is finally upon us, and I will be in the same room as Macy for the first time since we talked about the situation at the winery. Josie has been covering the smaller events, so I've been dealing with the day to day operations at The Oaken Tribune. Luckily, the book reading at the library went off without any incident, though Josie did mention how weird she thought it was that Harper wore sunglasses indoors and spoke barely loud enough for her to hear her from the back.

Macy and I haven't seen much of each other, relying on nightly FaceTime calls to get our fix of each other, and I can't wait to surround myself with her again. I miss her, and I am looking forward to seeing her after this damn dinner is over. It feels like it's been ages since I've been able to bask in her glow, and I am starved for her attention and the feel of her skin on mine. In reality, it's been three days, but fuck if that doesn't feel like that amount of time might just kill me.

I shoot her a text, letting her know just how excited I am to see her tonight when all of this is over. She's been knee deep in preparations for the concert tomorrow, so I'm sure she'll be stressed, but I plan on working some of that off of her in creative ways.

Giving myself a once over in the mirror, I run my hands through my hair one last time, making sure it's in the right place. It's not every day you have to pretend you don't know that your girlfriend is a secret pop star.

The dark jeans and white t-shirt topped with a tan leather jacket aren't the nicest items of clothing that I wear, but I figure this is more of a casual meet and greet anyway. Besides, the way the shirt hugs my muscles, I think I look pretty fucking good, and I am sure Macy would agree. That is, right before she would tear my shirt off of me and put her tongue all over my abs.

I grab my keys, and head out the door, jumping in my car and making my way to the mayor's house. When I arrive, I can already see that there's a few blacked out SUVs parked along the extended driveway, indicating that Macy and her team are already here. I wonder if she's inside already, or if they're waiting in the car for the rest of the guests to arrive. I would think she'd want to be the last one to arrive, right? What the fuck do I know about pop stars though. I guess it will be a learning curve I will have to figure out over time.

I park my car and head inside. As I walk through the door, I notice Josie standing there. She's been a little cagey with me for the last few days, seeming lost in some sort of internal conflict. Macy already told me she may have recognized her at the grape crushing, so I assume she's doing her best to convince herself she's not totally bonkers.

I haven't pressed her to talk about it, so hopefully she gets over it soon. It'd be nice if her head was in the game as we finish our plans. Paper sales have been skyrocketing over the last week, though I will admit there was minor snag I wish we would have foreseen.

At the grape-smooshing event or whatever it's called, Macy – or *Harper* – took a hard fall out of the barrel of grapes. Josie was kind enough to not publish anything about it since Chase is doing us a solid by giving us all of the exclusive rights to interviews and everything, but what we should have foreseen is that the slippery fuck known as Leopold Regis was still skulking around town look for a story.

Unfortunately, we don't have the power to totally bar him from the events of the festival, so he was there doing a story for his gossip site and caught everything on camera as well. He clearly had no such decency to not post anything about it, so of course Harper ended up catching some heat for that. At least it was pretty minor in the grand scheme of things, but it still pissed me off that he was just out here to make her look bad. Fucking prick.

"Hey, Jos," I say, walking up to her. "Are Harper and her team here yet? Or are those giant SUVs for some other celebrity I don't know about?"

She glances up at me, seeming to not have realized that I arrived. "Huh? Oh, no, she's not here yet, but I think some of her people came early to scope things out and make sure that no crazy fanatics pop up. To be honest, I think they're all on edge since that asshole Regis is still lurking somewhere in the shadows. I really hate that guy."

Her face scrunches up at that, and I hum a sound of agreement. He really is the worst.

"She should be arriving anytime though. You haven't had the chance to meet her yet, have you?" she asks, giving me a cautious look. Since Macy hasn't revealed her secret yet, I play innocent with her, so she won't suspect anything more than she already has.

"Not yet. Why? Is she a total diva or something?"

"No, nothing like that. I was just wondering," she trails off, looking around the room. She opens her mouth to speak again, but that's when the entire entourage surrounding Macy, as Harper Bloom, rolls into the room.

The dining room of the mayor's house is massive, so I don't get a great look at her from this point, but I already know my girl is stunning. Her bold red hair is styled in large curls, flowing down her back, nearly to her natural waist. Her curves are killer in the red sequin, high waisted pants she's wearing with a tiny bra-like crop top covering her ample chest. Her bronze skin seems to glisten when it hits the light, and every eye in here turns to take her in. It's like every light in the room is hyper-focused on her, so I can't say I blame them. My song-bird is the light of every room she walks into, regardless of whether she's donned in sequins or denim.

The mayor steps toward her to introduce himself, blocking her from my view. She turns her beaming grin on him and shakes his hand. He says something to her that makes her laugh, and I can't help but smile right along with her joy. That laugh is killer, and I can't wait to spend the rest of my life memorizing the sound of it. After a moment of chatting with her, the mayor turns and addresses the rest of the room.

"Alright, now that we're all here, I think it's time we get the drinks flowing! In honor of our *very* special guest, we have a margarita station ready to go. Harper, I heard you're quite the fan of tequila, is that right?"

She smiles and rolls her eyes but answers his question. "I guess you could say that."

"Wonderful! I will have one of our servers bring one over to you, and the rest of you can fend for yourselves. We have seating arrangements around the table, so be sure to locate your name card and take a seat. The first course will be served in five minutes."

With that, he claps his hand and ushers Macy toward her

seat at the head of the table. I'm sad to see that my place card is nearly the furthest from her it could be. I guess I can't be too surprised since everybody assumes that we barely know each other outside of the minimal time we've spent together for the paper.

I snag a beer from the bar set up in the corner of the room and make my way to my seat to prepare for the first course. I briefly catch Macy looking my way, but before I can wave at her, she looks away, turning to Stella and whispering something at her. I make a mental note to punish her for that slight later.

* * *

The dinner goes smoothly, with several courses coming and going and easy conversations continuing to flow. Macy seems to be engrossed in some sort of discussion with the mayor, and Stella is right there with her hyping her up. Whatever they are talking about seems to have the mayor completely enthralled, not that I can say I am surprised. Macy and Stella together really do know how to draw in everyone around them, like moths to flames. A perk of living life in the spotlight, I suppose.

I have spent a majority of the night chatting with Josie and Chase, who took up residence on my other side when he arrived. He came in after Macy, and I assume he had previously been running around trying to make sure everything would run smoothly. He might not be the same carefree guy I grew up with anymore, but he is sure as shit good at what he does now. I have to admire how easily he stepped into this new version of himself, and I feel a pang of jealousy that I don't expect. Maybe after this week is all wrapped up, I will walk through my role with the same ease again. It's either that or start making some changes, which doesn't scare me nearly as much as it would have before.

After the final course comes and goes, and we all have a few post-dinner drinks, the mayor stands up, clinking his glass to gain everyone's attention at the table.

"If you don't mind, I'd like to propose a toast." He smiles, and we all raise our glasses in preparation for whatever speech he has prepared for this event. I briefly glance in Macy's direction again, locking eyes with her and giving her a wink before she blushes and trains her gaze on the mayor once more.

"Ms. Bloom," the mayor starts. "It is an honor to have you with us here in our small corner of the world. I know you haven't always had the best reputation with the press, but coming here in good faith and doing such incredible things in our town makes me realize just how little of you we all actually get to see in the tabloids. I hope you take a piece of us with you when you leave. To Harper!"

"To Harper!" We all echo, and we take sips of our drinks as one.

The mayor sits back down, but people have started milling about the room rather than sitting for a formal dinner, so there's an open seat next to him. Taking my chance at getting to spend a little bit of time with Macy, I make my way over and fill the open seat.

"My apologies. I hope it's okay that I'm intruding on your conversation, Mr. Mayor," I say, clapping him on the shoulder like we are best buddies. I am hoping he won't dismiss me, and my hopes are answered when he responds.

"Not at all! Harper, I assume you've met Brody McAllister? He's the editor of the paper you've been working with here in town. I can tell you've made an impact on the *Oaken Tribune* with your arrival. It seems like every person I run into around town has a copy tucked somewhere on them. And people say print media is dying," he finishes, chuckling at his own joke. I laugh along slightly, though his comment still hits a little close to home with how much we were struggling before Macy's arrival.

I also have to remind myself not to blurt out just how well the two of us know each other. I honestly don't know how Macy keeps all of it straight when she has to play two roles, but I will admit there is a slight thrill to having this secret just between the two of us.

Before I can say anything incriminating, Macy jumps in with a smile on her face to greet me as if we are meeting for the first time.

"Not officially, but yes I know who you are. Nice to finally meet you," she says, reaching out to shake my hand professionally. I take her hand in mine and rub my thumb along the top of it secretly so the mayor doesn't notice, eliciting a blush on her cheeks.

"It's absolutely my pleasure, Harper. So, how have you been liking Oaken so far? Probably a far cry from what you're used to, I would imagine."

"I love it here! You'd be surprised at how familiar this all seems," she says wistfully. "Plus, it doesn't hurt that I've had some time to decompress after everything."

"Ah yes, the small town life isn't so bad," the mayor replies, interjecting himself back into the conversation. "What has been your favorite part of your time so far, Harper? I can't imagine it was the tumble you took at the grape squishing event. That was certainly something to behold, that's for sure." He chuckles recalling the event. I have the urge to reach over and punch him for bringing up an embarrassing moment for my girl.

To her credit, Macy just giggles her laugh that makes me damn near weak in the knees and waves him off.

"No, I can honestly say that will not be going into my scrapbook of favorite memories," she says, laughing slightly at the reminder of her fall. "I think my favorite part of being back here was visiting the roller rink." Her eyes meet mine, and I swear I fall a little more in love with her at this moment, recalling just how meaningful our date at the rink was for the two of us. The heat that fills her gaze has me wanting to ditch this whole event and remind her just how in love with her I am.

Before I can follow up with a question of my own, though, Josie makes her way over and inserts herself into our conversation as well.

"The roller rink? When did you have time to go there?" she asks. "Your schedule has been so packed, I'm amazed that you had any time at all to check that out. How were you able to get in there without being swamped by people?" Josie eyes Macy up, clearly trying to figure something out in her head. My gaze swings to Macy, and I can tell that she's anxious about how suspicious Josie is being at this moment, especially after nearly figuring out it was her at the winery. I try to cut in and help her out, but Macy beats me to it once again.

"Oh, um—" Macy starts, trailing off, panic lacing her tone. She laughs, but it doesn't hold the same level of humor as it did before, seeming to be more of a nervous tick than actual laughter. "I guess I must just be remembering a different time or something."

"Yes, but you've never been here before, right? I think I would have remembered the most famous woman in the world walking the streets of my small town," Josie asks, suspicion still lacing her tone. It's clear that she's trying to get Macy to admit something, and I have half a mind to wring her damn neck for making Macy so uncomfortable.

"Uh," Macy lets out, her breathing starting to turn shallow and her eyes wide with anxiety.

I want to reach over and grab one of her hands to help ground her in the room but think better of it, knowing we are supposed to have only just met. Her panicked gaze still meets mine, and I try to steer the conversation away.

"What's with the third degree, Josie?" I ask her, annoyance lacing my tone. She glares at me, just as annoyed that I'm not letting the questions slide.

"I'm just being curious, Brody. Besides, I'm sure Harper is used to journalists wanting answers," she finishes, and she looks back over toward Macy, who is still visibly uncomfortable.

Without commenting on Josie's statement, Macy abruptly stands up from her chair, nearly knocking it over in her haste, and backs away from the table.

"I'm sorry, I just," she says, trailing off again slightly, "I need some air. Excuse me."

With that, she flees the dining room, leaving the room in a stunned sort of silence. After a second, I stand up and excuse myself, following her out of the room.

macy

I'M A SECRET POP STAR?

OH, fuck. Oh fuck me sideways with the handle of a rusty spoon that was plucked out of week old dirty dishwater. Just fuck me in every way a person can be fucked.

"I need some air. Excuse me." I stand up abruptly, damn near knocking my chair over as I try to get out of this situation with Josie. I rush out of the room, paying no mind to the puzzled looks of the other people at the dinner table.

I rush down the hallway, finding an alcove that I can just panic in. I seriously cannot believe I let something like that slip with everyone in the room. How could I be so stupid? Josie was already suspicious, and I basically gave her every bit of evidence to confirm her theory about me. I should have just come clean with her from the start. I mean, she's never given me any reason not to trust her, and she's basically in the inner circle now anyway. Maybe it's time to let her in on the secret.

I drop my head into my hands, leaning back against the wall and allowing the panic to overtake me for a minute. I am so lost in my stress that I don't realize someone has walked up to me hiding here until there are hands on my shoulders.

I gasp, stiffening at the sudden contact, not quite sure who's touching me right now, with my head still in my hands. Part of me thinks it could be Stella, coming to reassure me that nobody noticed my tiny confession. However, the sheer size of the hands lets me know that it's definitely not my petite friend and is someone decidedly more muscly and smelling of smoke and rum.

Brody.

I peek out at him through my fingers, not dropping my hands, not wanting him to see just how much I'm freaking out about this. His blue eyes show nothing but concern and pierce me all the way down to my soul. Having his eyes on me in this way reignites my panic, and I instantly start hyperventilating. I've never been so careless with this secret before, and I'm worried that not only will other people put two and two together, but that I may have fucked up my friendship with Josie too.

Taking as deep of a breath as I possibly can, I do my best to pull it together enough to ease his concern.

"Hi! I'm fine, nothing to worry about. I'm good. All good. Just casually freaking out that everyone's going to know that it's me and that my secret will be blasted all over the world. And not only that, but Josie's going to hate me forever, and–"

"Hey, hey, hey! Macy, relax! Breathe, songbird!" Brody says, cutting off my blubbering that he can probably only half understand anyway with my hands still covering most of my face.

"But–"

"It's going to be okay," he says, moving his body closer to mine and pressing against me, his hand curling around my hip while his other tucks a lock of my red hair behind my ear. "You didn't say anything incriminating. Josie's just being nosy. Even if she thinks she knows, she wouldn't tell anyone. I promise."

I lower my hands from my face and stare directly into his eyes, a deep sense of calm rushing over me from the love I can see shining in them. I take a couple of deep breaths before I am able to say anything, doing my best to fully calm down after my panic attack.

"You're right. It's going to be fine, right?" I ask, trepidation still lacing my tone.

"It's going to be fine. I promise. We'll figure out what to say to Josie together, okay?"

"Okay. I love you, Brody," I whisper, choking on the sudden lump in my throat. He leans his forehead down to mine.

"I love you, Macy," he says, and he finally closes the distance between us, capturing my lips with his own.

It starts out as an innocent enough kiss, but before long, I find my lips opening to allow him full access into my mouth. He wastes no time and deepens the kiss, groaning. I moan along with him and wrap myself around him as much as I can. I run my hands up his sides, bunching his shirt, while he tangles his fingers in my hair and angles my head to bring us even closer.

I'm about two seconds away from pulling him into an empty room and taking him on whatever available surface is in there when someone exclaims loudly.

"I fucking KNEW it!"

Brody and I break away from each other abruptly, whipping around to come face to face with a very smug looking Josie who's staring directly at us with her arms crossed.

"Josie, I–" I start, but she holds her hand up to stop me from speaking.

"No. Explanation please. Now," she demands, and I finally see the demanding side of her that Brody is always telling me she exhibits at the office.

"So, um..." I trail off, not really sure how to drop the "so I'm a secret pop star" bomb. I look to Brody in hopes that he will have a better idea of how to handle the situation, especially since my heart is still racing, not just from our kiss but from being caught.

Brody blows out a breath and turns to face Josie. "So, Macy is Harper Bloom. Surprise?"

"Smooth, babe. Super smooth," I say, sighing and turning back to Josie, who's still waiting on a further explanation from the two of us.

"Um... yeah. I'm kind of a secret pop star?" I let out more as a question than a statement, giving her an apologetic look that I hope smooths over the sting of the revelation.

"Yes, I gathered that. In fact, I vividly recall asking you about this at the winery when you lost your sunglasses, and you totally made me feel like I was just seeing things. What the hell, Macy?" she asks, demanding more of an explanation from me, which is well deserved.

"I'm—" I start, but she cuts me off again, turning her disappointed gaze on Brody.

"And you! How long have you known about this and kept me out of the loop?"

Brody gives her a sheepish look and says, "A while. It wasn't my secret to tell."

I speak up again, snagging her attention once more. "I'm so sorry, Josie. It's just that I've been keeping my life a secret for so long, and I've always kept my inner circle so small, it's hard for me to let others know. I never know if someone is going to use it against me or sell me out to the tabloids. I should have known you would never do that and should have just been honest with you from the start."

She lets out a deep sigh, rolling her eyes toward the sky and muttering something under her breath before addressing me again. "Yes, you should have. I know we haven't always been very close, but I would never betray your trust like that, Macy. What you're doing for Brody, and for the paper, is amazing, let alone all of the wonderful things you've done this week around town. I will always have your back. Trust that, okay? I will never tell a soul."

Her words and voice are so heartfelt and sincere that I feel tears prick at the corner of my eyes, and I rush forward to wrap her in a giant hug.

"Thank you, Josie. Welcome to the club," I say to her, kissing her cheek quickly, and she pulls out of our hug to smile at me.

"Thanks. But no more secrets, okay? I swear I was convincing myself I had completely lost my marbles this week after the winery incident!"

"Pinky promise," I say, nodding at her sincerely. "And hey, now you can help us figure out the Regis situation!" I add brightly. Maybe Josie will have some better ideas of how to take that prick down.

"Still? God, he's the worst," she says, exasperated. "Okay, one thing at a time. First, back to the party before everyone thinks you skipped town again, then we can address the Regis problem. I'll let you two get decent again, and meet you back in there." With that, she twirls away and heads back into the dining room.

"She's probably right. We should get back," he says, grabbing my hand to drag me out of the hallway. Just before we get back to the door for the dining room, he grips the hips of my sequin pants, stopping me in my tracks, and leans down to whisper in my ear. "I can't wait to see these on my floor later as I make you scream my name. That was just the warm up, songbird. Get ready for the finale."

With that, he gently swats me on the ass and heads back into the dining room, leaving me to follow.

It takes me a minute to compose myself, but after a minute, I take a deep breath and make my way in. After all, I am a fucking professional.

brody

I'VE GOT A PLAN

AFTER THE DEBACLE at the mayor's dinner, we've thrown almost all of our energy into prepping for the concert and working out ways to get rid of Regis. Josie has been a huge help, and Macy and I both realized that we probably should have told her much sooner rather than letting her find out on her own. You live and you learn, I guess. Unfortunately, we haven't come up with a solid plan yet, but we are getting close.

Currently, we are sitting at my office, waiting until Macy needs to start getting ready for the concert later. Despite the fact that I am not usually a concert lover, I find myself anticipating tonight. I've seen just how magnetic Macy is on stage when I was doing my research on her earlier this summer, but seeing something on video isn't the same as experiencing it in real life. I can't wait to see my songbird completely in her element, letting her love of performing shine through in everything she does.

I'm putting some last minute edits on the article that will run tomorrow, while Macy sits on the sofa in my office, absently scrolling on her phone. I'm surprised she hasn't left yet to get ready, but then again, since her secret is no longer such a secret, she's had no reason to avoid hanging out around the office, and we have spent every waking second together since last night. I can't say I'm complaining.

I just finish up with one of the paragraphs I was working on when Macy scares the fuck out of me by shouting loud enough to wake the dead.

"You've got to be fucking kidding me!" she exclaims, shooting up to sitting, ramrod straight.

"Jesus, songbird, don't fucking do that!"

"Goddamn it! That slimy, skeevy, conniving, slippery–"

"What the hell is all of the shouting about in here?" Josie asks, bursting into the room.

Despite being asked a direct question by Josie, Macy is still glued to her phone and is continuing her stream of rather colorful insults at whatever she is seeing on the screen.

"Macy!" I say, cutting her off. "Will you stop with the descriptors, and tell us what's going on?"

She thrusts her phone in my direction, pointing directly to the screen that is far too small for me to see from the distance from my desk to the sofa. "Leopold Fucking Regis is what's going on! Look!"

She tosses me her phone and crosses her arms across her chest, huffing as she does. I scan through the article and notice that not only is Harper Bloom pictured, but Macy and myself are there. I am in both photos, seemingly getting "cozy" with both of them at separate times. The first photo is of me with Macy at the local diner on one of our dates from a few weeks ago. The second is from last night, of me and Harper embracing in the hallway of the mayor's house after her panic attack. This one is through the window, but there's no doubt who's in the photo.

"What the fuck?" I whisper, to no one in particular. Macy lets out a scoff anyway, clearly just as annoyed as I am.

I continue reading the article, trying to figure out just what Regis is trying to do with this trash. Apparently, he's trying to insinuate that Harper is up to her old ways of whoring around and not taking her break seriously. Not only that, but she's gotten herself involved in a love triangle with a local, no doubt in order to leave a string of broken hearts in her wake. God, I hate this fucking guy.

I finish reading and look over at Macy, noticing her fuming on the couch, shaking her head as if she can physically remove the memory of Regis from her brain by the motion. I let out a sigh and pass the phone over to Josie so she can read for herself what has Macy so worked up.

"What I don't get," Macy starts, "is how he manages to be everywhere all at once! How does he even know when he should be spying on us? And why does he always have to be picking on me? It's getting really fucking old."

I ponder her words for a minute. She's right, he does have an uncanny ability to predict where Harper is going to be, and when she's going to be up to something he deems article worthy. This week, it's not hard to know where she'd be, given we printed her itinerary in the paper and he would have access to it the same as anyone else, but it is weird that he manages to be wherever she is, even when he's not invited. He's got to have something weird going on to be able to be everywhere all at once.

"You know what?" I say, capturing both her and Josie's attention. "You're right. I wouldn't put it past the slimy fuck to be up to something weird, especially with how often he's been able to catch you in a scandal. I mean, he's been after you for years, right?"

It was a rhetorical question, but she nods anyway, curling her lip in disgust. "Unfortunately. I swear, it's like he's a fucking stain that I can't seem to get rid of, no matter how hard I try."

"My point exactly. How is he always just... *there*? He's gotta be up to something, and I'm going to figure out what it is."

She and Josie share a look of disbelief, not quite following my line of thinking. Josie speaks up first.

"What are you thinking?" She asks.

"I'm thinking, he has to be getting his information from somewhere, right? Somebody close to Macy is obviously feeding him some information, and I'm going to figure out who. After that, we just have to hit Regis where it hurts, and get him the fuck out of our lives for good," I say definitively, a plan already forming in my head.

Macy rolls her eyes and exasperatedly throws her head back on the sofa like she can't quite imagine how I would be able to make this happen.

"Yeah, but how? It's not like he's just going to spill all of his secrets to you, Brody. He's not exactly known for being someone who just does things out of the goodness of his heart," she scoffs, throwing her hands in the air.

I make my way over to sit by her on the sofa, wrapping her in my arms, and force her head to lean against my chest. I breathe in her scent for a second, getting lost in it before speaking again.

Josie makes a disgusted noise and mutters something about how we need to wait to be in love until she's not around before quickly exiting my office. After she's gone, I press a kiss to the top of Macy's head and speak directly into her ears.

"Don't you worry about that, songbird. Leave it to me, and I will get this asshole to leave Harper Bloom alone for the rest of her career. For now, you have a concert you've got to get ready for."

"But—"

I press a finger to her lips, cutting her off. "No buts, love. Do you trust me?"

She nods her head, nothing but tentative hope shining in her green eyes.

"Good girl," I whisper, and I lean down to press my lips against hers. Before things can escalate too far and I fuck her so hard she won't be able to walk straight, I pull away and lean my forehead against hers. "Now, time to go, songbird. I'll see you at the show. Leave the rest to me."

IT'S SHOWTIME

"OH MY GOD, girl! You seriously need to chill out!" Stella snaps at me, dropping her head back in frustration. "All of your jittery movements are making it damn near impossible for me to get your wig on straight. Do you *want* to give Regis something to write about tonight?"

I scowl at her, sticking my tongue out, but do my best to settle down. I've been on edge all afternoon since leaving Brody's office. He didn't tell me a damn thing before I left, and I'm kind of freaking out about whatever plan he came up with. Of course I trust him, I just don't like not knowing what's going on. Makes me all jumpy. I check my phone for the hundredth time, only to find that I still don't have any updates from him.

"Ugh, I just wish he would text me back! I mean, seriously, how hard is it to type a few words into a phone? The man is a damn editor for God's sake! You'd think a text would be easy!"

Stella swats me on the shoulder, and I turn back to glare at her again.

"Ace, seriously, chill. The man is totally in love with you. You think he's going to do anything to jeopardize that? He probably just doesn't want to be distracted when he's in take down mode. Give him a chance to get it done before you work yourself into another panic attack."

"Fine," I say, tossing my phone away from me so I can focus on the finishing touches to my costume before I have to head out onto the stage. "But if you're forcing me to calm down, you better at least tell me you've got some liquid courage around here somewhere. I'm not going to give up on our tradition of a pre-show shot just because I'm performing in my hometown!"

Stella squeals, hugging me around the shoulders. "Now that's what I'm talking about! Two shots coming right up!" She dances away toward the back corner of the tent that's serving as a makeshift dressing room.

Oaken isn't exactly a prime destination for concert venues, so we had to make do with tents and a build as you go stage. It will work for what we need it for, even if I am used to a fancier set up than this. It's not bothering me as much as it would have prior to spending the last few months living as a regular person again. Apparently I'm back to my humble roots and all that.

Stella pours the shots and brings them both over so we can take them together. I put the finishing touches on my look and admire myself in the mirror. I am impressed with how well I am able to step back into my role as Harper. I have loved the break from being in the spotlight, but I am ready to hit that stage again, disguise and everything. I think the extended time away from the limelight has actually been eye opening for me and has made me appreciate both parts of my world again.

"To absolutely crushing Leopold Fucking Regis and to knocking the socks off a certain grumpy paper editor in that outfit!" Stella says, clinking her shot glass with mine before we both throw them back like they're water. Okay, not exactly like water – the burn of tequila never really goes down that easily – but well enough for two well-practiced party girls.

"Cheers, babe," I rasp out, sucking on a lime to chase the lingering alcohol flavor down. I shake off the lingering anxiety I feel about Brody's mystery plan and make my way toward the exit of the tent so I can head toward the stage. "Let's go put on a show!"

* * *

The sound of my final song echoes across the stage, and the roar of the crowd fills my ears. It's not exactly the same as when I am playing to a crowd of thirty-thousand, but knowing I am performing for all of the people I grew up with makes this even more special. Even if they don't actually know it's *me* they're cheering for. Maybe someday I will feel ready to share that secret with the world, but for now, I'm happy getting to be both versions of myself when I choose to.

I give my final goodbyes to the fans, and the stage goes dark as I exit while the band continues playing instrumentals behind me to signify the end of the show. I will do an encore after another few minutes, but it's always best to leave the crowd in a little bit of suspense.

I flounce off stage, feeling the high of performing for a live audience again. Even though it's been nice being back in my hometown and getting to be a normal person for a while, I have seriously missed the thrill of singing my heart out in front of people and getting to just let everything go on that stage.

"Eeeeeek! Girl, that was amazing!" Stella bounds over to me and wraps me up in a bear hug, forcing me to bounce along with her in her excitement. She's always been my best friend and my biggest hype girl, and tonight, she doesn't disappoint. She seems to ride the same level of high that I do when I perform, even though she's only standing off stage watching from the sidelines. To her, she may as well be on that stage with me, and I love having her there to greet me with her off the charts excitement when I am finished with my sets. Though, I'd be lying if I said I didn't miss a certain broody presence waiting backstage as well. Hopefully whatever Brody is doing is worth the loss I feel at not having him here when I finish my set.

"Thanks, Stel! It felt really good to be able to don the sequins again," I say, smiling at her. "Karaoke was great and all, but there's nothing quite like that," I say, nodding my head back toward the stage to indicate my meaning. We make our way back toward my little dressing tent, razzing each other along the way and gushing about how great the set was, even if it wasn't my typical larger than life level of performance.

As we make our way over, something catches my eye, and I pull Stella off to the side to get out of view as quickly as possible.

"What the hell, Ace? What's going on?" Stella asks, unsure of my change in demeanor. I cut her off with a shush and motion for her to follow me.

I nod over toward where two figures are chatting quietly near another tent, filled with what I assume is equipment for the stage. With how many tents we have set up around here, nobody even notices them lurking back there, aside from me.

"Tell me you're seeing what I'm seeing," I whisper to Stella, my eyes locked in the direction I want her to look.

"Holy fuck," she whispers. "Is that Brody? Talking to Leopold Fucking Regis?"

My brows crease together at her confirmation that I'm not seeing things, and I just nod along, unsure of what to say. I am just as confused as she is, especially since Brody hasn't bothered to text me back all day. What could he possibly be doing here, at my concert, with Regis? I hope that whatever it is will be the ticket to getting him off of my back for good.

I'm just about to say something else when Brody gestures for Regis to go into the tent they are lingering by. I don't even think — I just grab Stella's hand and rush toward the tent as quickly, yet quietly, as possible.

"Come on. Let's go see what he's up to," I say, dragging her along with me. I slow my pursuit as we get closer to the tent and creep up to the small opening. I can't quite hear what they're saying inside, just some low mumbling, so I gesture for Stella to go to the other side, the two of us leaning as close to the opening as possible so we can catch what they're talking about.

Hearing the words that come out of his mouth, I fall even more in love with Brody than I ever thought possible.

brody

GOTCHA, MOTHERFUCKER

JUST BEING in the presence of this fuck makes me want to throw up in my mouth a little bit. But if it means I can get him out of Macy's life for good, then I will suck it up until I get something on him to force the issue. Still, it's an effort not to knock the fucker out and be done with it altogether. Depending on how this conversation goes, it might still be an option.

Gesturing for him to head into the equipment tent, I follow him in and lean against one of the many boxes that I imagine are used for stage props when they break everything down. The main concert ended a few minutes ago, but Macy always does some sort of an encore, so at least we have a few minutes of extra time before someone will come bursting in carrying all manner of bedazzled stage equipment.

He turns to look at me, shooting me a smarmy look that says he knows in his heart that he's better than me. I could knock his fucking teeth out for that look alone, but I steel my features to ensure I don't give him any reason to run for the hills before I get what I want out of him. It definitely won't get me anything but an assault charge if I don't reign it in just a little bit.

"Soooooo," he starts, dragging the word out for dramatic effect. Annoying prick. "I assume you didn't invite me here to take inventory on Harper Bloom's stage bullshit. What is it that you want?"

I clench my jaw, willing myself not to lash out at him for starting the conversation out like that, and give him a brief smirk instead.

"Well, I've been thinking," I say, running my hand along my jaw to accentuate my thought. "The recent success of the paper has been great, but it won't be long before all of this hype dies down, and I am once again scrambling to keep it alive. To be honest, it's getting to be a little exhausting busting my ass to find a story in this small patch of nothing town, knowing one probably doesn't exist. So, maybe it's time for me to branch out and try something a little more... *inviting* for my readers." I emphasize in a way that I know will tickle his sleazy mind. This man is nothing if not predictable in his interest in seeking out the most career damaging stories on people.

He cocks his head and raises a brow. I've definitely piqued his interest. "Oh, yeah? And what exactly did you have in mind?"

"Well, I can't help but notice that you have a loyal following of people who read your online gossip. Looking more into the online avenue seems to be the best route to take for me at this point, and I am tired of writing stories that nobody reads. I'd like to finally write something that captures some attention, so I'm thinking it's time for me to reach for the *stars*, if you catch what I'm saying."

He takes a minute to scrutinize me, eyeing me up and down, disbelief swirling in his eyes. "And why should I tell you anything? Last I checked, you were seen cozying up to my favorite walking trainwreck. You're telling me that you're really going to turn your back on Harper Bloom and her little assistant to rifle through the dirty laundry of celebrities for a living? I doubt it."

I laugh at his words, with very little humor in my tone, leaning into the act, even if it makes me feel physically ill to do so. "Well, to be honest, it's been fun chasing after the party pop princess herself. I mean, who wouldn't want a taste of some of the action that you caught in that audio clip, right? But that was just me trying to get myself on the map to launch my online career. I suppose I really should be thanking you for assisting me in that plan." I wink at him, trying to convince him that we are already in league together, even if he hasn't yet agreed to work with me.

Every word out of my mouth feels like a massive betrayal to all of the moments I've spent with Macy, but it serves as a means to an end. If I can get this prick to tell me some damning piece of evidence, I can leverage him to leave Harper alone for good, which means we can live without a target on our backs every day. I can't allow him to chase us all around the world, fucking up Macy's life with every scathing piece he writes.

He takes in my words, his jaw working as he does. I do my best to keep the disgust off of my face and a smug smirk plastered across my lips. I clench my fists, the only sign I will allow to show through, if only to keep them from reaching out to wrap around this guy's throat. Yeah, I think it's safe to say this guy brings out my inner psycho.

After another minute, he starts laughing and moves forward to clap me on the shoulders. "Who knew you had it in you? Seems like you've got a little of me in you after all. Cozying up to Harper Bloom just to stab her in the back to get what you want? Yeah, you're going places, kid. I might even have to make a play for you to come work at *The Regis Report*." He says this last bit with an edge of hope, like he knows I will make an excellent addition to his team of assholes.

"We'll see. I didn't work this hard to get in with Harper's team just to work for somebody else. But we can talk about it," I say to him. "What I'd really like to know is how you manage to get the scoop on everything the way you do? I mean, to be able to catch the infamous Harper Bloom with her pants down, literally, is quite the feat. How did you do it?"

I've already narrowed down my list of suspects on who's feeding him information, and I've figured out it's likely one, or more, of Macy's security team members. I just need this guy to tell me the who and the how and then I'll personally demolish every person who ever thought they could betray the trust of my songbird.

A slippery grin splits across his face, and he leans his head to the side like we are in on a secret together. I can't believe he's making it this easy, but I can't imagine he has many people in his corner, so maybe he's been itching for someone to confide in. His mistake.

"Well, since we're in league now, I suppose it wouldn't hurt to let a few of my skeletons out of my closet," he says, leaning in even further to speak quietly in my ears. "Well, I do have a pretty extensive network of sources working in Hollywood, but the tricky part has been getting them to place a few bugs in a few key places."

"Bugs?" I ask, my face contorting in confusion. He seriously can't mean that he is secretly recording people in their intimate moments, right?

He scoffs, rolling his eyes like I'm a total amateur for not understanding.

"You know, a *bug.* One of those tiny devices that records

conversations and things. I usually try to get them just in the general vicinity of whoever my victim is at the time, but I had my shining moment with Harper and her sexcapades. Even I couldn't have imagined I'd get something so juicy on tape." He finishes with a gleeful laugh, like he managed to stumble upon the cure for cancer, rather than illegally recording someone having sex without their knowledge or consent.

"How did you do it? I can't imagine it was that easy to just slip into her dressing room. You had to have someone let you in, right?" I've already gotten enough information to take him down, but I need to know who's been helping him.

"See, now that's where you need to take a lesson from me, young grasshopper. Anyone can be a pawn in the game, if you're willing to pay for their loyalty. Harper may be the biggest pop star in the world, but even her roadies can be easily bought with a few dollars and promises of future favors." He nudges me with a wink, confirming my suspicion that it was someone on her security team. That person better count their fucking days.

"So, you're saying, you pay people off to plant bugs so you can catch them on something? Who would take the risk?" I ask, trying to get him to admit it in his own words that he does, in fact, violate people's privacy in this way.

"Well, you have to be willing to cross a few lines to get what you want. But I suppose you've already done that. You'll just have to step up your game even more if you're going to make it in this industry," he says, conspiratorially. "Yes, I pay people to do my dirty work, and then I use the information I get to write my stories. This time, I managed to catch some-thing worth just posting directly to the site, but most times, it's more like a lead for a story I know I will catch later. Either way, it's a win-win for me. As for the who, I'd never name my sources. Let's just say that Harper should invest in a higher end security firm. Bodyguards just aren't what they used to be."

I nod along, as if I am following his train of thought and agreeing with him. I shoot him a winning smile and clap him on the shoulders, squeezing just enough to be painful. He flinches, shooting me a confused look at the level of pressure I am currently placing on his shoulders.

"Thank you, Regis. I think I've got just about everything I need," I say, and then I reach into my pocket to grab out my phone. "You and I are even more alike than you thought."

I turn the phone so he can see the screen. The screen that has been on, and recording, for the last ten minutes of our conversation, getting every piece of damning evidence we need to force him out of Harper's life for good. Using his own tactic against him gives me my own sense of satisfaction.

"What–" He starts, but I stop him with my hand in the air and a shake of my head.

"Nope. You don't get to ask questions," I snap, glaring at him. "See, this is how this is going to go now. You just confessed to knowingly paying people to plant recording devices in the private areas of celebrities. Not necessarily illegal, but it doesn't look good for you, that's for sure." His jaw snaps shut, and he returns my glare, crossing his arms over his chest. He doesn't seem to realize that he no longer has the upper hand in this interaction, but I will clear that up for him.

"But where you really fucked up was admitting to knowingly recording and posting an audio of a sexual act that occurred in a private area, which *is* illegal in most states. That is, if neither of the parties were aware of the recording device being in the room, which doesn't appear to be the case here."

He pales at my words, his mouth opening and closing like a fish. Clearly, I've managed to stump him, which he must not be used to. I stare him down and wait for him to make his next move. He finally steels his features and glares at me.

"What do you want?" he asks, his voice wavering in his anxious state.

Got you, fucker.

I put the phone back in my pocket, ensuring that he can't just take it from me and run, before speaking. Never can be too careful around someone this sketchy.

"What I *want* is for you to find a better outlet for your small dick energy. What I want is for you to get the fuck out of my town and never come back. What I want is for you to forget that Harper Bloom ever existed and for you to leave her damn name off of your site. That is, if you don't want to find yourself getting your ass kicked before you end up behind bars. Get me?"

He nods, furiously, as if he's a bobble head that a small child is knocking around at full force.

"Good," I say, reaching out to grab hold of his shirt and pulling him close to my face. "And if you *ever* so much as think about writing another article about Harper or anyone who even slightly knows her, you'll not only have the legal repercussions of your shady choices to deal with, you'll also have to deal with me, and I can promise you that I won't be happy to see your toad face again. Understand?"

"Y-yes. Fine. No more Harper content," he stammers out, and I release him. I can almost feel slime coating my hands from the brief contact. I wipe my hands on my jacket, just to be sure.

"Now get the fuck out of here before I change my mind about being nice," I growl at him, and he high tails it out of the tent like his ass in on fire. Good fucking riddance.

I huff out a sigh and make my way toward the tent opening with intentions of finding Macy and relaying the good news.

I make it about two steps out of the tent when I am forced to catch someone in my arms as they launch themselves at me. I catch the whiff of someone familiar and bury my face in her hair.

"Songbird."

macy

OH, SWEET RELIEF

I LAUNCH myself at Brody and bury my face in his neck, wrapping my legs around his waist. To his credit, he barely seems surprised to find me in his arms, simply sliding his hands beneath my thighs to hold me to him and pressing his face into my hair, hugging me close. I briefly take note of Stella's footsteps and small giggle as she heads off somewhere else and lets us soak in this moment together.

The relief I feel after hearing his final words to Regis is near soul crushing, and I find myself fighting back tears as I cling to him. I never imagined that he would have used me, but I admit that he was pretty convincing in the first part of the conversation. Thank God I didn't burst in there, fists flying, or I would have ruined everything.

I lean back enough so I can look him in the eyes and run my fingers through his hair, lightly tugging on the ends near the base of his skull.

"Jesus, Brody, you had me worried all day. Why couldn't you just tell me that was your plan?" I accuse him, though even I can hear that there's no real venom to my tone. I am mostly flushed with relief, so it makes it hard to really be angry with him for not including me in the plan. Well, I'm still a little angry, but that's more for being left out than anything.

He presses a quick kiss to my lips before answering my question.

"Because you would have wanted to get involved, and I wanted to be sure I could get him without risking him doubting me before I could really get to the thick of it," he says. I want to argue with him, but he's right. I would definitely have wanted to help, and apparently his plan worked better with less people in the middle. I guess it's justified. Mostly.

"Yeah, well, I've had enough secrets to last a damn lifetime, so next time please don't leave me hanging!" I say, shoving him slightly in jest.

"Next time, you can be in charge. Promise. Besides, you had a concert to get ready for, and there was very little time to make this happen," he explains further, though I am truly beyond caring at this point. "I needed to make sure that slippery fuck got what was coming to him. To be honest, he deserves a lot worse, but for now I guess I'll be satisfied knowing he won't be sniffing around you anymore. We can live in peace knowing our secrets are, for the most part, safe."

My heart swells at his words, focusing solely on one word in particular.

"We?" I ask, hope blossoming in my chest. We haven't exactly ironed out all of the details of what we are going to be after I step back into the spotlight, and I haven't been able to totally let go of my fear that he won't want to be under the microscope with me.

His expression softens, letting go of all of the anger he had built up while dealing with Regis. His eyes bore straight into mine, and my breath catches in my throat. Goddamn him for being so beautiful.

"I already told you, songbird. You're mine. In every way. In every sequin covered costume and plain white tee shirt. With raven black curls and a shiny red wig. In Oaken and in Malibu. You're it for me, and I am never letting you go," he says, pouring every bit of emotion he possesses into the words. A beaming smile breaks across my face, and he meets it with his own. "I love you, songbird. I love you as Macy White. I love you as Harper Bloom. I love you in every single way, and I will spend the rest of my life falling in love with every different version of you that you choose to be."

In lieu of speaking, I bend down and press my lips to his in a bruising kiss, infusing every bit of my own emotions into the motion. I moan against his mouth, and he takes the opportunity to tangle his tongue with mine, deepening the kiss even further. I am about two seconds away from ripping his clothes off right here, when he pulls away, pressing his forehead against mine in the way I love.

My eyes remain closed while I catch my breath, and I whisper, "I love you, Brody."

Thank God he's still holding me up because the smile that breaks across his face turns my legs to jelly. I'd for sure be on the floor if I were standing on my feet. He just locks eyes with me and kisses me again, solidifying the feelings we are both lost in.

After another minute of hardcore making out, he sets me on my feet.

"Come on," he says. "It's been long enough, and I think your audience is ready for an encore."

"I mean," I start, "we could just skip the encore and make a quick getaway back to your place. I doubt anyone would even notice if I didn't come back out."

He barks out a laugh, though it's husky, reading the innuendo in my words. You can't blame me for trying, right?

"Something tells me that if the most famous pop star in the

world didn't make her reappearance for the encore, more than a few people would notice. I'd hate for Chase to send the FBI after you or something and ruin all of our fun. When I get you alone again, I don't want any interruptions for at least a few hours, minimum."

My blood heats at his words, my thoughts delving into fantasies about the type of fun we could get into.

Reading my thoughts, he pulls me into him again, moving so his lips are right by my ear.

"Come on, songbird. Get your cute ass out there, and sing your damn song," he growls, directly into my ear, "so I can get you home and fuck you so hard you'll be too sore to perform again for weeks."

I whimper softly, itching to say "fuck it" and just let him drill me into the floor right here, right now. But he kisses the top of my head and gently pushes me back toward the stage with a quick swat on my ass.

I flash him a glare but turn back toward the stage, taking a deep breath. I lean into my feelings of pure and utter adoration for Brody, allowing it to fill me up until I am grinning from ear to ear, and make my way back in front of the crowd with a wave.

THE BEST OF BOTH

LUGGING the last of my suitcases down the stairs, I drop it at the bottom with a large thud. Even though I only brought a small portion of my things with me from Malibu, nobody could ever accuse me of traveling light.

"Jesus, Ace," Chase says, exasperation lacing his tone. He's currently helping me carry my bags out to the truck so we can make our way back to Malibu. "Next time we come back here, you have to try not to bring your entire closet with you. I mean, seriously. Did you even need half of this stuff?"

"First of all, this *is* me packing light. It's not like you gave me much notice when you were dragging me across the country against my will."

He scoffs at my words, rolling his eyes.

"It may have started that way, but you're not convincing anyone that you didn't enjoy the break from stardom. You totally loved being back home, soaking up life in the slow lane. Plus, you got to connect with Brody again, right? It's been a successful trip if you ask me."

I ignore his words even though he's right. When I first got back home, I was ready to spill all of my secrets. Since being here, and getting to connect with Brody as just Macy, I realized that I loved having the chance to really lean into who I am as a normal person, too. I would do it all over again in a heartbeat.

"Second of all," I continue, not giving him the satisfaction of admitting that he was right, "you never know what you might need, and I like having options. The point isn't to wear everything I bring with me but to be able to choose what I want and what feels right in the moment. You simply wouldn't understand, Mr. 'I wear the same outfit in different colors every day because it's easy but definitely boring.'"

He glares at me, curling his lip like he wants to stick out his tongue but won't allow himself to sink to my childish level. He turns away, and I do just that to his back as he goes, adding a middle finger for good measure.

"Macy Mae White!" Nana admonishes from the kitchen doorway, slinging a dish towel over her shoulder and putting her hands on her hips. I shrug sheepishly at her, and she just smiles and rolls her eyes, letting me off of the hook for my rude behavior. Knowing her, she probably would have done the same thing if she were me.

I go to grab one of my bags to bring out to the truck and help Chase, at least a little bit, when familiar rough hands wrap around the handle, beating me to it. I look up and my gaze meets Brody's ice blue ones, a slight fire behind them as he takes me in. I swear, we are always turned on around each other, and I can't say that I'm even slightly mad about it.

"I got this one," he says, smacking a quick kiss to my lips, and heads out to the truck. On the way, he grabs a black suitcase that I don't recognize, which makes me pause.

"Um," I pause, "that one's not mine."

He glances over his shoulder at me but continues his progression toward the truck. "I know. It's mine."

"Yours?"

"Yes. Mine," he says, matter of factly, making me even more confused.

"But–"

He cuts me off before I can ask any more follow up questions. "I've already told you. I'm not giving you up. I'm not letting you go. I'm coming with you, so grab your damn bags and let's go. We're not having this conversation again, songbird."

"But, what about the paper? You can't just pick up your life and leave everything behind, Brody. We have to make plans and figure out all of the logistics, right?" I follow him out the front door, all the way to Chase's truck.

He sighs, putting the bags in the bed of the truck and turning to face me. He pulls me into his arms, bringing his hands up to wrap around the sides of my neck, his thumbs pressing into my jaw to tilt my face toward his.

"Well, I may have been acting a little bit at the time, but I was serious about wanting to take on a more digital role with the paper. Josie can handle the day to day back here, and I can do my work from anywhere. I signed the rights of editor over to her this morning, so I'm free to follow you wherever you go. The logistics have all already been figured out, plans have already been made, so there's nothing left to worry about."

My mind reels with this new information. We didn't have much time to talk about what life was going to look like for us, and I should be annoyed that he made decisions without me, but I'm not. I'm far too elated that he's coming with me to really be bothered by being left out of planning again.

"So," I say, tripping over the word slightly while I work to contain my emotions. "So, you're coming with me? To Malibu? Like... right now?"

He shakes his head, confusing me further. "No, songbird. Not just to Malibu. I'm coming with you everywhere. When you travel the world as Harper Bloom and when you need a break as Macy White. I will be with you every step of the way. I even went out and bought myself a disguise and everything."

I pull my head back from him with an incredulous look on my face, "Really?"

"Really," he says, and lets me go to reach back into the truck bed where I find another bag. He hands it to me, gesturing for me to look at the contents inside. I shoot him a look, and open the bag, pulling a few things out.

First, I pull out a blonde wig that I am sure he got from a Halloween costume store. Next, I find a pair of aviator sunglasses. The last item, though, forces a laugh from me.

"A fake mustache?" I ask, holding it up in the space between us. His face lights up with humor as he smiles at me.

"I told you I'd wear one if it meant I got to follow you around the world," he says, pulling me close to him again. "And I always keep my promises."

My eyes pinball between his as I take all of this in. I can't believe he's doing all of this just to be with me. I feel my blood heating with excitement, imagining all of the possibilities our crazy double life will bring us. My lips tug up in a beaming smile, and I lock eyes with him.

"So, you're doing the double life thing with me? It can get a little wild. Are you sure you're ready for that level of crazy?"

"Always, songbird. I'm always ready for your brand of crazy," he says, and then he closes the distance between us, sweeping me off of the ground into a passionate kiss. I sigh into the motion, and let myself truly lean into the euphoria of this moment.

He holds me there, and we lose ourselves in the vision of knowing we are truly getting the best of both. Always.

epilogue brody:
one year later

"HARPER! Watch your–" I shout at her, seconds before she rails her head against the top of the stage elevator for what seems like the millionth time. I rush over to her to check and make sure this time she didn't do serious damage. She's hit her head on that damn thing at every concert she's done for the last year, and it's starting to worry me that she's going to end up with some head trauma.

Thankfully, by the time I make it over to her, she's laughing.

"Damn it, songbird! You have to start being more careful. I don't want you to end up with a concussion or something," I snap, though it doesn't take long before I am laughing right along with her.

Her laughter trails off, and she says, "Don't worry, babe. Nothing I can't handle." She shoots me a wink and then pulls me in for a hard kiss. Almost instantly, she pulls away with a groan.

"You know," she starts, pinning me with a hard look, "I thought the whole mustache thing would be sexy. But honestly, it's just itchy and uncomfortable. New rule: You're not allowed to kiss me with that sandpaper thing on."

I laugh at her words but pull her in for another kiss, disregarding her new rule.

"Come on, songbird. You love it. Besides, I didn't hear you complaining when I was giving you a mustache ride about fifteen minutes ago," I tease her and watch her cheeks burn a scarlet color in her embarrassment.

"Br-Stanley!" she whisper-shouts my chosen fake name, almost fucking it up and calling me by my actual name. I probably could have come up with something more Hollywood-esque, but I didn't have the luxury of time to think about it before we were forced to introduce my persona to the world.

Last year, when we got to Macy's house in Malibu, there was a huge crew of paparazzi awaiting our arrival. Thank God I had had the forethought to get into my disguise on the plane, or we would have been royally fucked right from the start. We made a brief statement about Harper's return to stardom, as well as her new relationship status, and then proceeded into her house to hide out for the weekend until we had to really get her back into the spotlight.

For me, it's been a huge learning curve navigating all of the craziness that comes with Macy's life as a pop star. Everywhere we go, we are under a microscope, and it can be overwhelming at times. But that's part of the beauty of living the double life, and I can see now why she decided to keep her private life totally anonymous. We've been able to take a step back a few times, and just be us for a while, and those are my favorite memories from the last year.

With that being said, I'd be lying if I said it wasn't a dream getting to experience the world through the lens of a superstar. The paper has flourished with the addition of the online blog, and we've been able to go more national with it. Josie is still running the local office, but it's become much bigger than we could have ever imagined. Macy tells me all the time how proud she is of me, and how she knows that my parents are proud of me, too, wherever they are now.

I know Macy was worried I would regret my choice to follow her and leave my easy life behind, but that couldn't be further from the truth. I told her I would go anywhere with her, and I have never once regretted that decision. I could never regret any of the choices that allow me to be with her every day.

Pulling myself back into the moment, I gaze into Macy's eyes, letting all of my love for her shine through. Her skin still holds the pinkish tone from my words earlier, but it only makes her even more beautiful than she already is. She may be covered in makeup and sporting her signature red hair, but she is every bit my songbird, and I am slightly dumbstruck by her beauty.

She flashes me a confused look, and asks, "What?"

"I just get distracted by how goddamn beautiful you are sometimes, songbird. It's enough to bring me to my knees," I say, allowing some husk to coat my tone. Her face softens at my words, and she leans forward to kiss me again, despite her earlier declaration of not kissing me with the mustache on.

"I love you," she whispers against my lips, and then she pulls back, pushing me away from the elevator slightly when it starts to rise slowly. "Now, get the fuck out of here! I have a concert to get to, you know."

"I love you, Macy," I whisper, knowing it's quiet enough that no one around me will hear me use her real name. I pull back and let her rise up to the stage knowing that I'm the reason for her stunning smile tonight.

* * *

"Oh my God! Fuck, Brody!" Macy cries out as she rides me on the sofa. We are currently in the process of defiling her dressing room in whatever city she was performing in tonight. Honestly, I can't quite figure out how she keeps all of them straight with how often she moves around, but it's the last thing on my mind as I continue to push her to the brink with my cock. Watching her perform for thousands of people knowing that I am the one who gets to greet her afterwards is a crazy turn on for me, and rushing back to her room to tear her sparkly dresses off of her has become somewhat of a tradition as we make our way through her tour dates.

"Jesus, songbird. Your pussy was absolutely made to take my dick. Look at how good you take me," I groan out, watching my cock slide in and out of her perfect pussy. With one hand, I reach up and gently wrap it around her neck, squeezing gently. With the other, I reach down and rub softly against her clit, making her moan loudly.

"You're so close, Macy. I can feel the way your pussy is already starting to choke my cock." I punctuate my point with a couple of thrusts from below, filling her as deeply as I possibly can. I feel her clench down against me, not quite reaching her peak yet, but nearly.

"Please. Please, Brody," she pleads, and I can tell it's nearly the only thing she has enough breath to say while I continue to slightly cut access to her air. Never one to deny her a damn thing that she wants, I pick up my pace from below and begin rubbing her clit in earnest. She rewards my efforts with another slew of curses and nearly screams in her effort to reach her orgasm.

"Come for me, songbird," I rasp out, leaning forward to lick and nip along her throat, pressing down one last time on her clit and slamming myself up into her as I feel her flutter around me in earnest. She goes boneless as she shouts my name, and I continue my thrusts into her to prolong her orgasm until I am right there and we are coming together.

She slumps against me, and I continue kissing along her neck and soothingly running my hands along her bare back. We just lay there for a few moments, soaking in our love for one another and enjoying the feeling of being close to each other.

After our breathing has slowed and the sweat on our bodies has cooled, I pat her on the ass and lift her off of my cock.

"Alright, love. I'd be shocked if Chase wasn't stomping around the stadium looking for you to make your way to the meet and greet," I say, standing up and pulling my clothes back on.

"Ugh, of course he is. Always out here stealing my fun," she pouts, but rushes to get her meet and greet outfit on. I'm sure we are late at this point, but it was well worth it.

After a few times of getting caught in the act, people started to pick up on our post-show ritual and learned to stay the fuck away for at least 20 minutes after we enter the dressing room. Ideally, I'd be in here all damn night making her scream, but unfortunately, she still has fans to please. At least I can let her go knowing that she's extra euphoric.

After she finishes getting her wig back into place, at least as much as it can be after I nearly tore it from her head, I pull her back into my arms to press my mouth to hers once more. We lose ourselves in the kiss for a minute, but she is on a schedule, so it's time to get going. I pull away and press my forehead against hers.

"Don't worry, songbird," I say, nearly growling with promise in my voice. "I swear, there's plenty more fun to come when we get home."

Home.

Not her home in Malibu, the one I have spent the last year getting comfortable in. No, we are headed back to the place where we fell in love to spend a couple of weeks, bringing ourselves back to Earth again. I, for one, can't wait to slow things down for a while before we have to head out on her international tour. The spotlight is great, but I am always looking forward to when I get to just be with Macy on our own terms. The whole double life thing is actually working out great for our relationship.

She lets out a rough breath, but pulls away from me, grabbing her bag.

"Alright, meet and greet. Then home. Ready?" she asks, making her way to the door.

"Always, songbird. Always."

Find out what happens after Brody's confession at the roller rink!

Join my newsletter to stay up to date on all future works, and to get a bonus spicy scene featuring our favorite Grumpy/Sunshine couple!

https://quiet-basil-60954.myflodesk.com/xuh3p2mups

acknowledgments

Not me trying to write these acknowledgements without crying. An impossible task, but I will do my best. First and foremost, I want to thank every one of my beta readers for taking the time to read the VERY rough first draft of this book. Without your feedback, it would not be what it is today, and I appreciate every second of your time and effort. On that note, my beautiful friend Paige is next. Your unerring love and support got me through the tough parts of writing this book, and I can't thank you enough. You made this book happen, and I can't tell you I love you enough! Morgan Elizabeth, you're up next babe. I truly don't think that I would have finished this book without your support and all of the writing sprints you did with me. I absolutely attribute the finished product of this book to you, and I can't even begin to express how much your love means. Same goes for you Rae! You are such an amazing person, and I am so grateful that you chose to spend the days in Vegas writing with me rather than going out and getting crazy. I am so excited to take on the indie author world with you! To my favorite person in the world and baby sister, Monica. You are by far my biggest cheerleader and fan and I love you so much. Even though you're going to ABSOLUTELY hate the spicy parts of this book, you still support my dreams and encourage me to reach for the stars every time. To my husband, I know you have your doubts about spicy books, but you still support me anyway and I appreciate your love as I work through this process. You are my number one book boyfriend, and you support me in all of my crazy, spontaneous, and somewhat scatterbrained ideas. I love you! Every one of you has made me the author I am today, and I can't tell you how much that means to me. I love you so much, and I can't believe I am lucky enough to know you!

Chelsie Lynn...doesn't even go here! <—Don't Listen to that, it's the imposter syndrome speaking. Anyways, Chelsie Lynn is a born and raised Minnesota girlie who freaking HATES the cold, and dear God why does anyone live here? Oh right... because...seasons. She has one husband, two fur babies, and LOADS of anxiety. But hey, 'tis the spice of life. She is a special educator by day, and the smootiest of sloots by night, turned author of nostalgic RomComs. You're freaking welcome, DCOM girlies. Half of the time she can't decide if she wants to channel her inner chaos Barbie, badass Scorpio witch, or wanna be 90s mom. But who needs to choose one way of being anyways, right? How boring life would be if we could only ever be one version of "us." She will forever be grateful that her love of reading led her to some of her favorite people and allowed her to discover her calling of being a writer.

Stay Smooty, Sloots <3